MAGNUM TENEBROSUM

The Abyss of the Mind

First published by Darkness Studios, LLC 2024

Copyright © 2024 by Magnum Tenebrosum

First edition

ISBN: 979-8-3302-4372-3

This book was professionally typeset on Reedsy.
Find out more at reedsy.com

To everyone from my past who contributed to the traumas in my life, this book is for you.

Thank you for the trials and darkness. Every painful moment and scar shaped who I am and fueled this book's creation.

Your actions made me confront the depths of the mind, uncover resilience, and find the strength to endure.

"The Abyss of the Mind" is a testament to the journey through pain and the stubborn power of hope.

With a hardened heart,

Magnum Tenebrosum

Contents

Foreword

Dear Reader,

This tale, like my life, is shadowed by mental illness, specifically Complex Post-Traumatic Stress Disorder (CPTSD). Like the protagonist, John, I have faced these shadows. This story reflects my journey, albeit through a darker, more fantastical lens.

CPTSD distorts reality, fractures the mind, and isolates the soul, making every day a battle. Through John's journey, I aim to reveal the harrowing realities of CPTSD—a struggle many endure, yet few truly understand.

This story isn't just about my battles; it's a call to action for understanding, compassion, and, above all, action. Mental illness isn't a choice or a sign of weakness; it's a silent battle fought by millions, often alone. But it doesn't have to be that way.

Sharing this story aims to shatter the stigma around mental health and inspire those struggling to seek help. Whether you are working or know someone who is, know there is hope, help, and a way forward.

Introduction to the Protagonist

Johnathan "John" Miller, our protagonist, is a man in his late 40s who bears the heavy burden of CPTSD. His life has been a relentless gauntlet of fear and pain, beginning in his childhood and continuing into his adult years. Despite the deep scars etched into his psyche, John makes a crucial decision to seek help. This story follows his journey through the darkness of his past and the glimmers of hope he finds along the way. John's struggles and resilience are at the heart of this tale, reflecting the silent battles many face daily.

Join me in John's tale and real life, where our actions can make a difference. Together, we can create a world where mental health is treated with the same urgency and compassion as physical health. It starts with understanding, empathy, and a willingness to reach out to those in need.

While you follow John's struggles, remember his story reflects the silent battles many face daily. Let it be a reminder that behind every smile, there may be hidden pain, and behind every facade of strength, there may be a fragile soul in need of support.

Talk to a friend, family member, or professional if you're struggling. There's no shame in asking for help. And if you know someone struggling, be there for them—listen, support, and let them know they're not alone.

With empathy and understanding,

Magnum Tenebrosum

I

Part One

The Awakening

Part One

1

The Survivor's Burden

Johnathan "John" Miller stared blankly out the window of his small apartment, the city skyline a blur of lights and shadows. In his late 40s, John's face bore the marks of a lifetime of hardship—lines etched into his forehead and around his eyes told stories of sleepless nights and relentless anxiety. His eyes, once bright with youthful dreams, now held a perpetual sadness, reflecting the haunted depths of his past.

John's childhood was a relentless gauntlet of fear and pain. His father's rage was unpredictable, turning everyday moments into potential minefields. One night, ten-year-old John hid under his bed, trembling as his father's drunken shouts echoed through the house. The bruises from the last beating hadn't yet faded, and he knew better than to make a sound. These experiences etched deep scars into his psyche, manifesting years later as Complex Post-Traumatic Stress Disorder (CPTSD). Flashbacks would strike him out of nowhere, vivid and paralyzing. Nightmares plagued his sleep, leaving him exhausted and wary of the night. Hypervigilance was his constant companion, making him jump at the slightest noise and scan every room for potential threats. The world was a minefield, and he walked through it with the cautious tread of a man who knew danger intimately.

Adjusting to adult life had been an uphill battle. Jobs came and went, and friendships flickered and died. The ghost of his past never let him settle or find peace. He moved through the world like a shadow, present but never fully engaged, his mind always half-anchored in the torments of his childhood.

A few years ago, another cruel twist of fate added to his burden. John had been the victim of a hit-and-run accident. The faceless driver left him broken in the street, resulting in severe injuries, brain trauma, and a minor stroke. The trauma compounded his already fragile state, intensifying his CPTSD symptoms to nearly unbearable levels.

Yet amid the turmoil, John made a crucial decision: he chose to seek help, a glimmer of hope amidst the darkness. He found Stephanie Thompson, a therapist known for her expertise in treating trauma. Her compassion and experience offered a lifeline. Stephanie's office, a serene space filled with soft light and calming decor, became his sanctuary. Here, he began to unpack his heavy burden, piece by painful piece.

John's life unfolded in a modern urban environment—a concrete and steel maze teeming with noise and activity that often left him feeling distracted and overwhelmed. His simple, sparsely furnished apartment reflected a life focused on survival rather than comfort.

As John sat in his small living room, he could feel the weight of his trauma pressing down on him. The memories, the pain, the constant fear—they were a part of him, as ingrained as his breath. But there was also a sense of determination. Seeking therapy with Stephanie was a step toward reclaiming his life, a fight to find some semblance of normalcy and peace.

Vivid imagery and sensory details painted John's world in stark colors. The smell of stale coffee in his apartment, the distant hum of traffic, and the flickering streetlights outside his window all anchored him to the present, even as his mind drifted into the past. The weight of his trauma was tangible, a heavy cloak that he wore every day. But with each session with Stephanie, he hoped to lighten that load, to find a way to live without being suffocated by his memories.

In this modern urban jungle, John's journey was a testament to the resilience of the human spirit. Despite the darkness that clung to him, he continued to fight, to seek help, and to hope for a better future. In that struggle, he embodied the silent battles fought by countless others, each step a defiance against the shadows of the past.

John's mornings began in a haze, the remnants of night-mares clinging to him like a second skin. He shuffled into his tiny kitchen, its tiles cold under his bare feet, and brewed a pot of coffee. The bitter aroma filled the air, a familiar and somewhat comforting scent. As he poured himself a cup, his hands trembled slightly, a side effect of the brain trauma from the accident. The mug felt heavy in his grasp; each sip a small victory against the tremors.

The city's sounds filtered through the thin walls of his apartment—honking horns, distant sirens, the chatter of people on the street below. John found these noises both grounding and overwhelming. They were reminders that life went on outside his bubble of pain, yet each sound could also trigger a flashback, dragging him back to the darkest corners of his mind.

One particular morning, the sound of children laughing

outside pulled John into a memory he had long tried to bury. He closed his eyes, and the scene unfolded with brutal clarity: a young boy, no more than eight, cowering in the corner of a dimly lit room. Shadows loomed large as an angry voice hurled insults and threats. The boy's small frame shook with fear, tears streaming down his face, but he dared not make a sound. The pain of those days, the feeling of being powerless and unloved, washed over John like a tidal wave.

John opened his eyes, breathing heavily, his heart pounding. The laughter outside had turned to screams of joy, but to John, they were echoes of past torments. He rubbed his temples, willing the memories to fade, but they clung to him stubbornly. Each day was a struggle to keep those memories at bay, not to let them define his present.

Despite these challenges, John made his way to Stephanie's office. The journey there was fraught with anxiety. Crowded streets and busy intersections triggered his hypervigilance. He walked quickly, head down, avoiding eye contact, his senses on high alert for potential danger. The hit-and-run had left him particularly wary of cars. Each honk or sudden movement sent a jolt of fear through him, a visceral reminder of the fateful day his body had been shattered.

Stephanie's office was a haven of calm in his chaotic world. The soft blue walls and gentle lighting starkly contrasted the harsh realities outside. As John settled into the plush chair, Stephanie greeted him with a warm smile, the kind that reached her eyes and seemed to light up the room. In her early fifties, with streaks of gray in her chestnut hair, she exuded a calm confidence. Outside the office, Stephanie found solace in painting, a hobby that allowed her to unwind from the emotional weight of her work. She often brought the same patience and meticulousness to her therapy sessions, carefully unpacking the layers of her patients' trauma.

John sat in the waiting room, his leg bouncing nervously. The sterile smell of antiseptic filled his nostrils, reminding him of hospitals. He clenched and unclenched his fists to keep the panic at bay. When Stephanie called his name, he stood, every muscle tensed as if ready for flight. In the office, he hesitated before sitting down, his eyes darting to the door. Stephanie noticed and offered a reassuring smile. "Take your time, John. This is a safe space."

John swallowed hard. "I don't know if I can do this."

Stephanie nodded, her voice gentle. "It's okay to feel that way. Just know that whatever you share here stays here. We'll go at your pace."

He nodded, a lump forming in his throat. For the first time in years, he felt a flicker of hope. He could find some relief. Her presence alone was a balm to John's frayed nerves.

"How are you feeling today, John?" Stephanie asked, her voice steady and soothing.

John took a deep breath, trying to find the words. "Rough morning," he admitted, his voice barely above a whisper. "The memories...they just won't let go."

Stephanie nodded, her expression one of empathy and concern. "It's okay to feel that way, John. These memories are a part of you, but they don't have to control you. Let's work through them together."

Their sessions were a lifeline for John. Stephanie's guidance helped him navigate the turbulent waters of his mind. They talked about his childhood, about the abuse and neglect that had shaped him. They explored the trauma of the hit-and-run, the physical pain, and the lingering psychological scars.

Stephanie taught him grounding techniques and ways to anchor himself in the present when the past threatened to pull him under.

"Remember, John," Stephanie said during one session, "healing is a process. It takes time, and it's okay to have setbacks. What's important is that you're here, that you're trying."

John nodded, absorbing her words. He knew the road ahead was long and fraught with challenges, but he felt a glimmer of hope for the first time in a long while. Stephanie's support gave him the strength to face each day, to confront the demons of his past with a renewed sense of determination.

As he left Stephanie's office, the city seemed less menacing. The sounds, the people, the bustling streets were still there, but they felt more manageable. John knew he had a long way to go, but he was no longer walking that path alone. With Stephanie's help, he began to see a future where his trauma did not define him, where he could find peace amidst the chaos.

His burdens were still heavy, but John was learning to carry them step by step with more grace. His journey was beginning, and though the scars of his past would always be with him, he held onto the hope that one day, they would no longer have him captive.

The evenings were the hardest for John. As dusk settled over the city, shadows crept into his apartment, filling every corner with reminders of his past. The dim light seemed to invite the phantoms of his memories, making the air feel thick with tension. John often found himself pacing the small living room, trying to outrun the relentless onslaught of his thoughts.

His apartment was a modest one-bedroom, sparsely furnished, reflecting his transient existence. The walls were bare, save for a few photographs of landscapes—places he had never been but dreamed of visiting one day. The room was filled with remnants of his life before the accident: items that now seemed unfamiliar and distant.

One evening, John sat on his worn-out couch, a bottle of painkillers on the coffee table in front of him. His head throbbed, a lingering consequence of the brain trauma. He rubbed his temples, trying to alleviate the pain, but it was useless. The physical pain often mingled with the emotional, creating a storm inside him that was hard to weather.

His mind drifted back to the day of the accident. He had been walking home from a late shift at the warehouse, the night air crisp and cold. The street was quiet, the kind of quiet that made him uneasy. Out of nowhere, the blinding headlights of a speeding car bore down on him. There was no time to react. The impact was swift and brutal, throwing him into the air like a ragdoll. He remembered the sound of his body hitting the pavement, the blinding pain, and then darkness.

When he awoke in the hospital, the doctors spoke in hushed tones about his injuries—a broken leg, several fractured ribs, brain trauma, and a minor stroke. They told him he was lucky to be alive, but John didn't feel lucky. The accident had left him more broken than ever, adding layers of trauma to an already fragile psyche.

As he stared at the bottle of pills, John's thoughts grew darker. He wondered if the pain would ever end and if he would ever feel whole again. The weight of his trauma, both past and present, felt unbearable at times. But then he thought of Stephanie and the progress he had made in therapy. Her words echoed in his mind, reminding him that healing was possible and that he was not alone in this fight.

Determined not to succumb to despair, John pushed himself off the couch and grabbed his jacket. He decided to walk, hoping the fresh air would clear his mind. The city streets were a blur of lights and movement, starkly contrasting the stillness he craved. He wandered, letting his feet guide him, trying to focus on the present moment.

As he passed a park, he heard the distant sound of children playing. Their laughter was a bittersweet reminder of the innocence he had lost. He paused by the entrance, watching them chase each other around, their joy untainted by the world's harshness. He allowed himself to smile momentarily, feeling a glimmer of hope.

John continued his walk, his mind slowly calming. The city, despite its chaos, began to feel less intimidating. He reminded himself of his progress, his strength to seek help, and his support for Stephanie. Each step was a small victory, a testament to his resilience.

When he returned to his apartment, the shadows seemed less menacing. He settled back on the couch, the bottle of pills now a distant thought. He picked up a book from the coffee table, one Stephanie had recommended. It was about overcoming trauma and finding inner peace. John wasn't sure if he believed in such things, but he was willing to try.

As he read, the words resonated with him. They spoke of pain but also of healing, of the possibility of a life beyond trauma. John felt a sense of connection to the author's journey and a shared understanding of their struggles. It gave him hope that his story could have a different ending.

The night grew late, but John continued reading, feeling a sense of purpose he hadn't felt in a long time. The city outside grew quieter, the sounds of nightlife fading into the background. John found solace in the stillness, a rare moment of peace in his turbulent life.

He knew the road ahead was long and fraught with challenges, but he felt equipped to face it for the first time. With Stephanie's help and his newfound determination, John believed he could find a way to carry the survivor's burden with more strength and grace. His journey was far from over, but he was ready to take the next step.

Morning light filtered through the thin curtains of John's apartment, casting a soft glow that contrasted sharply with the harsh fluorescents of the night before. John stirred in his bed, the remnants of his troubled dreams clinging to him like cobwebs. He forced himself to get up, knowing that lingering in bed would only lead to darker thoughts.

The kitchen was small but functional. John reached the counter, where a half-empty cereal box sat next to a chipped mug. As he poured himself a bowl, his mind drifted back to his therapy session with Stephanie the previous week.

"Remember, John," she had said, her voice calm and reassuring, "it's about taking small steps. Healing isn't a straight line, and it's okay to have setbacks. What's important is that you keep moving forward."

He appreciated her words, but living by them was another matter entirely. Each day felt like an uphill battle, the weight of his past dragging him down. Yet, there were moments—fleeting but precious—where he caught glimpses of what life could be without the constant shadow of his trauma.

John sat down at the tiny kitchen table, the cereal crunching loudly in the silence. He knew he had to get ready for his appointment with Stephanie. Therapy days were both a relief and a challenge; they brought him face-to-face with his demons but also offered a path to understanding and, hopefully, peace.

After breakfast, John showered and dressed, his movements mechanical but steady. He avoided looking at his reflection too long, not wanting to confront the eyes that had seen too much. With a deep breath, he grabbed his jacket and stepped outside.

The therapy center wasn't far, but John preferred to walk, using the time to prepare himself mentally. The bustling streets of the city contrasted sharply with his internal turmoil. He watched people go about their day, wondering how many carried burdens like his.

As he approached the building, John's heart rate quickened. He paused at the entrance, taking a moment to steady himself before heading to the second-floor sanctuary of Stephanie's office. The receptionist greeted him warmly, and he walked down the familiar hallway.

Stephanie's office was a comforting space, filled with soft colors and gentle lighting. The walls were adorned with artwork that spoke of hope and resilience. John sat in the well-worn armchair, trying to calm his racing thoughts.

Stephanie entered, her presence immediately putting him at ease. She sat across from him, expressing genuine concern and empathy.

"How are you feeling today, John?" she asked, her voice a soothing balm to his frayed nerves.

John took a deep breath. "I've had better days," he admitted. "But I've also had worse."

Stephanie nodded, understanding the weight behind his words. "That's progress, John. You're acknowledging your feelings, and that's an important step."

They talked about his week, the constant struggle to stay afloat amidst the waves of his memories. Stephanie guided him through his thoughts, helping him untangle the knots formed over years of pain and neglect.

They revisited the accident, the hit-and-run that had changed his life. "It's not just about the physical recovery," Stephanie reminded him. "Your brain went through significant trauma, and it's okay to feel the way you do. What's important is that you're here, willing to work through it."

John listened, absorbing her words. He trusted Stephanie; her insights and compassion were a lifeline in his darkest moments. Despite everything, she helped him see that his survival was a testament to his strength.

The session moved to a close, and John felt a sense of relief mixed with exhaustion. Therapy was draining, but it also brought a clarity that he desperately needed.

As he left Stephanie's office, the sun had risen higher in the sky, casting a warm glow over the city. John paused for a moment, taking in the bustling scene around him. The world kept turning; life went on, and he was part of it.

The walk to the bus stop felt lighter, his steps more purposeful. He still had a long way to go, but he felt a flicker of hope for the first time in a while. He was not alone in this journey. With Stephanie's support and determination, he slowly, steadily found his way forward.

John's journey home was quiet, and the bus ride was a time for reflection. He stared out the window, watching the city blur past, his mind replaying the session with Stephanie. Her words resonated with him, offering hope amidst the pervasive darkness. He knew his path to healing would be arduous, filled with setbacks and challenges, but he was determined to persevere.

As the bus approached his stop, John gathered his belongings and stepped off, the familiar surroundings of his neighborhood greeting him. The sun was high in the sky now, casting long shadows that danced across the pavement. He strolled, taking in the sights and sounds of the city around him, a reminder that life continued despite his struggles.

When he reached his apartment, he unlocked the door and stepped inside, the quiet interior a stark contrast to the bustling streets outside. He set his things down and made his way to the small desk by the window, his journal lying open where he had left it. He sat down, staring at the blank page, the weight of his emotions pressing down on him again.

With a deep breath, John picked up his pen and began to write. He poured his thoughts onto the page, the ink flowing freely as he documented his fears, pain, and hopes. Each word was a cathartic release, a step toward understanding and acceptance.

He wrote about the accident, the moments of terror and confusion, the blinding pain, and the struggle to survive. He described the hospital stay, the long months of rehabilitation, and the lingering effects of the brain trauma and stroke. The memories were raw and painful, but he faced them head-on, determined to make sense of his experiences.

As the words filled the page, John felt a sense of clarity emerging. His trauma did not define him, but it was undeniably a part of him. Accepting that truth was difficult, but it was also empowering. He had survived, and that survival

14

meant something.

The sun began to set, casting a warm, golden light into the room. John paused, looking out the window at the vibrant hues painting the sky. It was a beautiful reminder that there could be moments of beauty and peace even in the darkest times.

John closed his journal, feeling a sense of accomplishment. Today had been a small victory, a step forward on his path to healing. He knew there would be more difficult days ahead, but he also knew he had the strength to face them.

As he prepared dinner, the simple cooking brought a sense of normalcy to his day. He moved through the motions, chopping vegetables and stirring the pot, the rhythmic actions grounding him in the present moment. When the meal was ready, he sat down to eat, savoring each bite and allowing himself to enjoy the small pleasure.

After dinner, John settled into his favorite chair with a book, the familiar weight of it comforting in his hands. He lost himself in the story, the words transporting him to another world, if only for a little while. It was a welcome escape, a brief respite from the heavy burden he carried.

As the night grew darker, John prepared for bed, his body tired but his mind more at ease. He lay down, the sheets cool and crisp against his skin, and closed his eyes. For the first time in a long time, he felt a glimmer of hope for the future.

He knew his journey was far from over, but he also knew he was not alone. With Stephanie's guidance and his newfound determination, he was finding his way through the darkness, one step at a time. As he drifted off to sleep, the promise of a new day awaited him, filled with possibilities and the hope of healing.

And so, John embraced the night, ready to face whatever challenges lay ahead, his heart bolstered by the knowledge that he was a survivor.

2

The Therapist's Approach

Stephanie Thompson's office was a sanctuary of calm amidst the chaos of the city. Soft, soothing colors adorned the walls, and comfortable chairs invited clients to settle in and share their burdens. The bookshelves, filled with literature on psychology and trauma, hinted at Stephanie's dedication to her field.

When John first arrived at Stephanie's office, he was greeted by her warm smile and gentle demeanor. Stephanie's presence immediately put him at ease, and he felt a flicker of hope that she could help him. As they began their session, Stephanie's empathetic gaze encouraged him to share his story.

John was hesitant at first. Years of burying his emotions had made him wary of opening up to anyone, let alone a stranger. He was accustomed to keeping his guard up, to pushing people away before they could get too close. But something about Stephanie's gentle demeanor made him want to trust her, to let her in.

Stephanie listened attentively, her empathy shining through in every word and gesture. She never rushed or pressured him to share more than he was comfortable with. Instead, she offered a listening ear and a reassuring presence, allowing him to lead their conversations.

In those early sessions, Stephanie focused on building trust and establishing a safe space for John to explore his emotions. She knew that healing from trauma required a delicate balance of patience and persistence, and she was committed to guiding him through the process at his own pace.

Stephanie's personal life mirrored her professional calm. Outside the office, she found solace in painting, a hobby that allowed her to unwind from the emotional weight of her work. Her small studio apartment was filled with canvases of vibrant landscapes, a stark contrast to the often sad nature of her job. She brought this sense of peace and creativity into her therapy sessions, encouraging John to explore art as a form of expression.

One particular session stood out in John's memory—a breakthrough that marked the beginning of his healing journey. Stephanie had introduced Cognitive Behavioral Therapy (CBT) as a way to help John recognize and challenge the negative thought patterns that had taken root in his mind.

"John," Stephanie began gently, "let's talk about some of the beliefs you have about yourself. You mentioned feeling worthless and undeserving of happiness. Where do you think those beliefs come from?"

John shifted uncomfortably in his seat. "I don't know. Maybe it's just who I am."

Stephanie shook her head. "Those beliefs are not inherent to who you are. They're learned, often from past experiences. Let's try to identify some specific instances where you felt this way."

After some hesitation, John spoke about his childhood and his father's relentless verbal abuse. "He always said I was a burden, that I'd never amount to anything."

Stephanie nodded, her expression one of understanding. "Those words were incredibly hurtful, and it's understandable that they've stuck with you. But let's challenge them. Can you think of a time when you felt valuable or accomplished, even in a small way?"

John thought for a moment. "There was this one time at work... I stayed late to help a coworker finish a project. We met the deadline because of my help."

"How did that make you feel?" Stephanie asked.

"I felt... useful. Like I mattered," John replied slowly.

Stephanie smiled. "That's significant, John. It shows that you are capable and valuable. Let's write that down and remember it the next time you feel unworthy."

This exercise was a turning point for John. For the first time, he began to see the resilience and strength that had kept him going despite his struggles. The CBT sessions gradually helped him replace negative beliefs with more constructive and empowering thoughts.

Another significant breakthrough occurred when John learned about grounding techniques. During a session, Stephanie introduced him to these methods as a way to manage his anxiety and flashbacks.

"John, grounding techniques can help you stay connected to the present moment," Stephanie explained. "They're particularly useful when you're feeling overwhelmed by memories or emotions."

John was skeptical but willing to try. Stephanie guided him

through a simple exercise. "Let's start with deep breathing. Inhale slowly through your nose, hold for a few seconds, and then exhale through your mouth. Focus on the sensation of your breath."

As John followed her instructions, he felt a slight sense of calm wash over him. "Now," Stephanie continued, "let's try a sensory exercise. Look around the room and name five things you can see, four things you can touch, three things you can hear, two things you can smell, and one thing you can taste."

John took in his surroundings, focusing on the details he often overlooked—the texture of the chair, the sound of distant traffic, the faint scent of lavender in the room. By the end of the exercise, he felt more anchored in the present, the intrusive memories receding into the background.

The most profound breakthrough came during an EMDR (Eye Movement Desensitization and Reprocessing) session. John had always avoided discussing the hit-and-run accident in detail. The memory was too painful, and he feared reliving the trauma. But with Stephanie's gentle guidance, he decided to confront it.

"John, EMDR involves recalling traumatic events while focusing on a specific external stimulus," Stephanie explained. "It helps reprocess the memory and reduce its emotional impact. Are you ready to try it?"

John nodded, albeit nervously. Stephanie instructed him to follow her finger movements with his eyes while recalling the night of the accident. "Take your time, John. Just let the memory come naturally."

As John focused on Stephanie's hand moving back and forth, the memory began to surface. He saw the blinding headlights, felt the impact of the car, and heard the screeching of tires. His heart raced, but Stephanie's calm presence kept him grounded.

"Keep following my fingers, John," she encouraged. "What else do you remember?"

"I remember... the pain. The feeling of being thrown to the ground. Everything went dark," John said, his voice trembling.

Stephanie nodded, continuing the movements. "You're doing great. Now, let's reprocess that memory. Imagine a different outcome—what if you had been able to get out of the way in time?"

John struggled at first, but gradually, he began to imagine himself avoiding the car. The feeling of helplessness started to fade, replaced by a sense of control. By the end of the session, the memory no longer held the same paralyzing power over him.

With each breakthrough, John made tangible progress. The frequency of his flashbacks and nightmares decreased, and he found himself better equipped to manage daily anxiety. He started to see Stephanie's office as a sanctuary where he could confront his past without being overwhelmed.

The improvements in therapy extended to John's personal life. He began to reconnect with old friends, cautiously reaching out and explaining his absence. Some relationships rekindled, providing him with a broader support network. Additionally, he revisited hobbies he had abandoned, like woodworking, finding solace and satisfaction in creating something tangible.

Stephanie's support was crucial, but she also encouraged John to build a broader support network. Integrating insights from his support group into therapy sessions allowed him to address his issues in a more holistic way. Maria and Dave from the support group became key figures in his life, offering companionship and understanding.

John also began forming new, healthy relationships. With Stephanie's guidance, he learned to set boundaries and communicate his needs, fostering connections based on mutual respect and support.

John's journey with Stephanie was a testament to the transformative power of therapy. Through CBT, grounding techniques, and EMDR, he learned to navigate his trauma and rebuild his life. With each session, he grew stronger, more resilient, and more hopeful about the future.

3

The Weight of Debt

The relentless buzz of John's alarm clock was a harsh reminder that another day had begun, bringing the weight of unfulfilled responsibilities and mounting debt. He groggily rose from his sagging mattress, the bed creaking in protest, and shuffled to the small kitchen of his rundown apartment. The smell of stale air and faint mildew clung to every corner, a constant reminder of his deteriorating situation.

John's gaze drifted to the stack of unopened envelopes on the kitchen table, each a silent accusation of his financial failures. He knew what they contained: overdue bills, final notices, and persistent reminders from his landlord, Dave Richardson. John's hand trembled as he picked up the latest letter from Dave, the words "Final Notice" glaring back at him in bold red ink.

He sank into a chair, feeling the crushing weight of his debt pressing down on his chest. Dave Richardson was a no-nonsense landlord known for his strict adherence to rules and deadlines. Their interactions were brief and cold, Dave's strict demeanor leaving no room for empathy or leniency.

John could still recall their last conversation a few days prior.

"John, you're two months behind on rent," Dave had said, his voice devoid of compassion. "If you don't pay up by the end of the week, I'll have no choice but to start the eviction process."

John tried to explain and plead for more time, but Dave's response was a curt dismissal. "It's not my problem. You either pay, or you leave."

Now, as John stared at the letter, the memory of Dave's stern face and harsh words replayed in his mind, amplifying his anxiety. He felt trapped, the walls of his apartment closing in on him, suffocating him with the inescapable reality of his debt. The rent money was nowhere to be found, and time was running out.

The knot in John's stomach tightened, his thoughts swirling in fear and despair. His financial struggles were not just a matter of money; they were a constant, gnawing presence that eroded his mental health, feeding his anxiety and deepening his sense of hopelessness. Each day was a battle against the crushing weight of debt, and John was losing ground, inch by painful inch.

John forced himself to get dressed, trying to shake off the oppressive thoughts that clung to him like a dark cloud. He needed to face the day, though the prospect seemed almost unbearable. His steps felt heavy as he made his way to the door, his mind replaying the events that had led him to this point.

The streets outside were bustling with activity, a stark contrast to the stillness of his apartment. John walked with his head down, avoiding eye contact with anyone who might recognize him. He couldn't bear the thought of running into a friend or acquaintance, someone who might ask about his well-being or why he looked so worn down. Isolation had become his shield, a way to protect himself from the pity or judgment of others.

As he neared the corner store, John's thoughts drifted back to the accident—the pivotal moment when everything had changed. It was a late evening, the sky darkening with the approach of a storm. John was crossing the street, preoccupied with worries about his job and bills, when a car came barreling towards him out of nowhere. The impact had been sudden and brutal, his body thrown onto the pavement like a ragdoll.

John remembered the cold, wet asphalt against his skin and the searing pain that followed. The driver had sped away, leaving him broken and bleeding in the street. The aftermath of the accident had been a blur of hospital lights, the beeping of machines, and the distant murmur of doctors discussing his condition. Severe injuries, brain trauma, and a minor stroke—those were the cold, clinical terms used to describe the damage done to his body and mind.

The physical scars had healed, but the trauma lingered, an ever-present reminder of his vulnerability. John's world had shrunk since that night; his life was reduced to survival tactics and desperate attempts to keep the darkness at bay. The financial burden of medical bills had only added to his woes, pushing him deeper into debt and despair.

At the store, John picked up the few essentials he could afford, his mind barely registering the items he placed in his basket. Each step felt like trudging through quicksand, every movement an effort against the invisible weight dragging him down. The cashier greeted him with a perfunctory smile, but

John couldn't muster the energy to respond. He paid for his groceries in silence, and the meager contents of his wallet were a stark reminder of his precarious situation.

Back in his apartment, John set the groceries on the counter and sank into a chair, exhaustion washing over him. The day's simple tasks had drained him, each a battle against the encroaching tide of his financial and emotional burdens. He leaned back, closing his eyes, trying to find a moment of peace in the chaos of his thoughts. But peace was elusive, and the specter of debt loomed large, casting a long shadow over his fragile existence.

John's solitude deepened as the days passed, each blending into the next. His apartment, once a refuge, now felt like a prison. The walls seemed to close in on him, echoing the relentless ticking of the clock—a constant reminder of the rent due date that loomed ever closer.

The knock on his door that afternoon was sharp and insistent. John knew who it was before he even opened it. Dave Richardson stood there, his face a mask of impatience.

"John," Dave began without preamble, "it's been a week. Do you have the rent?"

John's heart pounded in his chest. He had nothing, no money to offer, no solutions to propose. He opened his mouth to speak, but the words caught in his throat.

"Look, I don't want to have to do this, but you're leaving me no choice," Dave said, his tone cold and final. "If you don't have the money by tomorrow, you'll have to vacate the premises."

John felt the ground give way beneath him, his grip on the doorframe the only thing keeping him upright. He tried to explain, to ask for more time, but Dave's expression hardened.

"I'm running a business, John, not a charity. You need to understand that."

With that, Dave turned and walked away, leaving John standing in the doorway, the weight of his words settling heavily on his shoulders. He closed the door and leaned against it, feeling the crushing pressure of his predicament. He was out of time, and there were no options left.

Desperation clawed at him as he moved to the kitchen table, the unopened bills still mocking him. He grabbed one of the envelopes and tore it open, the printed words blurring before his eyes. Electricity, water, credit card—the debts were endless, each a brick in the wall that trapped him.

The familiar ache in his leg flared up, a reminder of the hit-and-run that had derailed his life. The accident had left him with more than just physical scars; it had stripped him of his independence, his ability to work, and his sense of security. Now, every step he took was a painful reminder of his fragility.

As the sun set outside, casting long shadows across the room, John felt the weight of his isolation more acutely than ever. The few friends he had once confided in had drifted away, unable or unwilling to deal with his relentless negativity and despair. Even his family had grown distant, their offers of help dwindling as his situation worsened.

John's thoughts spiraled as he sat there, the darkening room mirroring the growing darkness in his mind. He felt trapped in a cycle of anxiety and hopelessness, each day a struggle to keep his head above water. The mounting pressure of his financial difficulties was suffocating, and he saw no way out.

The noise from the street below filtered through the thin walls, a distant hum of life that felt worlds away from his own. John was alone, caught in a relentless storm of debt and despair, his mind a battlefield of fears and memories. The weight of it all pressed down on him, a suffocating blanket of hopelessness that threatened to crush what little strength he had left.

In the quiet of his apartment, John stared at the ceiling, feeling the overwhelming burden of his existence. He was adrift in a sea of debt, with no lifeline in sight, and the relentless waves of his past traumas threatened to pull him under.

The night descended like a shroud, wrapping John's apartment in darkness. He lay on his bed, staring at the cracked ceiling, his mind churning with relentless turmoil. Sleep eluded him, chased away by haunting memories and the ever-present fear of what tomorrow would bring. The accident replayed in his mind with brutal clarity: the blinding headlights, the screech of tires, and the sickening thud as his body hit the pavement. The physical pain had been indescribable, but the emotional agony of being abandoned lingered even longer.

John shifted restlessly, his leg aching with a dull throb that never entirely went away. The doctors had done what they could, but the injuries were severe. The brain trauma and minor stroke had left lasting effects, subtle at first but growing more pronounced over time. His memory was patchy, his thoughts often muddled, and the simplest tasks sometimes seemed impossible.

John had tried to pick up the pieces in the months following the accident. He'd gone through physical therapy, struggled to regain his strength, and fought to reclaim some semblance of normalcy. But the medical bills had piled up, each a stark reminder of his vulnerabilities. The financial burden and his inability to work had pushed him to the brink. Isolation became his refuge, a way to shield himself from the world that had shown him so little mercy. Friends and family had offered help initially, but their patience had worn thin. They couldn't understand the depths of his despair, the way his mind seemed to turn against him, whispering insidious thoughts that he was worthless, that he'd never escape the shadows of his past.

John rolled over, his gaze landing on a small, framed photo on his nightstand. It was a picture of him with his parents, taken at a family gathering years ago. They looked so happy, so carefree. But the truth was far from the smiling faces in the photograph. His childhood had been a battleground, where safety was an illusion and love was conditional. His father's harsh words and his mother's cold indifference had carved deep wounds in his psyche. The constant fear of doing something wrong, of being punished for the slightest mistake, had left him anxious and wary. He'd learned early on that the world was unsafe and that trust was a luxury he couldn't afford.

As he lay there, the weight of his childhood traumas mingled with the recent horrors of his adult life. The isolation, the financial struggles, the lingering pain from the accident— they were all part of the same, unending nightmare. He felt like he was drowning, each breath a struggle against the overwhelming tide of his fears and regrets.

John's thoughts drifted to the future, or rather, the lack of one. He couldn't see a way out of his predicament. The eviction notice was a looming threat, and without a job or any means to pay his bills, he faced the genuine possibility of homelessness. The thought of losing even this tiny, decrepit apartment was terrifying. It was all he had left, the last vestige of stability in a life torn apart.

Despair settled over him like a suffocating blanket, the darkness closing in from all sides. He felt utterly alone, adrift in a sea of memories and fears, with no lifeline in sight. As the night wore on, John lay in the darkness, his mind a battlefield of past traumas and present struggles, the weight of his debt and isolation pressing down on him with relentless force.

Morning arrived with an unwelcome harshness, the dim light filtering through the grimy windows doing little to dispel the darkness within John's mind. The weight of another sleepless night pressed on him as he dragged himself out of bed, his body aching and his thoughts muddled. The kitchen was a mess of unopened bills and empty food wrappers, a silent testament to his descent into despair.

He sat at the table, staring at the latest eviction notice, the bold red letters blurring before his eyes. It felt like a physical blow, a confirmation of his failure. He was out of options, with no money and no one left to turn to. Desperation gnawed at him, a relentless presence that he couldn't escape.

John picked up his phone, his hand trembling as he dialed the number he'd memorized by heart. The line rang several times before a gruff voice answered.

"Yeah?"

"Dave, it's John," he said, his voice barely above a whisper.

There was a pause, then a sigh. "What do you want, John?"

"I… I need more time. Please, just a little more time. I'm trying to get the money together."

Dave's tone was impatient, bordering on annoyance. "John, I've given you more time than I should have. You're way past the deadline. I can't keep waiting. You have until the end of the day to come up with something, or you're out."

John's heart sank, his last shred of hope slipping away. "Dave, please…"

But the line had already gone dead. John stared at the phone in his hand, feeling the crushing finality of Dave's words. There was no more time. He was out of chances.

He dropped the phone on the table and buried his face in his hands, the overwhelming sense of helplessness washing over him. His thoughts spiraled, each one darker than the last. He thought about the accident, the pain, and the struggle to recover. He thought about his childhood, the constant fear, and the lingering scars that had never really healed.

A knock at the door startled him, pulling him out of his reverie. He stood slowly, his legs like lead as he approached the door. Opening it, he found a woman standing there, her expression a mix of concern and determination.

"John? It's Maria from the support group."

John blinked, trying to process her presence. He hadn't been to the group in weeks, too ashamed and overwhelmed to face anyone. Maria had always been kind, one of the few people who seemed to care genuinely.

"Maria, what are you doing here?" he asked, his voice rough.

She looked at him with a softness that made his chest ache. "I've been worried about you. You stopped coming to the meetings, and no one has heard from you. I thought I'd check in."

John stepped aside, letting her into the cluttered apartment. Maria glanced at the scene, her concern deepening.

"John, you don't have to go through this alone," she said gently. "There are people who want to help. You just have to let us."

Her words broke something in him, the fragile barrier he'd built to keep everyone out. He sank into a chair, the weight of his burdens too much to bear alone. Maria sat beside him, her presence a small but significant comfort.

As they talked, John opened up, sharing pieces of his story that he'd kept hidden for so long. The accident, the debts, and the relentless fear of losing everything spilled out in a torrent of pain and frustration. Maria listened without judgment, her compassion a balm to his wounded soul.

"We can find a way, John. Together, we can find a way."

Her words offered a glimmer of hope, a small but vital light in the darkness surrounding him. For the first time in what felt like forever, John thought he wasn't alone in his struggle. He realized that there might be a way out, however slim. Maria promised to return the next day to help him make calls and fill out applications.

As the evening wore on, Maria left with a promise to return, leaving John with a sense of cautious optimism. He moved to the window and looked at the city, the distant lights twinkling against the encroaching night. The world outside seemed vast and indifferent, but a tiny spark of determination within him hadn't been there before.

The next day, true to her word, Maria returned. Together, they spent hours on the phone, navigating bureaucratic hurdles and filling out seemingly endless forms. John's anxiety spiked at the thought of sharing his story with strangers. Still, Maria's steady presence helped him push through the discomfort. They hit several roadblocks—applications denied, long waiting lists, unhelpful responses—but Maria remained undeterred. She reminded John that this was just the beginning and that persistence was vital.

They secured a few small victories: a reprieve from eviction and a meeting with a social worker specializing in housing assistance.

Amid this flurry of activity, John found moments of introspection. He thought about his parents, his father's harsh discipline, and his mother's cold detachment. These early experiences had shaped him and made him wary of seeking help and trusting others. But here was Maria, a beacon of kindness, challenging those ingrained beliefs with unwavering support.

The conversation with the social worker was a turning point. The woman was sympathetic but practical, laying out a realistic path forward. She helped them draft a plan that included temporary housing assistance, medical support, and vocational rehabilitation. It wasn't a perfect solution, but it was a start, giving John a tangible goal to work towards.

That night, after Maria left, John sat alone in his apartment, a sense of cautious hope blossoming. The weight of his debt and the specter of his past traumas still loomed large, but he felt a spark of resilience for the first time in a long time. He knew the road ahead would be difficult, filled with setbacks and challenges, but he also knew he wasn't facing it alone.

The days that followed were a blur of activity and emotion. John felt himself oscillating between hope and despair, moments of clarity punctuated by bouts of anxiety. Maria's continued presence was a grounding force, her belief in him a constant reminder that he had value and was worth saving.

One evening, as they reviewed yet another stack of paperwork together, Maria broached a topic that John had been avoiding.

"You should consider therapy again," she said gently. "I

know it's been hard, but having someone to talk to, someone who can help you navigate all of this—it could make a big difference."

John hesitated, the old fears and doubts rising to the surface. Therapy had always felt like an admission of failure, a reminder of his weaknesses. But Maria's words resonated with him, her concern and care evident in her eyes.

"Maybe," he said quietly, the thought taking root. "Maybe I'll give it another try."

Maria smiled, a look of relief washing over her features. "I think that's a great idea, John. One step at a time, right?"

As John nodded, he felt a tentative sense of resolve. The journey ahead would be long and fraught with obstacles, but he was beginning to see that he didn't have to face it alone. With Maria's support and the small victories they'd already achieved, he was starting to believe in the possibility of a future beyond the darkness that had enveloped him for so long.

The following week, John took a step that once seemed impossible: he made an appointment with a therapist. The decision was fraught with anxiety, but Maria's encouragement and the small victories they'd achieved gave him the strength to move forward. Walking into the therapist's office, he felt trepidation and cautious hope.

Dr. Whitaker, a calm and composed woman in her forties, greeted him with a warm smile. Her office was a soothing space, filled with soft lighting and comfortable furniture. John settled into a chair, his heart racing, but Dr. Whitaker's demeanor put him at ease.

"John, it's good to meet you," she began. "Why don't you start by telling me a little about what brought you here?"

John took a deep breath and began to talk, his words halting at first but gradually flowing more freely. He spoke of the accident, the financial struggles, and the crushing weight of his childhood traumas. Dr. Whitaker listened intently, her gaze steady and compassionate, making notes occasionally but never interrupting.

As the sessions progressed, John found himself opening up in ways he hadn't expected. Dr. Whitaker's insightful questions and gentle guidance helped him unpack the layers of pain and fear built up over the years. They delved into the complexities of his relationship with his parents and the unresolved anger and hurt that still festered within him.

One day, during a particularly intense session, John recounted the night of the accident in vivid detail. The therapist's office seemed to fade away as he described the blinding headlights, the terror that gripped him, and the unbearable pain that followed.

"It was like the world stopped," he said, trembling. "Everything slowed down, and all I could think was, 'This is it. This is how I die.' But then, I didn't die. I woke up in the hospital, broken but alive. And I didn't know what to do with that."

Dr. Whitaker nodded, her expression thoughtful. "Survivor's guilt can be a heavy burden to carry, John. It sounds like you've been through so much, and you've had to navigate it all on your own. But you're not alone now."

Those words lingered with John, echoing in his mind as he left the office. He realized that his isolation had been a defense mechanism to protect himself from further hurt. But it had also trapped him in a cycle of despair. Allowing himself to be vulnerable and to seek help was the first step towards breaking free.

As John continued therapy, he noticed subtle changes in his outlook. The overwhelming sense of hopelessness began to lift, replaced by a tentative sense of possibility. He started to reconnect with old friends, reaching out tentatively and finding that many were willing to offer their support.

Maria remained a steadfast presence, and her friendship was a constant source of strength. They spent more time together, sharing meals and discussing their hopes and fears. Maria's laughter was infectious, a reminder that there was still joy in the world.

One afternoon, as they walked through a nearby park, Maria broached a subject on her mind. "John, have you thought about what you want to do moving forward? I mean, beyond just getting through each day?"

John considered her question, a sense of uncertainty mingling with a burgeoning sense of purpose. "I used to love working with my hands," he said slowly. "Before the accident, I was really into woodworking. Maybe I could get back into that."

Maria's eyes lit up. "That's a wonderful idea, John! You're so talented, and doing something you love could be really healing."

Encouraged by her enthusiasm, John decided to take the plunge. He found a community center offering woodworking classes and signed up excitedly and apprehensively. The first class was daunting, and his hands were unsteady as he reacquainted himself with the tools. But as the weeks passed, he found peace in the rhythmic motions, the smell of freshly cut wood a balm to his troubled mind.

Creating something tangible, something beautiful helped ground him in the present. It became a form of therapy, complementing his sessions with Dr. Whitaker. The support he received from Maria and his burgeoning sense of community at the center provided a foundation upon which he could rebuild his life.

As the end of the eighth week approached, John found himself reflecting on the journey he'd undertaken. The weight of his debt and the shadows of his past were still there, but they no longer defined him. He was learning to live with his scars, both physical and emotional, and to find strength in his vulnerability. Most importantly, he was rediscovering a sense of hope. It was fragile, like a young sapling growing amidst the ruins, but it was there. And with the support of his friends, his therapist, and his resilience, John knew he could nurture it into something solid and enduring.

John's days began to take on a new rhythm, each filled with small, meaningful steps forward. His mornings were no longer consumed by dread and despair but were marked by purpose. He would rise early, enjoy a quiet cup of coffee, and prepare for his day anxiously.

Therapy sessions with Dr. Whitaker became a cornerstone of his week, each one offering new insights and helping him navigate the labyrinth of his past traumas. They worked through his lingering fears and anxieties, particularly those rooted in his childhood and the accident. Each breakthrough was a victory, no matter how small, and Dr. Whitaker's unwavering support made all the difference.

Woodworking classes at the community center became a source of solace and joy. The scent of sawdust, the feel of wood beneath his fingers, and the satisfaction of creating something with his hands provided a sense of accomplishment that had been missing from his life for so long. He formed connections with others in the class, people who shared his passion and offered their camaraderie.

One evening, as John sat in his apartment, surrounded by the beginnings of his woodworking projects, he felt a sense of peace. Once a prison of his own making, the apartment slowly transformed into a sanctuary. The walls no longer closed in on him; instead, they offered a safe space where he could heal and grow.

Maria's visits were a highlight of his week. They shared meals, laughter, and long conversations that ranged from the mundane to the profound. Her presence reminded him he wasn't alone and had people who cared about him and believed in his potential.

One day, Maria gave him a set of high-quality woodworking tools. John's eyes widened in amazement as he unwrapped the carefully chosen items, each symbolizing her belief in his talent and future.

"Thank you, Maria," he said, his voice thick with emotion. "This means more to me than you can imagine."

Maria smiled, her eyes shining with warmth. "You deserve it, John. You're doing incredible work, and I can't wait to see what you create."

With newfound determination, John threw himself into his projects. He began crafting functional and artistic pieces, each a testament to his journey of healing and self-discovery. His confidence grew with each completed project, and he even considered selling his work or showcasing it at local art fairs.

As the weeks turned into months, John continued to recover. While still challenging, his financial situation became more manageable thanks to the assistance programs and careful budgeting. He was no longer just surviving; he was beginning to live again.

One exceptionally bright afternoon, John stood in his apartment, admiring a finished piece of furniture—a beautifully crafted wooden table that he'd spent weeks perfecting. It represented more than just his skill; it symbolized his resilience and the progress he'd made.

He felt a profound sense of accomplishment as he traced his fingers over the smooth surface. He recalled the dark days when he felt trapped by his debt and haunted by his past. Those memories were still there, but they no longer had the power to dominate his life. He had found a way to move forward, to carve out a future filled with hope and possibility.

The chapter on financial struggles and overwhelming debt drew a close, but John's story was far from over. He had faced his demons and emerged more robust and determined to build a life he could be proud of. The support of friends like Maria, the guidance of Dr. Whitaker, and his inner strength had brought him to this point.

John felt deeply grateful as the sun set, casting a golden glow over the city. He knew challenges would still be ahead but was ready to face them. With each step forward, he was reclaiming his life, piece by piece, and transforming his pain into something beautiful.

And so, with the weight of debt no longer crushing his spirit, John looked toward the future with renewed hope. He was ready to embrace the possibilities that lay ahead, confident in his ability to overcome whatever obstacles might come his way.

4

A Glimmer of Hope

The transition from surviving to thriving is often a gradual, almost imperceptible process. For John, the journey was marked by small victories, each building on the last, creating a foundation of resilience. His life had shifted from a relentless struggle against the tide of his past to a cautious exploration of the future's possibilities.

John's mornings began with a sense of purpose. He no longer dreaded the alarm clock's buzz but saw it as a signal to start a new day filled with potential. His routine included a healthy breakfast, a walk in the nearby park, and time spent in his small woodworking shop. The space, once cluttered and neglected, had transformed into a sanctuary of creativity and focus.

The rhythmic motions of woodworking provided John with a meditative escape. Each project was a testament to his progress, a tangible reminder of his ability to create and rebuild. He found joy in the scent of freshly cut wood, the hum of his tools, and the satisfaction of a piece well made. His workbench, once a place of frustration, had become a symbol of his recovery.

The support of his friends, especially Maria, was instrumental in this transformation. Maria's unwavering belief in John had been a beacon of hope during his darkest days. Her encouragement and practical assistance had helped him navigate the complexities of his financial situation and emotional recovery. Their friendship, once a lifeline, had evolved into a partnership built on mutual respect and shared goals.

Maria visited regularly, and their conversations often drifted to John's future. "You know, John," she said one evening as they shared a meal, "I think you could turn your woodworking into a business. People would love your work."

John smiled, the idea both exciting and daunting. "I've thought about it," he admitted. "But it feels like such a big step."

Maria's eyes sparkled with enthusiasm. "You've already taken so many big steps. What's one more? Plus, you're not alone in this. We can do it together."

Her words resonated with John, and he began to seriously consider the possibilities. With Maria's help, he researched starting a small business, from marketing to managing finances. The process was overwhelming at times, but Maria's presence provided reassurance.

One of the first steps was creating a portfolio of his work. John spent hours photographing his pieces, carefully selecting the best images to showcase his skills. Maria helped him design a website, and they worked together to write descriptions highlighting the craftsmanship and unique qualities of each item. The finished site was a testament to their hard work and collaboration, a digital storefront for

John's creations.

As the weeks passed, John's confidence grew. He started receiving orders through his website, each one a validation of his efforts. The feedback from customers was overwhelmingly positive, and he began to believe in the possibility of a sustainable future in woodworking.

The sense of accomplishment extended beyond his business. John's sessions with Dr. Whitaker continued to be a source of insight and healing. They delved into the deeper layers of his trauma, exploring the intricate web of memories and emotions that had shaped his life. Dr. Whitaker's compassionate guidance helped John develop coping strategies and build emotional resilience.

One day, during a particularly enlightening session, Dr. Whitaker introduced the concept of post-traumatic growth. "John," she said, her voice thoughtful, "you've shown incredible resilience in the face of adversity. Post-traumatic growth is the idea that people can experience positive change as a result of their struggles. It's about finding meaning and strength in what you've been through."

John considered her words, feeling a spark of recognition. "So, it's not just about surviving. It's about growing because of what I've been through?"

Dr. Whitaker nodded. "Exactly. It's about using your experiences to become stronger and more compassionate. It's clear that you're already on that path."

The idea of post-traumatic growth resonated deeply with John. He began to see his journey not just as a series of hardships but as a transformative process. His past, with all its pain and challenges, had shaped him into a person capable of empathy, creativity, and strength. This shift in perspective was liberating, allowing him to embrace his story with a newfound sense of purpose.

John's relationship with his parents also started to evolve. With Dr. Whitaker's encouragement, he initiated a conversation with them about his childhood and the impact it had on him. It was a difficult and emotional process, but it allowed for a level of honesty and understanding that had been missing for years.

His father, once a figure of fear and intimidation, listened with a mixture of regret and sorrow. "John, I know I wasn't a good father," he admitted, his voice heavy with emotion. "I didn't know how to handle my anger, and I took it out on you. I'm sorry."

John felt a mixture of relief and sadness. "I appreciate that, Dad. It's been hard carrying all of this, but I'm trying to move forward."

His mother's response was more reserved, but she too expressed a desire to rebuild their relationship. "I know I wasn't there for you the way I should have been," she said quietly. "I want to try and make things right."

These conversations were not a cure-all, but they were a significant step towards healing. John's parents began to make more of an effort to support him, and their relationship slowly started to improve. It was a fragile process, but it offered hope for the future.

As John's business grew, so did his sense of community. He became involved with local artisan markets, showcasing his work and connecting with other craftsmen. These interactions provided a sense of belonging and validation, reinforcing the idea that he had something valuable to offer.

One evening, as John prepared for an upcoming market,

Maria stopped by to lend a hand. They worked side by side, arranging his pieces and discussing their plans for the future.

"You know, John," Maria said thoughtfully, "you've come a long way. It's inspiring to see how much you've grown."

John smiled, a sense of pride and gratitude swelling within him. "I couldn't have done it without you, Maria. You've been there every step of the way."

Maria's eyes softened. "We're a team, John. And I'm so proud of you."

Their partnership, built on mutual support and shared dreams, was a cornerstone of John's recovery. With Maria by his side, he felt ready to face whatever challenges lay ahead.

The journey from survival to thriving was not a straight path, but John had learned to navigate its twists and turns with resilience and hope. He was no longer defined by his past but empowered by it, using his experiences to build a future filled with possibility and purpose.

As the market day arrived, John stood at his booth, surrounded by his handcrafted pieces. The sun shone brightly, casting a warm glow over the bustling crowd. He felt a sense of accomplishment and anticipation, ready to share his work with the world.

The day was a success, with many visitors admiring and purchasing his creations. Each sale was a testament to his hard work and perseverance, a tangible reward for his journey. John's heart swelled with pride as he interacted with customers, sharing the stories behind his pieces and connecting with people who appreciated his craft.

As the market wound down, John took a moment to reflect on how far he had come. The weight of his past no longer felt like an anchor dragging him down but like a foundation upon which he could build a new life. The struggles he had faced had forged a resilience and strength that would carry him forward.

John's journey was far from over, but he embraced the future with hope and determination. With the support of his friends, the guidance of his therapist, and his inner strength, he was ready to continue his path of recovery and growth. The market was just the beginning, a stepping stone towards a future filled with promise and possibility.

And so, as the sun set on the market day, John packed up his booth with a sense of fulfillment and optimism. The road ahead might still have its challenges, but he was no longer walking it alone. He had found his way from surviving to thriving, and the possibilities for his future were endless.

5

Reconnecting with Friends and Family

John stood at the edge of the park, nervously shifting from foot to foot. He had spent the morning mentally preparing himself for this moment, the first step in reconnecting with his old friends. His heart raced as he scanned the familiar faces gathered around a picnic table, their laughter and chatter a stark contrast to the turmoil inside him.

It had been years since John had seen them. His struggles had isolated him, and he had distanced himself from everyone, retreating into a solitary existence where the weight of his troubles was his alone to bear. But today was different. Today, he was taking a step towards healing, towards rebuilding the relationships that had once been so important to him.

He took a deep breath and walked towards the group, his palms sweaty with anxiety. As he approached, the laughter died down, and all eyes turned to him. For a moment, there was silence, and John felt the urge to turn and flee. But then, one of his friends, Emily, broke the tension with a warm smile.

"John! It's been too long!" she exclaimed, getting up to give him a hug.

The warmth of her embrace melted some of the tension in John's chest. He returned the hug, feeling a wave of relief. "Yeah, it has. I'm sorry for disappearing on everyone."

Emily pulled back and looked at him, her eyes filled with understanding. "We're just glad you're here now. Come, sit with us."

John took a seat at the table, his presence prompting a chorus of greetings from the others. There was Dave, his old college roommate, whose hearty laugh could lift anyone's spirits. Next to him was Sarah, a childhood friend who had always been the voice of reason in their group. And then there was Mike, a coworker from a previous job, who had shared many a late-night conversation with John about their dreams and fears.

The initial awkwardness soon gave way to easy conversation. They talked about their lives, their jobs, and the little things that had happened over the years. John found himself laughing at Dave's jokes and nodding along to Sarah's stories about her kids. It felt good to be a part of something again, to be surrounded by people who cared about him.

As the afternoon wore on, John felt a sense of belonging that he hadn't experienced in a long time. His friends' acceptance and warmth were a balm to his wounded soul. The fear that they would judge him for his struggles began to fade, replaced by a growing sense of hope.

Emily, sensing that John might be overwhelmed, gently steered the conversation towards lighter topics. "Remember that road trip we took to the beach?" she asked, her eyes sparkling with nostalgia. "We got lost and ended up camping in that weird little town."

John chuckled, the memory surfacing in his mind. "Oh, yeah. That was quite an adventure. I think we spent more time trying to find our way back than actually enjoying the beach."

The group laughed, and John felt a warm glow of contentment. These moments of shared memories and laughter were precious, reminding him of the good times they had shared and the bonds that had not been broken by time and distance.

As the sun began to set, casting a golden hue over the park, the group slowly dispersed. Emily walked with John to his car, her expression thoughtful. "I'm really glad you came today, John. We've missed you."

John nodded, feeling a lump form in his throat. "I've missed you all too. It's just... things have been tough."

Emily placed a hand on his arm, her touch gentle and reassuring. "You don't have to go through it alone. We're here for you, no matter what."

John looked at her, gratitude shining in his eyes. "Thanks, Emily. That means a lot."

As he drove home, John reflected on the day. Reconnecting with his friends had been a significant step towards healing. Their acceptance and support were invaluable, helping him feel less isolated and more hopeful about the future.

Back in his apartment, John felt a sense of calm that had been absent for so long. The darkness that had clung to him for years seemed a little less oppressive, the weight of his struggles a bit lighter. He knew there was still a long road ahead, but the first steps had been taken, and he was not alone on this journey.

The next day, John decided to reach out to his family. It had been even longer since he had spoken to them, and the prospect filled him with a mixture of anxiety and hope. He picked up the phone and dialed his sister's number, his heart pounding in his chest.

"Hello?" came her familiar voice, tinged with surprise.

"Hey, Liz. It's John," he said, his voice trembling slightly.

There was a pause, and then a rush of emotion. "John! Oh my God, it's so good to hear from you! How have you been?"

John took a deep breath, feeling the tightness in his chest begin to ease. "I've been better, Liz. But I'm trying to get back on track. I'd love to catch up if you're free."

Liz's voice was warm and inviting. "Of course, John. Let's meet up this weekend. We have so much to talk about."

As he hung up the phone, John felt a sense of relief. Reaching out to his friends and family was not just about reconnecting; it was about rebuilding the support network that he had once taken for granted. Their presence in his life was a source of strength, helping him face the challenges ahead with renewed determination.

In the weeks that followed, John continued to rebuild these connections. He met with Liz and her family, sharing stories and laughter that reminded him of the importance of family bonds. He reached out to other friends, rekindling old friendships that had been neglected.

Each interaction was a step towards healing, a reminder that he was not alone. His friends and family became his anchors, helping him navigate the turbulent waters of his life. Their support and love were the foundation upon which he could rebuild his life, one step at a time.

John's journey was far from over, but he no longer felt adrift. The darkness that had once consumed him was being replaced by a growing light, fueled by the love and support of those around him. With each day, he felt stronger, more capable of facing the challenges ahead.

As he looked towards the future, John knew there would be more obstacles to overcome. But he also knew he had the strength to face them, backed by the unwavering support of his friends and family. Reconnecting with them had been the first step in a long journey towards healing, and with each step, he moved closer to a brighter, more hopeful future.

John's journey of reconnecting with friends and family had begun to bear fruit. Each interaction, each shared moment, was a step towards healing the fractured bonds that had once been so strong. But rebuilding trust and fostering openness required more than just re-establishing contact; it demanded honesty, vulnerability, and time.

One Saturday afternoon, John sat in his living room, looking through old photo albums. The images were a mix of happy and bittersweet memories, a visual representation of the life he had distanced himself from. Determined to continue rebuilding these connections, he decided to invite some friends over for dinner. It was a small gesture, but one that symbolized his commitment to mending the past.

Emily was the first to arrive, her smile lighting up the room. "Hey, John! Thanks for inviting us over. It's been too long since we all got together like this."

John smiled, feeling a mix of excitement and nervousness. "Yeah, it has. I thought it was time to catch up and spend some quality time together."

As the evening progressed, the atmosphere grew more relaxed. Dave, Sarah, and Mike soon joined them, and the room was filled with the sounds of laughter and conversation. John felt a sense of warmth and belonging, the presence of his friends a comforting reminder of the support he had around him.

At one point, John took a deep breath and decided to share a bit more about his recent struggles. "I want to thank you all for being here tonight. I know I've been distant, and I'm sorry for that. Things have been tough... really tough. But I'm working on getting better, and I'm grateful for your support."

His friends listened intently, their expressions a mix of concern and encouragement. Emily reached out and placed a hand on his arm. "John, you don't have to apologize. We're just glad you're letting us in. We're here for you, no matter what."

Dave nodded, his usually jovial demeanor taking on a serious tone. "We all go through rough patches, John. The important thing is that you're not facing it alone. We've got your back."

Sarah chimed in, her voice gentle. "We care about you, John. And we're proud of you for taking these steps. It's not easy, but you're doing it."

Mike, ever the practical one, added, "If there's anything we can do to help, just let us know. Sometimes, just having someone to talk to can make a big difference."

John felt a surge of gratitude. These were the people who had known him at his best and his worst, and their unwavering support was a lifeline. He nodded, feeling a lump in his throat. "Thank you. It means a lot to me."

The evening continued with more stories and laughter, the bonds of friendship growing stronger with each shared moment. John realized that opening up and being vulnerable was not a sign of weakness, but a step towards healing.

The next day, John decided it was time to visit his sister, Liz, and her family. He hadn't seen them in years, and the thought of facing them filled him with a mix of anxiety and hope. As he drove to her house, he rehearsed what he wanted to say, hoping to bridge the gap that had grown between them.

Liz greeted him at the door with a warm smile and a hug that conveyed all the love and worry she had felt during his absence. "John, it's so good to see you. Come in, come in!"

John stepped inside, the familiar sights and sounds of his sister's home bringing back a flood of memories. Her husband, Tom, was in the kitchen preparing dinner, and their two kids were playing in the living room.

"Uncle John!" they shouted in unison, running to give him hugs. John's heart swelled with emotion. He had missed so much, but he was here now, ready to make amends.

As they sat down to dinner, John took a deep breath and began to speak. "Liz, Tom, I owe you both an apology. I've been distant, and I know I've missed a lot. Things have been really hard, and I didn't want to burden you. But I'm trying to change that."

Liz reached across the table and squeezed his hand. "John, you don't have to go through this alone. We're family, and we love you. Whatever you need, we're here for you."

Tom nodded in agreement. "You're always welcome here, John. Don't ever hesitate to reach out."

Their words were a balm to his soul. He felt a renewed sense of hope and determination. They spent the rest of the evening catching up, sharing stories, and making plans for future visits. The connection he felt with his family was a vital part of his healing process, a reminder that he was not alone in his journey.

Over the next few weeks, John continued to nurture these

relationships. He made it a point to call his friends regularly, to check in and let them know how much their support meant to him. He visited Liz and her family more often, enjoying the simple pleasures of being surrounded by loved ones.

Each interaction, each moment of openness, helped John rebuild his sense of self and purpose. He found that the more he shared, the lighter his burdens felt. His friends and family became his anchors, grounding him in moments of doubt and lifting him in times of despair.

One weekend, as he sat with Liz on her porch, watching the kids play in the yard, John felt a profound sense of peace. "I'm really glad we're reconnecting, Liz. I didn't realize how much I needed this."

Liz smiled, her eyes shining with tears. "Me too, John. You're family, and we've missed you. It's never too late to start again."

John nodded, feeling the truth of her words. It was never too late to rebuild, to heal, and to find hope. With the unwavering support of his friends and family, he knew he could face whatever challenges lay ahead. Their love and acceptance were the foundation upon which he could build a brighter future, one step at a time.

John's efforts to reconnect with his family had begun to show positive results. However, as with any family, the dynamics were complex and fraught with both tension and affection. Over the weeks that followed, John navigated these intricacies, working to rebuild the trust and openness that had once defined his relationships with his sister, Liz, and other family members.

One Saturday morning, John arrived at Liz's house for a family brunch. The smell of pancakes and bacon wafted through the air as he walked in, greeted by the laughter of his niece and nephew. Liz welcomed him with a warm hug, and Tom gave him a friendly pat on the back. It felt good to be included in these family gatherings again.

As they sat around the table, the conversation flowed easily. They talked about work, school, and upcoming plans. John enjoyed the normalcy of it all, the feeling of being part of a family unit. However, beneath the surface, there were unresolved issues that needed to be addressed.

After brunch, Liz and John found themselves alone in the kitchen, washing dishes. Liz glanced at John, her expression serious. "John, I'm really glad you're here. But I think we need to talk about some things. There's a lot we haven't discussed."

John nodded, feeling a knot form in his stomach. He had known this conversation was coming, but it didn't make it any easier. "I know, Liz. I've been avoiding it, but we need to talk."

Liz dried her hands and led John to the living room. They sat on the couch, the atmosphere heavy with unspoken words. "Why did you shut us out for so long?" Liz asked, her voice tinged with hurt. "We were worried sick about you, and you just disappeared."

John sighed, running a hand through his hair. "I didn't want to burden you. I felt like I had to deal with everything on my own. The accident, the financial troubles, everything… it was just too much."

Liz reached out and took John's hand. "We're family, John. We're supposed to help each other through the tough times. You don't have to carry this alone."

John looked down, feeling the weight of his sister's words. "I know, but I was ashamed. I felt like I had failed everyone, and I didn't want you to see me like that."

Liz squeezed his hand, her eyes filled with empathy. "You didn't fail us, John. We all have our struggles. What matters is that you're here now, and you're trying to make things better. That takes a lot of courage."

John felt a wave of emotion wash over him. Liz's acceptance and understanding were like a balm to his wounded spirit. "Thanks, Liz. I'm trying, really. It's just been so hard."

Liz nodded, her expression softening. "I know it has. But you don't have to do it alone anymore. We're here for you, every step of the way."

Their conversation marked a turning point in their relationship. The walls that had been built up over years of silence and distance began to crumble, replaced by a renewed sense of trust and openness. John realized that his family's support was a crucial part of his healing process.

Over the next few weeks, John continued to spend time with Liz and her family. They had dinners together, went on outings, and shared more conversations about their lives. Each interaction helped to rebuild the bond between them, making John feel more connected and supported.

One evening, as they sat on the porch watching the sunset, Tom joined them, bringing a sense of quiet strength to the conversation. "John, I've been thinking," Tom began, his voice steady. "You've come a long way, and I'm proud of you. But I think it's important for you to find a way to move forward, to create a new path for yourself."

John nodded, appreciating Tom's straightforwardness. "I've been thinking about that too. I've started reconnecting with old friends and finding new ways to cope. It's a process, but I'm getting there."

Tom smiled, his eyes reflecting a deep sense of understanding. "That's all we can ask for, John. Just keep moving forward, one step at a time."

The support and encouragement from Liz and Tom were invaluable. They helped John see that he was not alone in his struggles and that he had a network of people who cared about him. This realization gave him the strength to continue working towards his goals and to face the challenges ahead with renewed determination.

John's relationship with his parents was more complicated. His father, a stern man with high expectations, had always been difficult to please. His mother, while more nurturing, often sided with his father, leaving John feeling isolated and misunderstood. Reconnecting with them required patience and a willingness to confront painful memories.

One afternoon, John decided to visit his parents. As he drove to their house, his mind was filled with memories of his childhood—the good times and the bad. He knew this visit would not be easy, but it was necessary for his healing.

His mother greeted him at the door, her eyes lighting up with surprise and joy. "John! It's so good to see you. Come in, come in."

John stepped inside, feeling a mix of anxiety and hope. His father was in the living room, reading the newspaper. He looked up as John entered, his expression unreadable.

"Hi, Dad," John said, trying to keep his voice steady.

His father nodded, folding the newspaper. "John. It's been a while."

They sat in the living room, the air thick with unspoken tension. His mother tried to break the ice with small talk, but John knew they needed to address the underlying issues.

"Dad, Mom, I know I've been distant," John began, his voice shaking slightly. "I've been going through a lot, and I didn't want to burden you. But I realize now that I need your support."

His father's expression softened slightly, and his mother reached out to take his hand. "We've been worried about you, John," she said gently. "We just want to help."

John took a deep breath, feeling a surge of emotion. "I know. I've missed you both, and I want to rebuild our relationship. But we need to talk about some things, about the past."

His father nodded, his eyes reflecting a mix of regret and understanding. "I know I wasn't always the easiest person to live with. I had high expectations, and I pushed you hard. I thought it was what you needed, but maybe I was wrong."

John felt a lump in his throat, the pain of those memories still fresh. "It was tough, Dad. I felt like I could never measure up, like I was always letting you down."

His father looked down, his voice quiet. "I'm sorry, John. I never meant to make you feel that way. I just wanted you to be strong, to succeed."

John nodded, appreciating his father's honesty. "I understand that now. But it's important for me to find my own path, to figure out who I am and what I want."

His mother squeezed his hand, her eyes filled with love. "We're here for you, John. Whatever you need, we'll support you."

The conversation was a turning point, a step towards healing the wounds of the past. John knew there was still work to be done, but the openness and honesty they shared that day laid the foundation for a stronger, more supportive relationship.

In the weeks that followed, John made a conscious effort to spend more time with his parents. They had long talks about their past, their mistakes, and their hopes for the future. Each conversation brought them closer, helping to mend the fractures that had once seemed insurmountable.

John's journey of reconnecting with his family was far from over, but he felt a renewed sense of hope and determination. The support and love of his friends and family were his anchors, grounding him in moments of doubt and lifting him in times of despair. With their help, he knew he could face whatever challenges lay ahead and continue his path towards healing and personal growth.

John's journey of reconnecting with friends and family was progressing, but another crucial element of his healing was the support group meetings he attended regularly. These meetings provided a safe space where he could share his experiences, listen to others, and draw strength from the collective resilience of the group.

The support group met every Wednesday evening in a modest community center. The room was arranged in a circle, fostering an atmosphere of openness and equality. The walls were adorned with motivational posters and artwork created by group members, each piece telling a story of pain, resilience, and hope.

As John entered the room, he was greeted by familiar faces and a few newcomers. Stephanie, the group facilitator, welcomed him with a warm smile. "Good to see you, John. How have you been?"

John smiled back, feeling the comforting familiarity of the group. "I've been doing okay, Stephanie. It's been a journey, but I'm making progress."

Stephanie nodded, her eyes filled with empathy. "That's great to hear. Let's get started, shall we?"

As the group settled in, Stephanie began with a brief introduction for the newcomers. "Welcome, everyone. For those who are new, this is a safe space where we share our experiences and support each other. There's no pressure to speak, but we encourage you to listen and participate when you're ready."

John glanced around the circle, noting the diversity of the group. Each member had a unique story, but they were all united by their struggles and their commitment to healing.

One of the regulars, Dave, was the first to speak. Dave was a burly man in his early fifties with a gruff exterior that masked a deeply empathetic soul. He had served in the military and carried the scars of his experiences. "This week's been tough," Dave began, his voice steady but tinged with emotion. "I've been having a lot of nightmares. But coming here helps. It's good to know I'm not alone."

Maria, a soft-spoken woman in her late thirties, nodded in agreement. Maria had been a nurse during the war and had seen more than her fair share of trauma. Her dark, expressive eyes seemed to hold a universe of emotions. "I've been struggling with anxiety," she admitted. "But volunteering at the local shelter has been a lifeline. It helps me feel connected and useful."

As the discussion continued, John felt a sense of camaraderie and understanding. Each member's story resonated with him, reflecting different facets of his struggles. When it was his turn to speak, he took a deep breath and began to share.

"I've been reconnecting with my friends and family," John

said, his voice steady. "It hasn't been easy, but it's been worth it. There were a lot of unresolved issues and hurt feelings, but opening up and being honest has helped us start to heal."

The group listened attentively, their expressions encouraging. John felt a surge of gratitude for their support and understanding.

"I also want to introduce myself to the newcomers," he continued. "I'm John. I've been dealing with CPTSD from a hit-and-run accident and some difficult childhood experiences. This group has been a lifeline for me, and I'm grateful to be a part of it."

One of the newcomers, a young woman named Rachel, spoke up next. Her voice was tentative but filled with determination. "I'm Rachel. I've been struggling with depression and anxiety. It's been hard to reach out for help, but I'm glad I found this group. Hearing your stories gives me hope."

The group offered Rachel words of encouragement, welcoming her into their circle of support. John felt a sense of pride in being part of such a compassionate and resilient community.

Another newcomer, Ben, a middle-aged man with a weary expression, shared his story. "I've been dealing with the aftermath of a divorce and some financial troubles. It's been a rough road, but I'm trying to find my way forward. Being here, hearing your experiences, makes me feel less alone."

Stephanie guided the discussion with gentle questions and prompts, ensuring everyone had a chance to speak and feel heard. The meeting continued with members sharing their coping strategies, successes, and setbacks.

One of the highlights of the meeting was when Stephanie

introduced a new activity. "Tonight, I'd like us to try something different," she said, her tone encouraging. "We're going to do a grounding exercise. It's a technique that can help you stay present and manage overwhelming emotions."

Stephanie guided the group through the exercise, asking them to focus on their senses—what they could see, hear, touch, smell, and taste. John found the exercise calming, a way to anchor himself in the present moment and quiet the storm of his thoughts.

After the exercise, Stephanie invited the group to share their experiences. John was one of the first to speak. "That was really helpful," he said. "I've been dealing with a lot of anxiety, and this exercise gave me a sense of peace. It's something I can see myself using in my daily life."

Others echoed his sentiments, expressing gratitude for the new tool to add to their coping strategies. The meeting ended on a positive note, with members feeling more connected and supported.

As John left the community center, he reflected on the evening. The support group meetings were more than just a place to share his struggles; they were a source of strength and inspiration. The stories and experiences of others provided him with new perspectives and coping mechanisms, helping him navigate his own journey of healing.

In the weeks that followed, John continued to attend the meetings regularly. He developed deeper connections with the group members, finding solace in their shared experiences. The support group became an integral part of his healing process, offering a sense of belonging and understanding that was invaluable.

Through the support group, John learned the importance

of community and connection. The empathy and encouragement he received from his fellow members helped him see that he was not alone in his struggles. Together, they formed a network of support, each person contributing to the collective resilience of the group.

John's journey was still ongoing, but the support group meetings provided a beacon of hope. With each meeting, he felt more empowered to face his challenges and continue his path towards healing. The stories of his fellow group members were a reminder that, despite the darkness, there was always a glimmer of hope.

John's participation in the support group had been a source of strength and inspiration, but his journey towards healing was also deeply intertwined with his therapy sessions with Dr. Whitaker. These sessions were the cornerstone of his progress, providing him with the tools and insights he needed to navigate his complex emotional landscape.

One Wednesday afternoon, John walked into Dr. Whitaker's office, feeling a mix of anticipation and anxiety. The warm, inviting space had become a sanctuary for him, a place where he could explore his deepest fears and hopes without judgment. Dr. Whitaker greeted him with her usual calm and encouraging demeanor.

"Good to see you, John. How have you been feeling this week?" she asked as they settled into their chairs.

John took a deep breath. "It's been a mix of good and bad days. I've been reconnecting with friends and family, which has been really positive. But I still struggle with anxiety and flashbacks, especially at night."

Dr. Whitaker nodded, her expression thoughtful. "It's a big step to reconnect with loved ones. It sounds like you're making significant progress. Let's talk about the anxiety and flashbacks. Have you been using any of the grounding techniques we discussed?"

John nodded. "Yes, I have. The support group also introduced a grounding exercise that I found really helpful. Focusing on my senses helps me stay present."

"Excellent," Dr. Whitaker said, her voice filled with encouragement. "Grounding techniques are very effective. Let's build on that and explore some additional strategies."

Dr. Whitaker introduced John to cognitive-behavioral techniques to help him identify and challenge negative thought patterns. They worked on recognizing triggers for his anxiety and flashbacks and developing healthier responses. One particularly effective exercise involved writing down his thoughts and feelings, then examining them to find more balanced and rational perspectives.

During one session, they delved deeper into a specific incident that had been haunting John—the night of the hit-and-run accident. Dr. Whitaker gently guided him through the memory, helping him process the emotions associated with it.

"John, I want you to describe what happened that night," she said softly. "Take your time and focus on the details."

John hesitated, his heart pounding. "It was late, and I was walking home from work. The streets were almost empty, and I was lost in my thoughts. Suddenly, I heard a car approaching fast. The next thing I knew, there were headlights blinding me, and I felt this incredible impact."

Dr. Whitaker nodded, encouraging him to continue. "What were you thinking and feeling at that moment?"

"I was terrified," John admitted, his voice trembling. "I

thought I was going to die. Everything happened so fast, and then there was this excruciating pain. I remember lying on the pavement, unable to move, and feeling completely helpless."

As John recounted the experience, tears filled his eyes. Dr. Whitaker handed him a tissue, her expression compassionate. "You went through an incredibly traumatic event, John. It's understandable that you would have these feelings. Let's work on reframing this memory, focusing on your survival and strength."

They spent the next few sessions using Eye Movement Desensitization and Reprocessing (EMDR) therapy to help John process the trauma. This technique involved recalling the traumatic event while simultaneously focusing on external stimuli, such as moving lights or tapping. The goal was to reduce the emotional intensity of the memory and reframe it in a more positive light.

During one EMDR session, John experienced a breakthrough. As he focused on the memory of the accident, he began to see it not just as a moment of terror and pain, but as a testament to his resilience and will to survive.

"I survived," he said aloud, his voice filled with a newfound sense of empowerment. "I went through something horrific, but I came out the other side. I'm stronger than I realized."

Dr. Whitaker smiled, her eyes reflecting pride in his progress. "That's a powerful realization, John. Your strength and resilience are key components of your healing. Keep focusing on those positive aspects."

As the weeks passed, John continued to make significant strides in therapy. He learned to challenge his negative thoughts and replace them with more balanced perspectives. He developed healthier coping mechanisms for dealing with anxiety and flashbacks, such as deep breathing exercises and mindfulness practices.

One particularly impactful session focused on his childhood traumas. Dr. Whitaker helped John explore the lingering effects of his father's harsh discipline and his mother's emotional distance. They discussed how these experiences had shaped his self-perception and contributed to his feelings of inadequacy.

"You've internalized a lot of negative messages from your past," Dr. Whitaker observed. "But those messages don't define you. You have the power to rewrite your narrative and see yourself in a more positive light."

John nodded, feeling a mix of hope and determination. "I've been trying to do that. Reconnecting with my family has helped, and I'm starting to see that I'm not the person my father made me feel like I was."

Dr. Whitaker's guidance was instrumental in helping John navigate these complex emotions. Each session brought new insights and strategies, empowering him to take control of his mental health and well-being.

As John continued his therapy journey, he began to notice positive changes in his daily life. His relationships with friends and family deepened, built on a foundation of trust and openness. He felt more confident in social situations, less haunted by the shadows of his past.

One evening, as he sat with his sister Liz on her porch, John shared some of the breakthroughs he had experienced in therapy. "It's been challenging, but I feel like I'm finally making progress. I'm learning to see myself differently, to appreciate my strengths."

Liz smiled, her eyes filled with pride. "I'm so glad to hear that, John. You've always been strong, even if you didn't see it. I'm proud of you for taking these steps."

John's therapy sessions with Dr. Whitaker continued to be a source of strength and healing. Each breakthrough brought him closer to a place of self-acceptance and peace. The support of his therapist, combined with the love of his friends and family, created a solid foundation for his ongoing journey.

As John looked towards the future, he felt a sense of hope and possibility. He knew there would still be challenges and setbacks, but he also knew he had the tools and support to face them. His therapy sessions had given him the skills to navigate his emotions, and the unwavering support of his loved ones provided the strength he needed to keep moving forward.

John's therapy sessions with Dr. Whitaker and the support from his friends and family had laid a strong foundation for his ongoing journey of self-discovery and personal growth. However, the path to healing was not linear; it was marked by both triumphs and setbacks, each contributing to his evolution.

One sunny morning, John sat in his small but cozy apartment, reflecting on the progress he had made. His living space, once a symbol of his isolation and despair, had transformed into a haven of creativity and comfort. His woodworking projects adorned the shelves, each piece a testament to his resilience and newfound passion.

John decided it was time to take another step towards personal growth. He had always enjoyed nature, finding solace in its tranquility. Inspired by his therapy sessions and the grounding techniques he had learned, he decided to start hiking regularly. The idea of immersing himself in nature, away from the hustle and bustle of the city, appealed to him.

His first hike was a modest trail in a nearby park. As he walked, the sounds of rustling leaves and birdsong filled the air, creating a soothing symphony that calmed his mind. The physical exertion felt good, a reminder of his body's strength and resilience.

At the trail's end, John sat on a large rock, overlooking a serene lake. He took a deep breath, feeling a sense of accomplishment and peace. The hike had been a small but significant victory, a step towards reclaiming his life and finding joy in simple pleasures.

John's commitment to hiking became a regular part of his routine. Each trail he conquered symbolized his progress, both physically and emotionally. The act of moving forward, one step at a time, mirrored his journey of healing.

However, not all days were filled with triumphs. There were moments when John felt the weight of his past pressing down on him, threatening to pull him back into the darkness. On such days, the memories of the accident and his childhood traumas resurfaced with a vengeance, challenging his newfound stability.

One particularly difficult evening, John found himself overwhelmed by flashbacks. He sat in his apartment, his heart racing and his mind spiraling. The coping mechanisms he had learned seemed out of reach, and he felt himself slipping.

In desperation, he called Emily. Her voice, calm and reassuring, was a lifeline. "John, take a deep breath. You're not alone. Remember the grounding techniques we practiced? Let's do them together."

Emily guided him through the exercise, her presence a

steady anchor. Gradually, John's breathing slowed, and the panic subsided. "Thank you, Emily," he said, his voice filled with gratitude. "I don't know what I would do without you."

"You don't have to do this alone, John," Emily replied. "We're all here for you, every step of the way."

This setback was a reminder that healing was a continuous process. John accepted that there would be bad days, but he also recognized the importance of reaching out for support when needed. His friends and family were his pillars, their unwavering support helping him navigate the rough patches.

As time went on, John continued to grow and evolve. He decided to share his woodworking talents with others, offering to teach a class at the community center. The idea of helping others discover the therapeutic benefits of working with their hands excited him.

His first class was a mix of nervousness and excitement. As he demonstrated basic woodworking techniques to a small group of participants, John felt a sense of fulfillment. Teaching allowed him to connect with others in a meaningful way, turning his passion into a source of joy and healing for himself and others.

One evening, after a particularly successful class, John sat down with Dr. Whitaker for another therapy session. "I've been teaching a woodworking class," he said, a smile spreading across his face. "It feels good to share something I love with others."

Dr. Whitaker nodded, her eyes reflecting pride. "That's wonderful, John. Teaching is a powerful way to connect with others and reinforce your own growth. How has it impacted you?"

"It's given me a sense of purpose," John replied. "And it's

helped me see how far I've come. I still have bad days, but I feel stronger, more resilient."

Dr. Whitaker smiled. "You've made incredible progress, John. Remember, personal growth is about embracing both the triumphs and the setbacks. Each experience shapes who you are and brings you closer to your goals."

John left the session feeling inspired and hopeful. His journey was far from over, but he was equipped with the tools and support he needed to continue moving forward.

The culmination of John's growth journey was marked by a significant milestone—a reunion with his extended family. The event was held at his sister Liz's house, bringing together relatives he hadn't seen in years. The prospect of facing them filled him with both excitement and apprehension.

As he walked into the bustling house, filled with laughter and conversation, John took a deep breath. Liz greeted him with a warm hug, her eyes shining with pride. "I'm so glad you're here, John."

John smiled, feeling a surge of gratitude. "Me too, Liz. It's time to reconnect with everyone."

Throughout the evening, John engaged in heartfelt conversations with his relatives, sharing his journey and listening to their stories. The warmth and acceptance he received were overwhelming, reinforcing the importance of family bonds.

One moment stood out above the rest. As he spoke with his father, the man who had once seemed so distant and stern, John felt a shift in their relationship. "I'm proud of you, son," his father said, his voice filled with emotion. "You've shown incredible strength and resilience. I'm sorry for the times I didn't see that."

John felt tears welling up, his heart full. "Thank you, Dad.

That means a lot to me."

The evening was a testament to the power of connection and the possibility of healing old wounds. John realized that his journey had not only transformed him but had also brought his family closer together.

As John drove home that night, he felt a profound sense of peace and fulfillment. His journey towards self-discovery and personal growth was ongoing, but he was no longer defined by his past. He had reclaimed his life, finding strength in his vulnerabilities and joy in his passions.

John's story was one of resilience, hope, and the unwavering support of those who loved him. With each step forward, he embraced both the triumphs and the setbacks, knowing that they were all part of his journey towards a brighter, more fulfilling future.

And so, with the lessons he had learned and the love of his friends and family guiding him, John continued to move forward, one step at a time, towards a life filled with purpose, connection, and hope.

6

Discovering New Passions

John's life had taken a turn for the better with the support of therapy and the reconnection with his friends and family. Yet, it was his discovery of a new passion that truly ignited a sense of purpose and fulfillment within him: woodworking. This creative outlet not only provided a therapeutic escape but also became a meaningful part of his healing journey.

It all started with a simple, rustic bookshelf. One evening, feeling restless and anxious, John decided to take on a project to occupy his mind and hands. He had always been good with his hands, enjoying the tactile satisfaction of creating something from nothing. As he rummaged through his small workshop, he found some leftover wood and decided to build a bookshelf for his apartment.

With each cut of the saw and each drive of the nail, John felt a sense of calm wash over him. The rhythmic motions and the focus required for the task helped quiet his racing thoughts. As he worked, his mind wandered to memories of his grandfather, a skilled carpenter who had taught him the basics of woodworking. Those childhood days spent in his grandfather's workshop had been some of the happiest of his life, filled with the smell of sawdust and the satisfaction of creating something with his own two hands.

When the bookshelf was finally complete, John stepped back and admired his handiwork. It wasn't perfect, but it was his creation—a tangible symbol of his efforts and resilience. Placing the bookshelf in his living room, he felt a surge of pride and accomplishment. It was a small victory, but a significant one in his journey towards healing.

Encouraged by this success, John decided to take on more woodworking projects. He started with simple pieces: a coffee table, a set of shelves, and a few picture frames. Each project allowed him to immerse himself in the process, providing a therapeutic escape from the stress and anxiety that often plagued him.

Woodworking became a form of meditation for John. The act of shaping wood, sanding it to a smooth finish, and assembling the pieces into a cohesive whole required focus and patience. This process mirrored his own journey of piecing together the fragmented parts of his life. As he worked, he found himself reflecting on his experiences, gaining new insights and perspectives.

One day, John decided to create a piece that held deeper meaning. He designed a memory box, a small chest with intricate carvings on the lid. As he worked on the box, he thought about the memories he wanted to keep inside—photos of his family, mementos from his childhood, and letters from friends who had supported him. The process was both cathartic and symbolic, representing his efforts to cherish the positive aspects of his past while moving forward.

As John's skills improved, so did his confidence. He began

experimenting with more complex designs and techniques, pushing the boundaries of his creativity. The satisfaction of completing each project and seeing the tangible results of his efforts was incredibly rewarding. It gave him a sense of purpose and accomplishment that had been missing from his life for so long.

The therapeutic effects of woodworking extended beyond the workshop. John found that the skills he developed— patience, attention to detail, and problem-solving—translated into other areas of his life. He became more mindful and present in his interactions with others, appreciating the small moments and finding joy in everyday activities.

John's newfound passion also became a way to connect with others. He started sharing his projects with friends and family, their positive feedback boosting his self-esteem. His sister Liz was particularly supportive, often visiting his apartment to see his latest creations. They would sit together, admiring his work and discussing new ideas.

One afternoon, as they sat on the porch with a cup of tea, Liz suggested something that sparked a new idea. "John, your woodworking is amazing. Have you thought about teaching others? You have so much talent, and I'm sure there are people who would love to learn from you."

John considered her words, feeling a mix of excitement and apprehension. The idea of teaching others was daunting, but it also offered an opportunity to share his passion and help others discover the therapeutic benefits of woodworking.

Encouraged by Liz's enthusiasm, John decided to take the plunge. He approached the community center where he attended support group meetings and proposed the idea of a woodworking class. The staff was supportive and excited about the new program, and they quickly set up a schedule.

On the first day of the class, John felt a familiar mix of nerves and excitement. He welcomed a small group of participants, each eager to learn and create. As he demonstrated basic techniques and guided them through their first projects, John felt a profound sense of fulfillment. Teaching others not only reinforced his own skills but also provided a way to give back to the community that had supported him.

The class quickly became popular, with more people signing up each week. John's passion and dedication were evident in every lesson, and his students appreciated his patient and encouraging teaching style. He watched with pride as they completed their projects, their faces lighting up with the same sense of accomplishment he had felt.

As the weeks turned into months, John's woodworking class became a cornerstone of his new life. It was more than just a hobby; it was a source of joy, connection, and purpose. The therapeutic effects extended far beyond the workshop, influencing every aspect of his life and helping him build a brighter future.

As John's woodworking projects flourished, he found himself yearning to explore other creative outlets. The therapeutic effects of creating with his hands had opened a new world of possibilities, and he wanted to see what other forms of expression could bring him joy and peace.

One rainy afternoon, while browsing a local bookstore, John stumbled upon a section dedicated to painting. The vibrant colors and expressive brushstrokes on the covers of the books captivated him. He picked up a beginner's guide to watercolor painting, intrigued by the idea of playing with colors and creating something beautiful on a blank canvas.

That evening, John set up a small painting corner in his living room. With a set of watercolors, brushes, and paper, he began his first painting. The process was both challenging and exhilarating. He experimented with different techniques, blending colors, and creating abstract shapes. Each stroke of the brush felt like a release, a way to express emotions that words could not capture.

As he painted, John realized that art, like woodworking, required patience and attention to detail. It was a meditative process, allowing him to focus on the present moment and quiet his mind. The colors and shapes he created were reflections of his inner world, a visual representation of his thoughts and feelings.

Painting quickly became a regular part of John's routine. He found joy in the unpredictability of watercolors, the way the pigments flowed and blended on the paper. Each painting was a new adventure, a chance to explore different aspects of his creativity. He often painted late into the night, losing track of time as he immersed himself in the process.

John's newfound passion for painting also provided another way to connect with his friends and family. He shared his artwork with them, inviting feedback and encouraging them to join him in his creative endeavors. Liz, always supportive, decided to take up painting as well, and they often spent afternoons together, each working on their own projects while sharing tips and techniques.

One weekend, Liz suggested they visit a local art gallery. The experience was inspiring for John. He marveled at the diverse styles and mediums on display, from oil paintings to sculptures and mixed media. The gallery visit sparked new ideas and fueled his desire to experiment with different forms of art.

Back at home, John decided to try his hand at clay sculpting. He purchased some clay and basic tools, eager to explore this new medium. Sculpting proved to be a different kind of challenge, requiring precision and a keen sense of form and texture. As he molded the clay, he felt a deep sense of connection to his work, shaping it into various forms and figures.

John's explorations in art led him to discover another passion: photography. During one of his hikes, he brought along an old camera that had been collecting dust in his closet. Capturing the beauty of nature through the lens was a revelation. The world around him seemed to come alive in new ways, each frame telling a story of its own.

Photography became a way for John to document his journey, capturing moments of beauty and reflection. He created a photo journal, combining his images with personal reflections and poetry. This project became a powerful tool for self-expression and introspection, helping him process his experiences and emotions.

As John's artistic pursuits expanded, so did his sense of fulfillment and well-being. Each new creative outlet provided a unique way to explore his inner world and connect with the world around him. The joy of discovery and the satisfaction of creating something meaningful enriched his life in ways he had never imagined.

The support from his friends and family was instrumental in this journey. They encouraged him to pursue his passions and celebrated his successes. Emily, who had always been a source of strength, became his muse and model for many of his photographs. Her encouragement and belief in his talents gave him the confidence to keep exploring and growing.

John's artistic journey also brought him closer to the community. He joined local art groups and attended workshops, meeting fellow artists who shared his passion. These connections provided a sense of belonging and camaraderie, reinforcing the importance of community in his healing process.

One day, John received an invitation to participate in a local art fair. The prospect of showcasing his work to the public was both exciting and nerve-wracking. With the support of his friends and family, he decided to take the plunge. He selected a collection of his best paintings, sculptures, and photographs, each piece representing a part of his journey.

The art fair was a resounding success. John received positive feedback and appreciation for his work, and he sold several pieces. The experience was a validation of his talents and a testament to the power of creativity in healing and personal growth.

As John packed up his booth at the end of the fair, he felt a deep sense of accomplishment. His journey of self-discovery and creative exploration had brought him to this moment, surrounded by the fruits of his labor and the support of those who believed in him.

Looking back, John realized that discovering new passions had been a pivotal part of his healing journey. Each creative outlet, whether it was woodworking, painting, sculpting, or photography, had provided a way to express himself, find joy, and connect with others. These activities had not only enriched his life but had also helped him build a future filled with hope and possibility.

John's journey of personal growth and self-discovery

through woodworking, painting, and photography had brought immense joy and fulfillment into his life. However, he soon realized that sharing his passions with the broader community could deepen his sense of purpose and connection. Engaging in community activities and events became a new focus, helping him build new relationships and strengthen existing ones.

One of John's first steps into community engagement was through his woodworking class at the community center. The class had become a popular fixture, attracting a diverse group of participants who were eager to learn and create. John found immense satisfaction in teaching, guiding his students through the process of crafting their projects, and watching their skills and confidence grow.

As the class gained popularity, the community center staff approached John with an exciting proposal: to host a woodworking exhibition showcasing the works of his students. The idea thrilled John, and he eagerly accepted the challenge. He saw this as an opportunity to celebrate the creativity and hard work of his students and to bring the community together.

The weeks leading up to the exhibition were filled with bustling activity. John and his students worked tirelessly to prepare their pieces, refining their techniques and adding finishing touches. John also took on the role of curator, organizing the display and ensuring that each piece was presented in the best possible light.

The day of the exhibition arrived, and the community center buzzed with excitement. Friends, family, and community members gathered to admire the woodworking projects on display. John's heart swelled with pride as he watched his students receive praise and recognition for their work. The event was a resounding success, fostering a sense of accomplishment and camaraderie among all involved.

During the exhibition, John struck up a conversation with Rachel, a local artist who had been inspired by the woodworking class. Rachel invited John to participate in an upcoming community art fair, suggesting that he showcase not only his woodworking but also his paintings and photographs. Encouraged by the positive feedback from the exhibition, John agreed.

The community art fair was held in a spacious park, with colorful tents and booths set up under the shade of tall trees. Artists from all walks of life displayed their creations, and the atmosphere was vibrant with creativity and enthusiasm. John set up his booth, displaying a selection of his woodworking pieces, paintings, and photographs. Each piece represented a facet of his journey, a testament to his resilience and artistic exploration.

As visitors browsed his booth, John engaged in conversations about his work and the stories behind each piece. He was amazed by the positive reactions and the genuine interest people showed in his journey. Many visitors shared their own experiences and struggles, finding inspiration in John's story of healing through creativity.

One visitor, a woman named Karen, was particularly moved by John's photographs. She explained that she was a counselor at a local youth center and often worked with teenagers facing various challenges. Karen invited John to speak at the youth center and share his story, hoping that his experiences and creative outlets could inspire the young people she worked with.

John was deeply touched by the invitation and agreed to visit the youth center. A few weeks later, he found himself standing in front of a group of teenagers, sharing his journey of overcoming trauma and discovering new passions. He spoke about the therapeutic effects of woodworking, painting, and photography, encouraging the young audience to explore their own creative interests.

After his talk, John led a hands-on workshop, teaching the teenagers basic woodworking techniques. The energy in the room was infectious, and John felt a deep sense of fulfillment as he watched the young participants immerse themselves in the creative process. The experience reinforced his belief in the power of creativity to heal and transform lives.

John's involvement in community activities continued to expand. He joined local art groups, participated in community clean-up projects, and volunteered at the community center. Each engagement brought new connections and deepened his sense of belonging.

One memorable event was a neighborhood mural project organized by the local art collective. The project aimed to beautify a neglected wall in the community with a vibrant mural that celebrated the area's diversity and resilience. John was excited to contribute, bringing his woodworking skills to create decorative frames and elements that would be incorporated into the mural.

The mural project was a collaborative effort, with artists and residents of all ages coming together to paint, build, and create. As John worked alongside his neighbors, he felt a profound sense of unity and shared purpose. The mural took shape over several weeks, transforming the once-dull wall into a colorful testament to the community's spirit.

The unveiling of the mural was a joyous occasion, attended by local residents, artists, and community leaders. John stood back, admiring the finished piece and reflecting on the journey that had brought him here. The mural symbolized not only the community's resilience but also his own growth and transformation.

Through these community engagements, John built new relationships that enriched his life. He formed friendships with fellow artists, mentors, and neighbors who shared his passion for creativity and community. These connections provided a support network that bolstered his confidence and sense of purpose.

John's journey of self-discovery and personal growth had come full circle. From the depths of trauma and isolation, he had emerged as a resilient and creative individual, using his passions to connect with others and give back to the community. The relationships he built and the experiences he shared reinforced the importance of community and the power of creativity to heal and inspire.

John's journey through woodworking, painting, photography, and community engagement had transformed him in ways he had never imagined. As he sat in his apartment one quiet evening, he reflected on the incredible changes he had experienced over the past months. His life, once dominated by trauma and isolation, had blossomed into a tapestry of creativity, connection, and purpose.

John opened his journal, a habit he had picked up in therapy, and began to write. The act of putting pen to paper allowed him to process his thoughts and emotions, providing clarity and insight. As he wrote, he reflected on the key moments of his journey:

- **Therapy and Support**: The foundation of John's healing had been laid in his therapy sessions with Dr. Whitaker and the unwavering support of his friends and family. They had helped him confront his past, manage his anxiety, and build healthier coping mechanisms. The support group meetings had provided a safe space to share his struggles and find solace in the experiences of others.
- **Discovering Woodworking**: What started as a simple project to occupy his mind had grown into a profound passion. Woodworking had taught John patience, precision, and the joy of creation. It had become a therapeutic outlet, allowing him to channel his emotions into tangible works of art.
- **Exploring Art**: Painting and photography had opened new avenues for self-expression. The vibrant colors of his watercolors and the captured moments in his photographs were reflections of his inner world. These creative pursuits had enriched his life, bringing joy and a sense of accomplishment.
- **Community Engagement**: By teaching woodworking, participating in art fairs, and volunteering, John had found a deeper sense of purpose. These activities had connected him with others, fostering new relationships and reinforcing his belief in the power of community.

John closed his journal and looked around his apartment, filled with the fruits of his labor—wooden furniture, paintings, and photographs that told the story of his journey. Each piece represented a step towards healing and growth, a testament to his resilience.

As he looked to the future, John felt a mix of excitement and anticipation. He had come a long way, but he knew his journey was far from over. There were still challenges to face and new horizons to explore. Yet, he felt ready, equipped with the tools and support needed to navigate whatever lay ahead.

John's plans for the future were filled with hope and ambition:

1. **Expanding His Teaching**: Inspired by the success of his woodworking class, John planned to offer more workshops and classes, possibly branching out into painting and photography. Teaching others had been incredibly fulfilling, and he wanted to share the therapeutic benefits of creativity with as many people as possible.

2. **Community Projects**: John was eager to continue his involvement in community projects. He envisioned organizing more collaborative art initiatives, like the mural project, to bring people together and beautify the neighborhood. These projects not only enriched the community but also strengthened the bonds between its members.

3. **Personal Growth**: John was committed to ongoing personal growth. He planned to continue his therapy sessions with Dr. Whitaker, using them as a space to reflect on his progress and address any new challenges that arose. He also intended to keep exploring new hobbies and creative outlets, embracing the joy of discovery.

4. **Sharing His Story**: John realized that his journey could inspire others. He contemplated writing a memoir or starting a blog to share his experiences and the lessons he had learned. By being open about his struggles and

triumphs, he hoped to encourage others facing similar challenges to seek help and find their own paths to healing.

As John reflected on these plans, he felt a profound sense of gratitude. He was grateful for the support of his friends and family, the guidance of his therapist, and the strength he had found within himself. His journey had been difficult, but it had also been filled with moments of beauty and connection.

The evening sky outside his window was painted with hues of orange and pink, a reminder of the ever-changing nature of life. John stepped onto his balcony, taking in the serene view. He felt a sense of peace and fulfillment, knowing that he had transformed his life through creativity, community, and resilience.

With a deep breath, John made a silent promise to himself: to continue growing, to keep creating, and to always cherish the connections that had brought him this far. His journey was a testament to the power of healing and the endless possibilities that lay ahead.

John's story was one of transformation—an evolution from pain and isolation to joy and connection. It was a journey marked by the discovery of new passions, the rebuilding of relationships, and the unwavering support of a community that believed in him. As he looked towards the future, he carried with him the lessons of the past and the hope of new beginnings.

And so, with his heart full of gratitude and his spirit resilient, John stepped forward into the next chapter of his life, ready to embrace whatever came his way with creativity, courage, and an open heart.

7

Support Group Dynamics

The support group had become a cornerstone of John's healing journey, a place where he found understanding, empathy, and a sense of belonging. Each meeting brought together a diverse group of individuals, each with their own stories of struggle and resilience. As John became more involved, he learned about the lives of his fellow members, and he saw how their collective healing process unfolded.

One Wednesday evening, as John entered the community center's meeting room, he felt the familiar warmth and camaraderie that characterized these gatherings. Stephanie, the group facilitator, welcomed everyone with her usual grace and warmth. "Welcome, everyone. It's good to see you all here. Let's begin by checking in with each other."

The group settled into their chairs, forming a circle that invited openness and connection. Stephanie started by introducing two new members. "We have a few new faces tonight. Please welcome Thomas and Lila. Thomas is a retired firefighter, and Lila is an elementary school teacher. Would you both like to share a bit about yourselves?"

Thomas, a tall man with a rugged appearance, spoke first. His voice was steady but carried a hint of vulnerability. "I'm Thomas. I retired a few years ago after serving as a firefighter for over two decades. I've been struggling with PTSD and trying to find ways to cope. This group seems like a good place to start."

The group welcomed Thomas with encouraging nods and smiles, appreciating his courage in sharing his story.

Next, Lila introduced herself. She was a petite woman with kind eyes and a gentle demeanor. "Hi, I'm Lila. I teach first grade, and I've been dealing with anxiety and depression for a while. It's been challenging, especially trying to stay strong for my students. I'm hoping this group can help me find some balance."

Stephanie thanked them both for their introductions and then turned to the rest of the group. "Let's go around and do our usual check-in. Share something about your week, how you've been feeling, or anything else you'd like to talk about."

John listened as each member shared their updates. Dave, the veteran, talked about his ongoing battle with nightmares but also mentioned a new hobby he had taken up—gardening—which had brought him some peace. Maria, the nurse, spoke about her volunteer work at the shelter and how it helped her feel connected and purposeful.

When it was John's turn, he shared his recent experiences with his woodworking class and his exploration of painting and photography. "I've been finding a lot of joy in creating art. It's been therapeutic, and I've even started teaching a woodworking class at the community center. It feels good to give back and share something I'm passionate about."

The group responded with words of encouragement and

support, reinforcing the positive impact of John's journey on his well-being.

As the check-in continued, other members shared their stories:

- **Ben**, a middle-aged man dealing with the aftermath of a difficult divorce, talked about his progress in setting boundaries and rebuilding his life. He mentioned how attending the support group had helped him feel less alone and more hopeful about the future.
- **Rachel**, the young woman who had joined a few months ago, spoke about her ongoing struggles with depression but also highlighted the small victories she had achieved, like getting out of bed and going for a walk each day. She credited the group's support with helping her find the strength to keep going.
- **Karen**, a single mother juggling work and raising two children, shared her challenges in balancing her responsibilities while managing her anxiety. She expressed gratitude for the group's understanding and the practical advice they offered.

Stephanie then guided the group through a discussion about coping strategies. "Tonight, let's focus on the different ways we cope with our struggles. What techniques have you found helpful, and what are some new things you'd like to try?"

The conversation flowed naturally as members shared their coping mechanisms. Dave talked about how gardening had become a form of meditation for him, providing a sense of tranquility and accomplishment. Maria mentioned how volunteering gave her a sense of purpose and connection, helping her combat feelings of isolation.

Thomas, the new member, listened intently, absorbing the wisdom and experiences of the group. When it was his turn, he hesitated before speaking. "I've always been used to being the strong one, the one who helps others. It's hard for me to ask for help or admit that I'm struggling. But hearing all of you share your stories makes me realize that it's okay to be vulnerable."

Lila nodded in agreement. "I feel the same way. Teaching requires so much emotional energy, and I often feel like I have to keep it all together for my students. But I'm learning that taking care of myself is just as important."

Stephanie smiled, her eyes filled with empathy. "It's true. Self-care is crucial, and it's something we all need to prioritize. Remember, it's not a sign of weakness to ask for help or to take time for yourself. It's a sign of strength and self-awareness."

As the meeting continued, the group delved deeper into the various coping strategies they used. Some members mentioned mindfulness practices, like meditation and deep breathing exercises, while others talked about the benefits of physical activity, such as yoga and hiking.

John shared his experience with woodworking and how it had become a meditative practice for him. "When I'm working with wood, I feel completely present. The focus and attention to detail required help quiet my mind and bring a sense of peace."

Rachel spoke about her recent exploration of journaling. "Writing down my thoughts and feelings has been really helpful. It's like a release, a way to get everything out of my head and onto paper. Plus, it's something I can do whenever I need to, which is comforting."

Ben mentioned the support he found in online communities and forums. "There are some great online spaces where people share their experiences and offer advice. It's nice to connect with others who understand what I'm going through, even if we've never met in person."

The discussion was rich with insights and shared experiences, creating a sense of solidarity among the group members. As the meeting drew to a close, Stephanie encouraged everyone to continue exploring new coping strategies and to lean on each other for support.

"Remember, we're all in this together," she said. "Each of you brings something unique to this group, and your presence and participation make a difference. Let's keep supporting each other and finding new ways to heal and grow."

As the group dispersed, John felt a deep sense of gratitude for the collective healing process he was a part of. The support group had become a lifeline, offering a space where he could share his journey and draw strength from the resilience of others.

Walking home that evening, John reflected on the stories and experiences shared during the meeting. The connections he had formed with the group members were invaluable, each person contributing to the tapestry of healing and support. Together, they navigated the complexities of their struggles, finding hope and strength in their shared journey.

As the support group meetings progressed, John found himself forming deeper connections with several members. These relationships became an integral part of his healing process, providing mutual support and understanding that was invaluable. Each member brought their unique perspectives and experiences, enriching the group's collective journey.

One evening, after a particularly intense meeting, John lingered in the community center's hallway, gathering his thoughts. Maria, the nurse, approached him with a warm smile. "John, you did great today. Your story about teaching woodworking really resonated with me."

John smiled back, grateful for her kind words. "Thanks, Maria. It helps to share. I always find your stories about volunteering so inspiring. You give so much of yourself."

Maria nodded. "It's my way of coping, I suppose. Helping others makes me feel connected and purposeful. Do you want to grab a coffee and chat more about it?"

John agreed, and they headed to a nearby café. Over steaming mugs of coffee, they shared more about their lives outside the support group. Maria talked about her experiences as a nurse and how volunteering at the shelter helped her process her own trauma. John spoke about his woodworking classes and the sense of fulfillment he found in teaching.

Their conversation flowed easily, and John felt a growing sense of camaraderie with Maria. They agreed to make their coffee chats a regular occurrence, finding comfort and strength in each other's company. These meetings became a source of encouragement, a space where they could share their victories and struggles with someone who truly understood.

Similarly, John developed a strong bond with Thomas, the retired firefighter. Thomas had initially been reserved, but over time, he opened up about his experiences. One evening, after a meeting focused on coping strategies, Thomas approached John.

"Hey, John," Thomas began, "I was really moved by what

you said about finding peace in woodworking. I used to do a bit of wood carving myself, years ago. Maybe we could work on something together?"

John was thrilled at the idea. "I'd love that, Thomas. It would be great to collaborate on a project. How about we meet at the community center's workshop next Saturday?"

Thomas agreed, and their woodworking sessions became a regular part of their routine. As they worked side by side, they shared stories and insights, each piece of wood becoming a symbol of their healing process. Thomas found solace in the rhythmic motions of carving, and John appreciated the opportunity to bond over a shared passion.

Rachel, the young woman struggling with depression, also became a close friend. One afternoon, John noticed Rachel sitting alone in the park, looking lost in thought. He approached her gently. "Hey, Rachel. Mind if I join you?"

Rachel looked up, a small smile playing on her lips. "Of course, John. I could use some company."

They sat together, watching the children play and the leaves rustle in the breeze. Rachel spoke about her ongoing battle with depression and the small steps she was taking to manage it. John shared his own struggles and how the support group had been a lifeline for him.

"You know," Rachel said, "I've been thinking about trying something new, maybe joining your woodworking class. It sounds therapeutic, and I could use a creative outlet."

John's face lit up with enthusiasm. "I'd love to have you in the class, Rachel. It's a great way to focus your mind and create something beautiful. Plus, the community we've built there is really supportive."

Rachel decided to give it a try, and she quickly became

91

an enthusiastic participant in the woodworking class. The creative process helped her channel her emotions, and the sense of accomplishment she felt with each completed project was a boost to her self-esteem. John and Rachel's friendship deepened as they supported each other both in and out of the workshop.

Meanwhile, Ben, the man dealing with a difficult divorce, and Karen, the single mother, found solace in sharing their parenting experiences. They often exchanged advice and tips on balancing responsibilities while managing their mental health. One evening, after a particularly emotional group session, Ben suggested they organize a family day for the support group members and their children.

"It would be great for us to spend time together outside of these meetings," Ben said. "Our kids can play, and we can relax and enjoy each other's company."

The idea was met with enthusiasm, and a few weeks later, the group gathered at a local park for a picnic. The atmosphere was filled with laughter and joy as children played games and adults chatted and shared stories. John watched as the group members connected on a deeper level, their bonds strengthening with each interaction.

During the picnic, John found a quiet moment to speak with Thomas. "It's incredible how close we've all become," John said, looking around at the smiling faces. "I never imagined finding such a supportive community."

Thomas nodded, his expression thoughtful. "Yeah, it's been a lifeline for me too. It's amazing how sharing our stories and struggles brings us together. We all have different backgrounds, but we're united in our journey towards healing."

The relationships John had formed within the support

group were transformative. Each member contributed to his growth, offering different perspectives and insights. The collective healing process was powerful, creating a network of support that extended beyond the weekly meetings.

As John reflected on these deepening connections, he felt a profound sense of gratitude. The support group had not only helped him navigate his own challenges but had also allowed him to be a part of others' healing journeys. Together, they had created a community where vulnerability was met with compassion, and each step forward was celebrated.

The support group's strength lay not only in the sharing of stories but also in the various activities and workshops that fostered a sense of community and empowerment. These activities brought members closer together, providing them with practical tools for coping and opportunities to bond over shared experiences.

One of the most impactful activities organized by Stephanie was a mindfulness and meditation workshop. Held on a crisp Saturday morning, the workshop took place in a serene park with tall trees and a gentle stream flowing nearby. The setting itself was calming, providing the perfect backdrop for a day dedicated to inner peace and reflection.

As the group gathered on yoga mats and blankets, Stephanie introduced the session. "Today, we're going to focus on mindfulness and meditation. These practices can help us manage stress, stay grounded, and connect with our inner selves. Let's start with a simple breathing exercise."

The group followed Stephanie's guidance, closing their eyes and taking deep, deliberate breaths. The sound of the stream and the rustling leaves added to the atmosphere of tranquility. John found himself relaxing, the usual tension in his shoulders melting away. As they moved through different meditation techniques, including body scans and guided imagery, John felt a deep sense of calm and clarity.

After the meditation session, the group gathered in a circle to share their experiences. Rachel, who had been struggling with anxiety, spoke first. "I've never felt so relaxed in my life. The guided imagery exercise was especially powerful. I felt like I was truly in a safe, peaceful place."

Thomas agreed. "It's amazing how something as simple as breathing can have such a profound effect. I'm definitely going to incorporate these practices into my daily routine."

The mindfulness workshop was a resounding success, leaving everyone feeling refreshed and centered. Stephanie encouraged the group to continue practicing mindfulness at home, providing resources and suggestions for integrating it into their daily lives.

Another popular activity was the art therapy workshop, which combined creativity with healing. Held at the community center, the workshop featured various art supplies, including paints, clay, and collage materials. The group members were invited to express their emotions and experiences through art, guided by a local art therapist named Elena.

Elena started the session by explaining the therapeutic benefits of art. "Art allows us to express feelings that might be difficult to put into words. It's a way to process emotions and experiences in a safe and supportive environment. There's no right or wrong in art therapy—just creativity and self-expression."

The group eagerly dived into their projects, each member choosing a medium that resonated with them. John decided to work with clay, shaping it into abstract forms that represented his journey. He found the tactile nature of clay soothing, a reminder of his woodworking.

Rachel chose to paint, creating a vibrant canvas filled with swirling colors and shapes. "This is my way of expressing the chaos and hope I feel," she explained. "Each color represents a different emotion."

Maria and Karen worked on a collage together, cutting out images and words from magazines that reflected their experiences and aspirations. As they glued the pieces onto a large poster board, they chatted about their lives and the support they found in the group.

The art therapy session was filled with laughter, conversation, and moments of quiet introspection. At the end of the workshop, Elena invited everyone to share their creations and the meaning behind them. John felt a sense of pride and vulnerability as he explained his clay sculptures, and he was moved by the creativity and depth of the other members' artwork.

In addition to these workshops, the group also organized outdoor activities that combined physical exercise with social bonding. One of the favorite events was a hiking trip to a nearby nature reserve. John, who had discovered a love for hiking, was particularly excited about this outing.

The group met early in the morning, equipped with backpacks, water bottles, and a sense of adventure. The trail wound through lush forests, alongside sparkling streams, and up gentle hills that offered breathtaking views. As they hiked, the group members chatted and laughed, the natural surroundings providing a perfect backdrop for their conversations.

Thomas, who had been a bit reserved during the support

group meetings, opened up during the hike. "Being out here reminds me of the wilderness training we did as firefighters. It's therapeutic in its own way. I'm glad we're doing this together."

John nodded, feeling the camaraderie that had developed within the group. "It's amazing how nature can heal. I've found so much peace in hiking. It's great to share that with all of you."

As they reached the summit, the group took a break to enjoy the view and share a picnic. The sense of accomplishment and the beauty of the landscape filled everyone with a sense of joy and connection. Stephanie led a brief reflection exercise, encouraging everyone to share their thoughts on the hike and their journey with the support group.

Rachel spoke about the strength she drew from the group. "Every time we meet, I feel more empowered to face my challenges. Today's hike was a reminder that we're all on this journey together, and we're stronger because of it."

These activities and workshops played a crucial role in the collective healing process. They provided opportunities for the group members to explore new coping mechanisms, express themselves creatively, and build deeper connections. The sense of community and empowerment that emerged from these experiences reinforced the group's bond and supported their individual healing journeys.

John's involvement in these activities also deepened his relationships within the group. He found that sharing these experiences created lasting memories and fostered a sense of trust and solidarity. Each workshop and outing added another layer to their collective story, bringing them closer together.

As the group continued to explore new activities and workshops, they discovered the power of shared experiences. Whether through mindfulness, art, or nature, these activities enriched their lives and supported their healing in profound ways. The sense of community and empowerment that emerged from these experiences was a testament to the strength and resilience of the group, each member contributing to the collective journey of healing and growth.

Despite the progress made and the positive experiences shared, the journey of healing was not without its setbacks and challenges. The support group faced these obstacles together, finding strength in their collective resilience and growth. Each member encountered difficult moments, and it was the unwavering support of the group that helped them navigate these tough times.

One evening, the mood in the support group was somber. Rachel, who had been making significant strides in managing her depression, arrived looking particularly distressed. Her usually bright demeanor was overshadowed by a palpable sadness. As the group settled in, Stephanie gently addressed Rachel.

"Rachel, would you like to share what's been going on?" Stephanie asked, her voice filled with compassion.

Rachel took a deep breath, her eyes welling up with tears. "I've had a really tough week. My anxiety and depression have been overwhelming, and I've been struggling to get out of bed. I feel like all the progress I've made has just slipped away."

The group listened intently, their faces reflecting empathy and concern. John felt a pang of sadness for his friend, knowing how hard she had worked to overcome her challenges. He reached out, placing a comforting hand on her shoulder.

"Rachel, I'm so sorry you're going through this," John said softly. "Remember, setbacks are a part of the healing process. You've come so far, and we're all here to support you."

Thomas, who had been quiet, spoke up next. "Rachel, I've been there too. Sometimes it feels like you're taking one step forward and two steps back. But it's important to remember that even in those moments, you're still moving forward. We've got your back."

The group offered words of encouragement, sharing their own experiences with setbacks and how they had managed to overcome them. Maria suggested that Rachel revisit some of the coping strategies they had learned, such as mindfulness and journaling. Karen offered to accompany Rachel on walks, emphasizing the importance of staying active and connected.

Rachel wiped away her tears, visibly moved by the outpouring of support. "Thank you, everyone. It's comforting to know I'm not alone. I'll try to remember that this is just a temporary setback."

The group's collective support helped Rachel regain her footing, reminding her of her inner strength and resilience. Over the following weeks, she gradually found her way back to a more stable emotional state, bolstered by the unwavering encouragement of her friends.

Another challenging moment came when Ben faced a crisis with his ex-spouse over custody arrangements for their children. The stress of the situation had reignited his feelings of anger and helplessness, threatening to undo the progress he had made.

During one meeting, Ben shared his frustrations with the group. "I feel like I'm back at square one. The custody battle is taking a toll on me, and I'm struggling to keep my emotions in check. I don't know how much more I can take."

Stephanie guided the group in offering practical advice and emotional support. John, who had developed a strong bond with Ben, suggested focusing on self-care and setting boundaries to protect his mental health.

"Ben, it's crucial to take care of yourself during this time," John advised. "Lean on us for support, and don't be afraid to ask for help. Remember, you're not alone in this."

Maria chimed in, emphasizing the importance of seeking legal advice and ensuring that Ben's rights were protected. "It might help to talk to a lawyer who specializes in family law. Having someone knowledgeable on your side can make a big difference."

The group rallied around Ben, offering resources and support to help him navigate the legal and emotional challenges. Their collective resilience and practical assistance provided Ben with the strength to face the situation head-on.

In another instance, Thomas experienced a severe PTSD episode triggered by a loud noise at a community event. The incident brought back traumatic memories from his time as a firefighter, leaving him shaken and withdrawn. During the next support group meeting, he reluctantly shared his experience.

"It was like I was back there, in the middle of a fire. The noise just set me off, and I couldn't control my reaction," Thomas admitted, his voice filled with frustration and vulnerability.

The group responded with empathy and understanding, reassuring Thomas that his reaction was a natural response to his trauma. John shared his own experiences with triggers, explaining how he had learned to manage them over time.

"Thomas, it's okay to feel this way. It doesn't mean you're weak or that you haven't made progress," John said. "We all have triggers, and it's a part of the healing process to learn how to cope with them. We're here for you."

Stephanie suggested revisiting some grounding techniques that could help Thomas manage his PTSD episodes. She guided the group through a series of exercises, emphasizing the importance of staying present and focused on the here and now.

The group's support and the practical tools provided by Stephanie helped Thomas regain a sense of control. He felt reassured knowing that he had a network of friends who understood his struggles and were there to support him unconditionally.

As the group continued to face various setbacks, they found strength in their collective resilience. Each challenge brought them closer together, reinforcing the bonds of trust and solidarity. They learned to lean on each other, drawing on their shared experiences and the wisdom they had gained through their journey.

One of the most powerful moments of collective resilience occurred when the group decided to organize a charity event to raise awareness about mental health. The event, a community walkathon, aimed to bring people together and highlight the importance of support and understanding for those struggling with mental health issues.

The planning and execution of the walkathon required collaboration, creativity, and determination. Each group member took on a role, contributing their unique skills and talents. John helped design promotional materials, Maria coordinated with local businesses for sponsorships, and Thomas led the logistics team, ensuring everything ran smoothly.

On the day of the walkathon, the community came out in full force, showing their support for the cause. The event was a resounding success, raising funds and awareness for mental health initiatives. As the group walked together, surrounded by friends, family, and community members, they felt a deep sense of accomplishment and unity.

The walkathon was a testament to the power of collective resilience and the impact of community support. It reinforced the importance of coming together in the face of adversity and highlighted the incredible strength that could be found in shared experiences.

Through these moments of overcoming setbacks together, the support group members developed a profound sense of trust and solidarity. They learned that while individual resilience was essential, their collective strength was even more powerful. By supporting each other through the ups and downs, they created a foundation of mutual understanding and compassion that would carry them forward on their journey of healing and growth.

As the support group members continued their journeys of healing and growth, they recognized the importance of celebrating their milestones. These moments of achievement, both big and small, were testaments to their resilience and progress. Reflecting on their successes helped them stay motivated and hopeful about the future.

One evening, Stephanie suggested that the group dedicate a session to celebrating their accomplishments. "It's important to acknowledge how far we've come," she said. "Let's take some time tonight to share and celebrate our milestones."

The room buzzed with excitement as each member prepared to share their achievements. John felt a sense of anticipation, eager to hear about his friends' progress and to reflect on his own journey.

Rachel was the first to speak. "I've been able to manage my depression much better these past few months," she said with a proud smile. "I've been consistent with my therapy, and I've even started a blog to share my experiences and connect with others who are going through similar struggles."

The group applauded Rachel's bravery and dedication. Her blog had already gained a small following, and she was receiving positive feedback from readers who found comfort and inspiration in her words.

Next, Thomas shared his milestone. "I've been using the grounding techniques we learned, and they've made a huge difference. I've had fewer PTSD episodes, and when they do happen, I feel more in control. Also, I've completed a woodworking project with John, and it's been incredibly therapeutic."

John smiled, feeling proud of Thomas's progress. Their collaboration had strengthened their bond and provided a creative outlet for both of them.

Maria then took her turn. "I've continued volunteering at the shelter, and I've started a support group for the residents. Seeing them find hope and strength in each other has been incredibly rewarding. And I've learned so much from all of you, which I'm now able to pass on to others."

Karen shared her milestone next. "I've managed to find a better balance between work, parenting, and self-care. I've started taking yoga classes, and it's helped me manage my anxiety. The kids and I also have regular family game nights now, which has brought us closer together."

Ben spoke about his custody battle. "It's been tough, but with your support, I've been able to handle it better. I found a great lawyer who's helping me, and I'm making sure to take care of myself through this process. The group has been my rock."

Finally, it was John's turn. He took a deep breath and began. "I've discovered so much about myself through woodworking, painting, and photography. Teaching classes and participating in community projects have given me a sense of purpose. And I've formed incredible friendships with all of you, which has been the most meaningful part of my journey."

The group erupted in applause, celebrating John's achievements and the progress each member had made. Stephanie beamed with pride. "You've all come so far. It's inspiring to see how you've supported each other and grown together. Let's keep this momentum going as we look towards the future."

As the celebration continued, the group shared their hopes and plans for the future. Rachel talked about expanding her blog and potentially turning it into a book. Thomas expressed interest in starting a woodworking club for veterans, providing them with a creative and supportive space. Maria planned to further develop her support group at the shelter and organize more community events.

Karen was excited about pursuing further yoga training and possibly becoming an instructor to help others manage their anxiety. Ben looked forward to resolving his custody battle and focusing on building a stable and nurturing environment for his children.

John felt a renewed sense of purpose as he listened to his friends' aspirations. He shared his plans to host more art and woodworking workshops, to continue his personal creative projects, and to explore new ways of giving back to the community.

Stephanie encouraged everyone to stay connected and continue supporting each other. "Healing is a lifelong journey, and it's important to have a strong support network. Remember that we're all in this together."

As the meeting drew to a close, the group members exchanged hugs and words of encouragement. They left the community center that evening with a sense of accomplishment and optimism, ready to face whatever challenges lay ahead.

The journey of healing and growth had brought the support group members closer together, forging bonds that would last a lifetime. They had learned that, while setbacks were inevitable, their collective resilience and support could help them overcome any obstacle.

Looking ahead, John felt a profound sense of gratitude and hope. The support group had been a lifeline, guiding him through the darkest times and helping him discover his passions and purpose. With the unwavering support of his friends and the lessons he had learned, he was ready to embrace the future.

John's journey was a testament to the power of community, creativity, and resilience. As he stepped into the next chapter of his life, he carried with him the knowledge that healing was not a destination but a continuous process. And with each step forward, he was not alone but surrounded by a community of friends who shared his journey.

The support group's story was one of transformation and hope, a reminder that even in the face of adversity, there was always a path to healing and growth. Together, they had created a space of empathy, understanding, and empowerment—a sanctuary where they could all thrive.

And so, as the stars twinkled above and the night enveloped the city, John and his friends looked towards the future with optimism and determination. Their collective journey had just begun, and they were ready to embrace it with open hearts and minds, knowing that, together, they could overcome anything.

8

The Shadows Grow

John's descent into darkness was gradual, a slow unraveling of his sanity that began with subtle whispers and fleeting shadows. Initially, he dismissed them as remnants of his overactive imagination, mere phantoms conjured by stress and fatigue. But as days turned into weeks, these manifestations of his Shadow Self grew bolder, their presence in his mind more pronounced and impossible to ignore.

It started with a shadowy figure lurking at the edge of his vision, a dark silhouette that seemed to follow him everywhere. At night, as he lay in bed, it would stand at the foot of his mattress, watching him with hollow eyes. During the day, it would appear in reflections, in the glass of his office window, or the bathroom mirror. The figure never spoke, but its silent presence was a constant reminder of the darkness within him.

John's dreams, too, were invaded by these manifestations. They twisted into vivid nightmares that left him waking in a cold sweat, his heart pounding in his chest. In these dreams, the shadowy figure would loom over him, its form shifting and writhing like a mass of black smoke. It would reach out with long, clawed fingers, whispering incomprehensible words that filled him with dread and despair.

As the manifestations became more vivid, John found it increasingly difficult to distinguish between reality and illusion. He would see the shadowy figure in broad daylight, standing in his living room or the corner of his office. He would hear its whispers in the quiet moments of his day, a constant murmur at the back of his mind. The lines between his waking hours and his nightmares blurred, leaving him in a perpetual state of unease.

At work, John's performance began to suffer. He struggled to concentrate, his mind preoccupied with the shadowy figure that haunted him. His co-workers noticed his change, the way he would startle at the slightest sound or stare off into space. They offered words of concern and support, but John found it difficult to connect. The isolation he felt was suffocating, a heavy weight that pressed down on his chest and made it hard to breathe.

Even his relationship with Mark began to strain under the pressure. Mark, the supportive friend, noticed the toll the manifestations were taking on John. He would often find John staring at something only he could see, his eyes wide with fear. Mark tried to be there for him, to offer a shoulder to lean on, but John couldn't bring himself to explain the horrors that plagued him. How could he describe the shadowy figure that followed him everywhere, the whispers that filled his mind with dread? How could he make Mark understand the depths of his despair when he barely understood it himself?

The manifestations grew stronger daily, and their presence in John's life became more oppressive. The shadowy figure seemed to feed off his fear and anguish, growing larger and more menacing. John felt like he was losing his grip on reality, his mind unraveling as the shadows closed around him.

The toll on John's mental state was immense. He felt a constant sense of unease, a paranoia that gnawed at him from the inside. He would jump at every shadow, every creak of the floorboards, convinced the figure was lurking just out of sight. His sleep was plagued by nightmares, leaving him exhausted and on edge. The weight of his inner demons was crushing, a burden he could no longer bear alone.

In these dark moments, John's thoughts would turn to the possibility of escape. The idea of ending it all, of finding peace in the silence of oblivion, was seductive. But something always held him back, a small glimmer of hope that kept him tethered to the world of the living. This hope, fragile as it was, gave him the strength to keep going, to face another day with the shadowy figure at his side.

And so, John continued to fight his inner demons, even as the shadows grew darker and more menacing. He clung to the hope that he would someday find a way to banish the figure from his mind and reclaim the light lost to the darkness. Until then, he would endure, one day at a time, battling the shadows that threatened to consume him.

The shadowy figure grew bolder each day, its presence more intrusive and insidious. John's mind, once a sanctuary from external chaos, had become a battlefield where his sanity fought for survival. The manifestations were no longer content to lurk in the periphery; they now intruded into his most intimate thoughts and moments, warping his perception of reality.

At work, John's struggle to maintain composure became increasingly evident. His colleagues began to whisper among themselves, casting concerned glances in his direction. The once-familiar tasks he could perform with ease now felt insurmountable. His hands trembled as he typed, and his mind wandered, unable to focus on the simplest tasks. The shadowy figure was there, always watching, always waiting.

"John, you okay?" Mark's voice cut through the haze of John's thoughts, bringing him back to the present. John looked up to find Mark beside his desk, concerned.

"Yeah, I'm fine," John lied, forcing a smile that didn't reach his eyes. "Just a bit tired, I guess."

Mark didn't look convinced, but he nodded, respecting John's need for space. "If you need anything, just let me know, alright? We're all here for you."

John nodded, grateful for Mark's support but unable to voice the terror that gripped him. How could he explain the shadowy figure growing stronger each day? How could he make Mark understand the whispers that filled his mind, eroding his sense of self?

The manifestations began to infiltrate his daily routine. At the grocery store, he would catch glimpses of the figure in the aisles, its hollow eyes watching him from between the shelves. On his commute, it would appear in the reflections of the train windows, a dark silhouette that sent shivers down his spine. Every shadow, every flicker of movement, became a source of dread, blurring the lines between reality and hallucination.

John's evenings were no respite from the torment. The shadowy figure followed him home, its presence palpable in the dim light of his apartment. It would stand in the corners, its form shifting and undulating like smoke. The whispers grew louder at night, filling his mind with a cacophony of incomprehensible voices. Sleep was a fleeting escape, punctuated by vivid nightmares that left him gasping for breath.

He tried to distract himself with mundane tasks, hoping to drown out the whispers and banish the figure from his thoughts. But the more he tried to ignore it, the more persistent it became. The figure seemed to feed off his fear, growing larger and more menacing with each passing day.

His relationship with his co-workers became strained. They noticed his distracted demeanor, the way he would zone out in the middle of conversations, and his eyes glazed over with an unspoken fear. They tried to reach out, offering comfort and support, but John found it difficult to connect with them. The isolation he felt was suffocating, a heavy weight that pressed down on his chest, making it hard to breathe.

Mark, ever the attentive friend, was the only one who seemed to break through the barrier of John's isolation. He would often find John staring off into space, his eyes wide with fear, and gently coax him back to the present with a touch on the shoulder or a kind word. Mark's presence was a lifeline, a fragile thread that kept John tethered to reality.

"Hey, let's grab lunch together," Mark suggested one afternoon, sensing John's distress. "It'll do you some good to get out of the office for a bit."

John hesitated, the thought of stepping outside into the bustling city overwhelming. But Mark's genuine concern convinced him to agree. They walked to a nearby café, the familiar routine providing a semblance of normalcy.

As they sat down with their meals, Mark tried to engage

110

John in light conversation, steering clear of any topics that might trigger his anxiety. John appreciated the effort, though his mind remained clouded with thoughts of the shadowy figure that seemed to follow him everywhere.

Despite his growing paranoia and the ever-present dread, in moments like these, he provided a brief respite. He could almost forget the darkness lurking in his mind's corners. The camaraderie with Mark was a balm to his wounded soul, a reminder that he was not utterly alone in his struggle.

But as the manifestations grew stronger, these moments of peace became increasingly rare. The shadowy figure seemed to tighten its grip on John's mind, its whispers more insistent and malevolent. The line between reality and illusion blurred further, leaving John in perpetual fear and confusion.

John's world was unraveling, the shadows closing in around him. The manifestations were no longer just figments of his imagination but a tangible threat to his sanity. He felt himself slipping, the weight of his inner demons threatening to pull him under. And through it all, the shadowy figure watched a silent specter that fed off his fear and despair.

The days he has bled into each other, a monotonous haze of dread and anxiety. John's work performance continued to decline, and he found himself making mistakes he would have never made before. The shadowy figure's presence was relentless, and John began losing his grip on reality. His mind constantly teetered on the edge, the boundary between the real and the imagined dissolving into a murky abyss.

One particularly harrowing day, John was in the middle of a routine task when he felt the cold, oppressive presence of the figure behind him. He froze, the air around him thickening with tension. His heart pounded in his chest, and he could feel the eyes of the figure boring into the back of his head.

"John, you alright?" Mark's voice shattered the oppressive silence, but it took a moment for John to register the words.

John turned slowly, expecting to see the figure standing there, but there was nothing—just Mark's familiar, worried face. The sudden shift back to reality left John feeling disoriented and embarrassed. He smiled, trying to shake off the lingering sense of dread.

"Yeah, just… just tired," John mumbled, avoiding Mark's gaze.

Mark didn't push further, but the concern in his eyes deepened. "Why don't you take a break? Go for a walk or get some fresh air. It might help clear your head."

John nodded, grateful for the suggestion. He needed to escape the confines of the office, if only for a few moments. The walls seemed to close in on him, the shadows darker and more threatening. He quickly grabbed his coat and stepped outside, the cool air starkly contrasting the oppressive atmosphere.

As John walked, he tried to focus on the mundane details of the city around him: the chatter of pedestrians, the hum of traffic, the rustle of leaves in the trees. But the shadowy figure was never far from his thoughts, a dark cloud that followed him everywhere. Every shadow seemed to move, every flicker of light a potential harbinger of the figure's return.

In a small park, the relative quiet provided a reprieve from the chaos in his mind. He sat on a bench, taking deep breaths, trying to ground himself in the present. But the peace was short-lived. He saw it out of the corner of his eye—the shadowy figure stood beneath a tree, its form shifting and undulating like smoke, its empty eyes locked onto him.

Panic surged through him, and he gripped the edge of the

bench, his knuckles white. He squeezed his eyes shut, willing the figure to disappear. It was gone when he opened them again, but the fear lingered, a cold knot in the pit of his stomach.

John knew he couldn't keep living like this. The figure was consuming him, driving him to the brink of madness. He needed help, but the thought of confiding in someone, even Mark, filled him with shame and vulnerability. He was trapped in his mind, a prisoner to his fears and hallucinations.

The walk back to the office was a blur. John's thoughts were chaotic, the shadowy figure's presence still looming in the back of his mind. When he returned to his desk, he felt more exhausted than ever. The break had done little to alleviate his anxiety, and the figure's absence only made him more paranoid, knowing it could reappear at any moment.

Mark glanced up as John returned, offering a small, encouraging smile. "Feeling any better?"

John nodded, though the lie tasted bitter on his tongue. "Yeah, a bit. Thanks."

Mark didn't look convinced, but he didn't press the issue. Instead, he offered small gestures of support throughout the day—a cup of coffee, a word of encouragement, a shared joke. These moments were like lifelines, brief respites from the storm raging in John's mind.

Despite the growing darkness within him, John clung to these moments. They were reminders that not everything in his world was tainted by fear and despair. There was still light, however faint, and he had to hold onto it.

However, John's grip on that light became tenuous as the manifestations grew more robust and frequent. The shadows were closing in, and he felt himself slipping further into the abyss. The figure's whispers grew louder, its presence more menacing. John knew he was running out of time. If he didn't find a way to fight back, he would be consumed entirely, lost to the darkness forever.

The next few days, he brought little relief. The shadowy figure haunted John's every waking moment. He saw it reflected in shop windows, lurking in the corners of his apartment, and even standing behind him in the mirror. Each sighting chipped away at his sanity, making it harder to discern reality from hallucination.

At work, John's performance continued to suffer. His concentration was shattered, his mind constantly drifting to the figure and its oppressive presence. Tasks that had once been second nature now felt insurmountable. His supervisor began to question his reliability.

"John, we need to talk," his supervisor said one afternoon, pulling him aside. "Your work has been slipping. Is everything alright?"

John swallowed hard, fighting back the urge to tell the truth. He couldn't admit that a manifestation of his trauma was haunting him. "I've been dealing with some personal issues," he said carefully. "But I'm working on it. I promise it won't affect my work anymore."

The supervisor nodded, though his expression remained skeptical. "I hope so, John. We need you at your best."

As John returned to his desk, he felt the weight of failure pressing down on him. His attempts to hide his struggles were becoming less effective, and he feared it was only a matter of time before everything fell apart.

Mark noticed the tension and sat down beside him during their lunch break. "Hey, you seem more on edge than usual.

Anything you want to talk about?"

John hesitated, the instinct to protect his secret warring with his desperate need for support. He glanced around the break room, ensuring they were alone. "Mark, have you ever... seen something that wasn't there? Like, really seen it?"

Mark frowned, his concern deepening. "You mean hallucinations? Or something like that?"

"Yeah," John said quietly. "Something like that."

Mark leaned in, his voice gentle. "John, if you're seeing things, it's nothing to be ashamed of. It could be stress, or something else. But you don't have to deal with it alone. Maybe you should talk to someone—a professional."

The thought of confiding in a therapist filled John with a mix of relief and dread. He had already seen Stephanie for trauma, but the idea of explaining the shadowy figure felt overwhelming. "I've been seeing someone," he admitted. "But it's hard to talk about."

Mark nodded, his understanding palpable. "I get it. Talking about these things isn't easy. But it's a start. And I'm here if you ever need to vent or just need someone to listen."

It was profound, even if he couldn't fully express John's gratitude. "Thanks, Mark. I appreciate it. Really."

Despite the growing darkness in his mind, moments like this reminded John that he wasn't completely alone. Yet, the manifestations were becoming more vivid, more insistent. They started to bleed into his interactions at work, making him question his every move.

One evening, as he stayed late to catch up on his backlog, the office grew eerily quiet. The usual hum of activity had dwindled, leaving him alone with his thoughts. As he worked, he felt the familiar chill in the air—the unmistakable presence of the shadowy figure.

He looked up from his screen and saw it standing at the edge of the room, its form more distinct than ever. The figure seemed to pulsate with dark energy; its eyes—those empty voids—locked onto him. John's heart raced, and he felt a cold sweat across his forehead.

"No," he whispered to himself, his voice trembling. "You're not real. You're just in my head."

But the figure didn't waver. Instead, it began to move toward him, its form shifting and warping as it approached. John's breath quickened, and he felt the walls of the office closing in around him. He closed his eyes, willing the figure to disappear, but it stood beside him when he opened them again.

Panic surged, and he stumbled back, knocking over his chair. The figure loomed over him, its presence suffocating. John's vision blurred, and he felt himself teetering on the edge of consciousness. He couldn't take it anymore. The line between reality and illusion shattered, and he was trapped in a nightmare.

He fled the office in a desperate escape bid, leaving his work and belongings behind. He burst out into the night, the cool air a stark contrast to the oppressive heat of his panic. He ran, not caring where he went; he just needed to distance himself from the figure as much as possible.

But no matter how far he ran, he couldn't escape his mind. The shadowy figure was always there, lurking in the corners of his vision, whispering dark promises of despair and madness. And as John's world continued to crumble, he knew he was losing the battle against his inner demons.

John barely made it home, his legs trembling with exhaustion and his mind frayed from the relentless pursuit of the shadowy figure. He slammed the door behind him, locking it as if that could keep his inner demons at bay. His apartment, usually a place of solitude, now felt like a prison. Shadows seemed to lurk in every corner, each a potential hiding spot for the manifestation that haunted him.

He collapsed onto his bed, pulling the covers over his head like a child hiding from monsters. His breathing was ragged, each inhale and exhale a struggle against the overwhelming sense of dread that threatened to consume him. He tried to focus on something—anything—other than the figure. He recited mundane facts in his mind: his name, his age, his address. But nothing could distract him from the terror that clawed at his sanity.

The next morning, John awoke to the harsh reality of another day. His body ached from the previous night's exertion, and his mind felt on the brink of collapse. He dragged himself to the bathroom, splashing cold water on his face in a futile attempt to wash away the remnants of his nightmare.

Looking into the mirror, he saw his reflection and the shadowy figure standing behind him, its hollow eyes peering over his shoulder. He spun around, but the room was empty. His mind played tricks on him, and he couldn't trust his senses.

His phone buzzed with a text from Mark: "Hey, man. Just checking in. You okay?"

John stared at the screen, the words blurring together. He wanted to respond and reach out for the lifeline Mark offered, but he couldn't find the strength. Instead, he shoved the phone into his pocket and headed out, determined to finish the day without breaking.

At work, the atmosphere felt suffocating. Every sound seemed amplified, every movement a potential threat. The shadowy figure hovered at the edge of his vision, a constant reminder of his deteriorating mental state. He struggled to focus on his tasks, his hands shaking as he typed.

Mark appeared at his desk during a challenging moment, his presence a small comfort in the chaos. "John, you seem off today. Do you want to grab some coffee and talk?"

John hesitated, his instinct to isolate warring with his desperate need for connection. "Yeah, that sounds good," he managed to say, his voice barely above a whisper.

They found a quiet corner in the break room, away from the prying eyes of co-workers. Mark handed John a cup of coffee, the warmth seeping into his cold fingers. "What's going on, John? You can tell me."

John took a deep breath, trying to steady his nerves. "It's the... the things I see. They're getting worse. I don't know what's real anymore."

Mark's expression was one of genuine concern. "Have you talked to your therapist about this? Maybe she can help you make sense of it."

"I've tried," John said, his voice breaking. "But it's like my mind is unraveling. I don't know how to stop it."

Mark placed a reassuring hand on John's shoulder. "You don't have to go through this alone. We'll figure it out together. Just take it one step at a time."

For a moment, John felt a flicker of hope. Mark's unwavering support was a beacon in the darkness, a reminder that he wasn't completely lost. But as they returned to their desks, the shadowy figure was waiting. It loomed over John, a silent specter that refused to be ignored.

That evening, John sat in his apartment, the silence oppressive. He tried to distract himself with television, but every shadow seemed to move with a life of its own. He couldn't escape the feeling that the figure was watching him, waiting for him to break.

He reached for his journal, desperate to make sense of his thoughts. He wrote about the figure, about the fear and paranoia that consumed him. As he scribbled furiously, he felt a strange sense of detachment, as if observing his descent into madness from a distance.

The words on the page blurred together, his vision darkening. He felt the presence of the shadowy figure beside him, its cold breath on his neck. He dropped the pen, his hands trembling uncontrollably. "You're not real," he whispered to the empty room. "You're not real."

But deep down, John knew that reality had become a tenuous concept. The line between his inner demons and the outside world had dissolved, leaving him trapped in a nightmarish limbo. And as the shadows grew darker, he feared he would never return to the light.

John's torment continued through the night, the shadowy figure haunting his every move. He felt its presence even in his dreams, an inescapable entity that twisted his subconscious into a labyrinth of fear and despair. When he finally woke, drenched in sweat, he was more exhausted.

He dragged himself through his morning routine, the weight of his dread making every action feel monumental. The mirror in his bathroom reflected his face and the constant shadow hovering just behind him, a perpetual reminder of his slipping sanity. He splashed his face with cold water, hoping to jolt himself into a more transparent state of mind, but the chill only deepened his sense of isolation.

At work, he was a ghost of himself, his eyes vacant and his movements sluggish. His co-workers noticed but were too polite or afraid to comment. Only Mark dared approach, his concern evident in his brow furrow. "John, are you sure you're okay? You seem... worse."

John forced a weak smile, a brittle mask to hide the chaos. "Just a rough night, Mark. I'll be fine."

But Mark wasn't convinced. "Listen, why don't we get lunch together? My treat. It might help to get out for a bit."

John hesitated, his instinct to isolate clashing with the comfort Mark's presence offered. "Okay," he agreed finally, his voice a mere whisper.

The cafeteria was bustling with life, a stark contrast to the deathly quiet of John's mind. He picked at his food, unable to muster an appetite. Mark talked, filling the silence with mundane stories and small jokes, trying to lift John's spirits. For a moment, John felt the suffocating weight of his thoughts lighten, the normalcy of their interaction a balm to his frayed nerves.

But as they returned to their desks, the figure loomed more prominent in his peripheral vision. This dark specter refused to be ignored. John's hands trembled as he typed, his focus splintering under the relentless pressure. He could feel the figure's eyes boring into him, its silent presence a constant, gnawing fear.

The day he dragged on, each minute an eternity. When John finally stumbled into his apartment, he was a hollow shell of himself. The shadows in his home seemed to pulse with malevolence, each corner a potential hiding place for the figure that haunted him.

He collapsed onto his couch, his mind a tumult of fear and confusion. He reached for his journal, desperate to expel the darkness within. As he wrote, his thoughts spilled onto the page in a frantic scrawl, the act of writing a lifeline in the storm.

But the shadows crept closer, the figure's presence pressing against his consciousness. His pen slipped from his grasp, his vision narrowing as the room closed around him. "You're not real," he whispered, his voice a fragile plea.

But the figure loomed ever closer, its eyes hollow and unblinking. John could feel its cold breath on his skin, its silence a deafening roar in his mind. The line between reality and illusion was gone, leaving him adrift in a sea of shadows.

As the darkness enveloped him, John realized with a sinking heart that he could no longer fight it. The weight of his debt, his isolation, his fear—it all coalesced into the shadowy figure that now dominated his life. And as he sank into the abyss, he understood that confronting the shadows within was the only escape from this torment.

But at that moment, he lacked strength. The figure was too strong, its grip on his mind too unyielding. John closed his eyes, surrendering to the darkness that had claimed him, a silent promise echoing in his mind: tomorrow, he would find a way to fight back. Tomorrow, he would seek the light. But tonight, the shadows would reign.

9

Strained Relationships

Stephanie's voice cut through the haze of John's morning fog, her tone cheerful yet firm. "Come on, John, we've got to get going. You don't want to be late again." She was his therapist, dedicated to helping him navigate the relentless shadows of his trauma.

John grunted in response, forcing himself out of bed. His limbs felt heavy as if weighed down by the darkness inside him. Despite Stephanie's best efforts, the memories of his father's abandonment and the hit-and-run accident clung to him, feeding his despair.

The drive to work was quiet, punctuated only by Stephanie's attempts at conversation. John stared out the window, his mind a storm of intrusive thoughts. The scene from his past—the one that haunted him the most—played out in relentless loops: his father leaving, the screams, the slamming door. He was just a boy, too young to understand why the world had suddenly become so cold and unforgiving.

At work, the tension was palpable. Once supportive colleagues now regarded John with wary eyes. His behavior had become increasingly erratic due to internal battles spilling into his professional life. He lost track of conversations, snapped at minor infractions, and spent long periods staring into space, lost in the labyrinth of his thoughts.

Stephanie, always his beacon of light, shielded him from the worst of it. She intervened during his temper flares, smoothed over conflicts with their boss, and covered for him when his absenteeism became obvious. But even her unwavering support couldn't mask the growing strain.

"John, you need to pull it together," his boss, Mark, had said recently. "We're all trying to be patient, but you have to meet us halfway. This can't go on."

John had nodded, throat tight with shame and frustration. He wanted to explain the war in his mind but couldn't find the words. How could he convey the terror of waking each day, dreading the memories and fears that would inevitably come?

The isolation was suffocating. John felt like a ghost, drifting through the motions of his life while the real him was trapped in a distant, unreachable place. The more he tried to appear normal, the more glaring his differences became. He saw how co-workers avoided eye contact and how hushed conversations ended when he entered the room.

One afternoon, during a particularly stressful day, John snapped. A minor misunderstanding with a co-worker escalated into a full-blown argument, his voice rising to a shout. The office fell silent, all eyes on him, the weight of their judgment suffocating.

"John, calm down," Stephanie said, stepping between him and the others. Her voice was calm, but worry filled her eyes.

He took a deep breath, the realization of what he'd done

crashing down on him. "I'm sorry," he muttered, but the damage was done. The rift between him and his co-workers had widened, and he stood on the edge, staring into the abyss.

The morning sun filtered through the blinds, casting long shadows across the room as John prepared for another day. The once vibrant office, now a landscape of tension and suspicion, felt like a battlefield. Each step to his desk felt like a march into enemy territory.

Stephanie had offered to drive him again, but John insisted on walking. He needed the time alone to collect his thoughts and brace for the workday's gauntlet. Memories of his father's abandonment and years of neglect clung to him like a second skin, making every interaction a potential trigger.

When John entered the office, the usual chatter died down. Lively conversations turned to hushed whispers and sideways glances. John clenched his jaw, ignoring the growing paranoia whispering insidiously in his ear.

At his desk, he attempted to focus. Emails needed responses, and reports required compiling, but his mind's chaos made concentration impossible. His thoughts were a cacophony of past traumas and present fears, intertwining into a relentless din.

Lunchtime offered a brief respite. John retreated to the break room, hoping for peace. When Stephanie entered, sitting across from him, he sat alone, picking at his sandwich.

"How are you holding up?" she asked gently.

John shrugged, not trusting himself to speak. The walls felt like they were closing in, the pressure of maintaining normalcy almost too much.

"John, I know it's hard," Stephanie continued. "But you don't have to go through this alone. Let me help you."

He looked at her, seeing the sincerity in her eyes. "I don't know where to start," he admitted his voice barely above a whisper.

Stephanie took his hand. "One step at a time," she said. "We'll figure it out together."

Her words offered hope, but John knew the road ahead was long and challenging. The trauma of his past was relentless, and he would have to confront it to rebuild his life and mend relationships.

Afternoons were the hardest. The cumulative stress of the morning left him drained. As the clock neared three, the impending meeting loomed over him. He shuffled the papers Sarah gave him, trying to focus, but the words swam before his eyes.

The meeting room was stifling. John took a seat at the far end, hoping to blend in. Mark started the discussion, his tone brisk.

"As you know, we're on a tight deadline," Mark said. "I need everyone at the top of their game."

John felt the weight of those words, the unspoken implication that he was falling short. He saw it in how his co-workers avoided his gaze, their discomfort palpable. As the meeting progressed, his mind drifted to that day of the hit-and-run: the car, the pain, the helplessness. The driver was never caught, leaving him with fear and anger.

He heard the drone of the meeting, but his focus was elsewhere. He remembered the cold pavement, the sound of tires, the blinding pain. The psychological wounds were still raw.

By the end of the day, John's isolation felt more acute. His mental illness had grown into a monster, feeding on his fears.

He was slipping further into darkness despite Stephanie's support, unsure how to stop it.

"John, are you with us?" Mark's voice cut through his thoughts, pulling him back to the present. John blinked, realizing everyone was looking at him. His heart raced, and he felt a bead of sweat trickle down his back. "Uh, yeah. Sorry. Just a lot on my mind."

Mark's expression softened slightly, but there was an edge of impatience. "I understand, but we need you to stay focused. We're counting on you."

John nodded, feeling the pressure mount. He knew they were all watching him, judging him. The feeling of isolation intensified, a constant reminder that he was different, damaged. He wanted to scream, to tell them about the nightmares, the flashbacks, the relentless fear that gripped him every day. But he couldn't. The words wouldn't come.

As the meeting wrapped up, John gathered his things, eager to escape the scrutinizing eyes of his colleagues. Stephanie caught up with him in the hallway, her concern evident. "You okay?" she asked softly.

John sighed, running a hand through his hair. "I don't know, Steph. I'm trying, but it feels like everything is falling apart."

She placed a comforting hand on his shoulder. "You're not alone in this. We'll get through it together."

Her words were a balm to his troubled mind, but the underlying fear and anxiety remained. As they returned to their desks, John couldn't shake the feeling that he was a burden, a liability. His childhood trauma, the hit-and-run, the constant struggle with his mental health—it all felt like an insurmountable obstacle.

Back at his desk, John stared at his computer screen,

the blinking cursor a mocking reminder of his inability to function like everyone else. The weight of his past pressed down on him, each day a battle to keep his head above water. Despite Stephanie's unwavering support, he felt himself slipping further into the darkness, the isolation deepening with every passing moment.

The rest of the afternoon, he passed in a blur. John went through the motions, responding to emails and making phone calls, but his mind was elsewhere. The ghosts of his past were relentless, and the stress of maintaining his job and relationships was pushing him to the brink. He knew he couldn't go on like this but didn't know how to stop the downward spiral.

As the workday ended, John gathered his things, the exhaustion evident in every movement. Stephanie joined him, her presence a comforting constant in the chaos of his life. Together, they walked out of the office, the day's weight heavy on their shoulders.

"Do you want to talk about it?" Stephanie asked as they made their way to the parking lot.

John shook his head, too tired to delve into the complexities of his mind. "Maybe later," he said quietly.

She nodded, understanding his need for space. "Just know that I'm here for you, whenever you're ready."

John felt a flicker of hope as they parted ways, but the enormity of his struggles quickly overshadowed it. The road ahead was long and uncertain, and despite Stephanie's best efforts to keep him grounded, he couldn't shake the feeling that he was walking it alone.

The evening brought John a semblance of relief, a fleeting escape from the oppressive atmosphere of the office. He returned to his apartment, the familiar space offering a fragile sense of security. But the quiet only served to amplify the chaos in his mind. The apartment, once a sanctuary, now felt like a prison, the walls closing in as memories and fears flooded his thoughts.

He dropped his bag by the door and collapsed onto the couch, the weight of the day bearing down on him. The hit-and-run had left him physically damaged, but it was the psychological scars that tormented him most. The pain, the helplessness, the fear—they were constant companions, haunting his every moment.

John's phone buzzed, breaking the silence. It was a message from Stephanie: Hey, I'm just checking in. I hope you're doing okay. Let me know if you need anything.

He stared at the screen, the words blurring as tears filled his eyes. He wanted to reach out and let her know how much her support meant to him, but the fear of burdening her held him back. Instead, he typed a quick response: Thanks, Steph. I'm okay. I'm just tired.

Setting the phone aside, John closed his eyes, hoping to find some respite in sleep. But the nightmares were always waiting. He was back on that street, the car bearing down on him, the impact sending him sprawling. The pain was confirmed, the terror visceral. He woke with a start, drenched in sweat, his heart pounding.

The clock on the wall read 2:00 AM. Another sleepless night. He got up and wandered into the kitchen, the silence of the apartment oppressive. He poured himself a glass of water, his hands trembling. The memories of his childhood trauma resurfaced—his father's angry outbursts, the nights spent hiding in his room, the constant fear of doing something wrong.

These early experiences had shaped him, embedding a deep-seated anxiety that never thoroughly went away. The hit-and-run had only exacerbated it, adding layers of trauma that made everyday life a struggle. He felt like a ghost, disconnected and alone, drifting through his existence.

John's thoughts turned to his co-workers. He knew they talked about him behind his back, their whispers full of pity and suspicion. They didn't understand what he was going through, and he couldn't blame them. How could they? His behavior was erratic, and his moods were unpredictable. He was a shadow of his former self, and he hated it.

Back on the couch, he curled up, trying to find some semblance of comfort. The night he stretched on, each minute an eternity. He wished he could talk to Stephanie, but the fear of overwhelming her kept him silent. She was his lifeline, who seemed to care honestly, but he didn't want to drag her down with him.

The hours crept by, the darkness outside giving way to the first light of dawn. John felt a crushing sense of dread at the thought of facing another day. The weight of his traumas, both past and present, was suffocating. He didn't know how long he could keep up the facade, pretending to be okay when he was anything but.

Finally, he forced himself to get up and get ready for work. Each movement felt like an enormous effort, his body heavy with exhaustion. Looking at his reflection in the mirror, he barely recognized the man staring back at him. The haunted eyes, the lines of stress etched into his face—this wasn't who he used to be.

But he had no choice. He had to keep going, if not for

himself, then for Stephanie. She believed in him, which gave him the strength to face another day, no matter how difficult. With a deep breath, he gathered his things and stepped out into the world, the battle within him raging on, unseen and unrelenting.

The morning commute was a blur. John navigated through the bustling streets, his mind elsewhere. The honking horns, the chatter of pedestrians, and the rumble of the subway seemed distant, muted by the roar of his internal turmoil. He arrived at the office, barely acknowledging his co-workers as he made his way to his desk.

The day unfolded much like the previous ones, a monotonous grind punctuated by moments of acute anxiety. John buried himself in his work, trying to drown out the noise in his head. But the tension with his co-workers was palpable. He could feel their eyes on him, the judgment and unease clear in their glances.

Sarah approached him around mid-morning, a hesitant smile on her face. "Hey, John. Can you review these documents for the presentation tomorrow?"

John looked up, forcing a smile. "Sure, Sarah. I'll get right on it."

As she walked away, he felt a pang of guilt. Sarah had always been kind to him and patient even when he was at his worst. But the growing rift between him and the rest of the team was undeniable. His erratic behavior had made them wary, and he couldn't blame them. He was becoming a liability, a ticking time bomb.

Mark interrupted his thoughts by calling a team meeting. John joined his colleagues in the conference room, the atmosphere tense. Mark outlined the tasks for the upcoming project; his tone was clipped and efficient. John tried to pay attention, but his mind kept drifting back to the hit-and-run, the constant pain, and the struggle to keep his mental health in check.

"John, any updates on your end?" Mark's question jolted him back to the present.

John cleared his throat, trying to gather his thoughts. "Uh, yes. I've made some progress on the report. I'll have it ready by tomorrow."

Mark nodded, but there was a hint of skepticism in his eyes. "Good. We're on a tight deadline, so let's all stay focused."

The meeting ended, and John returned to his desk, the weight of his co-workers' expectations pressing down on him. He wanted to prove himself and show his capability, but the constant battle with his inner demons made it impossible.

Stephanie found him during lunch, and her concern was evident. "You seemed a bit off in the meeting. Everything okay?"

John shrugged, trying to brush it off. "Just a lot on my mind, you know?"

She didn't look convinced. "If you need to talk, I'm here. Don't forget that."

He appreciated her concern but couldn't shake the feeling that he was dragging her down with him. She had her own life and her challenges. He didn't want to be a burden. This thought gnawed at him constantly, creating a barrier even her kindness struggled to breach.

The afternoon was a struggle. John's mind was a battlefield, memories of the accident mingling with his childhood trauma. He remembered the nights spent cowering in his room, the fear of his father's wrath, and the constant sense of walking on eggshells. The sound of his father's shouting, the sting of a slap, the cold, hard floor where he often found refuge— these memories were etched into his psyche, impossible to escape. Those early experiences had shaped him, instilling a deep-seated anxiety that never entirely went away.

The hit-and-run had compounded his trauma, leaving him with physical and psychological scars that refused to heal. The pain was a constant reminder of his vulnerability, his helplessness. It colored every aspect of his life, from work to relationships.

As the day drew close, John felt the familiar exhaustion setting in. He gathered his things, avoiding the eyes of his co-workers as he made his way to the elevator. He sensed their whispers following him, their sidelong glances filled with suspicion and unease. It was as if they were waiting for him to unravel completely.

Stephanie joined him, her presence a comforting balm to his frayed nerves. "Want to grab a coffee?" she asked as they stepped onto the street.

John nodded, grateful for the distraction. They walked to a nearby café, and the evening air was cool and refreshing. Inside, they found a quiet corner, the hum of conversation and clinking cups creating a soothing backdrop.

Stephanie looked at him, her eyes filled with concern. "I'm worried about you, John. You're carrying so much on your own."

He sighed, running a hand through his hair. "I know. It's just... hard to talk about sometimes."

She reached across the table, squeezing his hand. "You don't have to go through this alone. I'm here for you, no matter what."

Her words brought a lump to his throat. He wanted to believe her, to lean on her support, but the fear of being a burden was ever-present. Still, her unwavering friendship gave him a glimmer of hope, a lifeline during his struggles.

John felt a small peace as they sat there, sipping their coffee. For a moment, the weight of his trauma lifted, and he allowed himself to believe that maybe, just maybe, he could find a way through the darkness with Stephanie by his side.

In the following days, he brought little reprieve. John moved through them like a ghost, his interactions with co-workers increasingly strained. The incident with the hit-and-run loomed large in his mind, a constant reminder of his vulnerability and the precariousness of his existence.

At the office, the tension was palpable. His colleagues' whispers followed him, their sidelong glances filled with suspicion and unease. He could sense their discomfort, their growing wariness. It was as if they were waiting for him to unravel completely.

One afternoon, as John was working on a particularly challenging task, Mark approached his desk. "John, we need to talk."

John's heart sank. He nodded, following Mark to a small meeting room. Mark closed the door, his expression serious.

"Look, John, I know you've been through a lot, and I understand things have been tough," Mark began, his tone measured. "But your performance has been slipping. The team is concerned, and frankly, so am I."

John swallowed hard, his mind racing. "I'm doing my best, Mark. It's just… it's been a rough few months."

Mark sighed, leaning against the table. "I get that. But we have deadlines, and we need everyone to be at their best. If you need time off or some help, we can discuss that. But we can't let the quality of work suffer."

John nodded, feeling a mix of shame and frustration. "I understand. I'll try to do better."

As he left the meeting room, he felt the weight of Mark's words pressing down on him. The fear of losing his job added another layer to his already overwhelming anxiety. He knew he needed to pull himself together, but the constant battle with his inner demons made it feel impossible.

That evening, he confided in Stephanie, and their usual coffee routine provided a safe space for him to vent his frustrations.

"Mark's right, you know," John admitted, staring into his cup. "I'm not pulling my weight. But I don't know how to fix it."

Stephanie listened patiently, her expression thoughtful. "You're dealing with a lot, John. Maybe it's time to get some professional help, someone who can guide you through this."

John shook his head. "I've tried therapy before. It helps for a while, but then everything just comes crashing down again."

She reached out, touching his arm gently. "This time might be different. And even if it's not, you don't have to go through it alone. We'll find a way together."

Her unwavering support was a lifeline, but John still felt the immense burden of his struggles. The hit-and-run, his childhood trauma, the mounting pressure at work—it all felt insurmountable.

As they parted ways that evening, John felt a flicker of hope. Stephanie's words had given him a glimmer of something to hold onto, a small light in the darkness. But the road ahead was still uncertain, and the weight of his demons threatened to pull him under.

Back at his apartment, John tried to find some semblance of normalcy. He went through the motions of his evening routine, but his mind was a whirlwind of anxiety and fear. Sleep, when it finally came, was fitful and filled with nightmares.

The following day, he awoke feeling more exhausted than before. But Stephanie's words echoed in his mind, urging him to seek help and find a way through the darkness. It was a daunting prospect, but the thought of losing everything—his job, friends, and sanity—pushed him to take that first step.

He called a therapist and set up an appointment. It was a small step, but it felt monumental. As he hung up the phone, he felt fear and relief. He wasn't sure what the future held, but he felt a sliver of hope for the first time in a long while. Maybe, with Stephanie's support and professional help, he could begin to heal and rebuild his life.

He provided a brief respite the evening at the café. Still, as John walked back to his apartment, the familiar weight of his troubles settled over him once more. Stephanie's words echoed in his mind, offering a fragile sense of hope. Yet, beneath that hope, the fear and pain persisted, a constant undercurrent threatening to pull him under.

As he reached his apartment, he dreaded the solitude that awaited him. The four walls, once a sanctuary, now seemed to close in on him, amplifying the chaos within. He dropped his keys on the table and sank into the couch, staring blankly at the ceiling. The quiet was oppressive, filled with the ghosts of his past.

John's mind wandered back to his childhood, to the nights spent hiding from his father's anger. The trauma of those early years had left deep scars, shaping his perception of the world and his place in it. The hit-and-run had only added to that burden, leaving him with a constant sense of vulnerability.

The relentless memories flooded his mind with images and sensations he wished he could forget. The sound of his father's shouting, the sting of a slap, the cold, hard floor where he often found refuge—these memories were etched into his psyche, impossible to escape.

He thought about his co-workers and the strained relationships that grew more distant daily. He knew they didn't understand what he was going through. How could they? His behavior was erratic, and his moods were unpredictable. He was a stranger to them, a source of unease in an otherwise orderly world.

But Stephanie… she was different. Her unwavering support was a lifeline, a beacon in the darkness. John clung to that support, even as he feared overwhelming her with his struggles. He wanted to be better and stronger for her and himself. But the road ahead seemed impossibly long, the obstacles insurmountable.

As the night wore on, John's exhaustion deepened. He longed for sleep, for the oblivion it promised, but the nightmares were always waiting. He closed his eyes, hoping for a brief respite, but the images of the hit-and-run, of his father's rage, were relentless. The pain was ever-present, a reminder of his frailty.

Finally, he rose from the couch and made his way to the bedroom, each step a monumental effort. He crawled into bed, pulling the covers around him like a shield. The darkness offered little comfort, but it was all he had. He lay there, staring into the void, wishing for a peace that seemed forever out of reach.

Morning came too soon, the first light of dawn creeping through the blinds. John felt like he hadn't slept, his body heavy with exhaustion. But he knew he had to face another day, to go through the motions even as the weight of his trauma threatened to overwhelm him.

John got up, moving through his morning routine with mechanical precision. Each action was a struggle. His mind fogged with fatigue and anxiety. But he had to keep going, if not for himself, then for Stephanie. Her belief in him was a fragile lifeline he couldn't afford to sever.

As he made his way to the office, the usual dread was still there, but a new sense of purpose tempered it. He would take it one day, one step at a time, fighting through the darkness. The road to healing was long and fraught with challenges, but he was no longer alone. And that made all the difference.

His co-workers' wary glances still stung in the office, but he held his head slightly higher. He focused on his tasks, pushing through the mental fog. When the anxiety threatened to overwhelm him, he remembered Stephanie's words, grounding himself in the knowledge that he had someone in his corner.

Throughout the day, he caught himself slipping into old patterns, the familiar anxiety gnawing at him. But each time, he pulled himself back, determined not to let his demons win. It was a constant battle, but he faced it with renewed vigor.

By the time the day ended, John felt a weary but satisfying sense of accomplishment. He gathered his things, ready to head home. As he left the building, Stephanie caught up with him, her smile a beacon of light in the twilight.

"How was your day?" she asked.

John shrugged, a small smile playing on his lips. "It was

tough, but I managed."

Stephanie nodded, her eyes reflecting her pride in his progress. "That's all we can do, John. Take it one step at a time."

He walked her to her car, the drizzle turning into a steady rain. As she drove away, John stood momentarily, letting the rain wash over him. The future was uncertain, and the path ahead was still shrouded in darkness. But for the first time in a long while, he felt like he had a fighting chance.

With a deep breath, he turned and returned to his apartment, ready to face whatever came next. The weight of his past was still heavy, but it was no longer insurmountable. With Stephanie's support, he believed he could find his way through the abyss of his mind, one step at a time.

Part 2
The Descent

II

Part Two

Part Two

10

The Breaking Point

The days had grown darker for John, and it wasn't just the winter evenings that came earlier. His mind, once a fortress of resilience, had crumbled into a battleground where shadows roamed freely. The manifestations of his fears, once confined to the edges of his vision, had now taken center stage, dancing mockingly in front of his eyes no matter where he looked.

John's apartment had become a prison, each wall closing in with a palpable weight. The silence was deafening, broken only by the whispers of his Shadow Self, a sinister echo of his darkest thoughts. No matter how hard he tried to drown them out with television or music, they always found a way through, creeping into his consciousness and settling there like an unwelcome guest. The air was heavy with the scent of stale cigarettes and the faint tang of fear, the corners of the room darkened by the creeping shadows that seemed to thicken and solidify with each passing day.

As John sat on his threadbare couch, his eyes were drawn to the dark corner of the room where the shadows seemed to thicken. He could almost see the outlines of figures shifting and coalescing, their forms hazy yet terrifyingly real. He closed his eyes, pressing his palms against them in a futile attempt to banish the visions. The pressure only brought more vivid images to the forefront of his mind—memories of the war, the faces of comrades lost, and the relentless guilt that gnawed at his soul. The echo of gunfire, the smell of blood and sweat, the haunting cries of those he couldn't save—they all played out in an endless loop, an unending torment that blurred the lines between past and present.

His phone buzzed on the coffee table, a brief reprieve from the relentless onslaught of his thoughts. John glanced at the screen and saw a message from Stephanie: "Just checking in, John. How are you holding up?" He stared at the words, his fingers hovering over the keyboard, but he couldn't bring himself to type a response. What could he say? That he was drowning in a sea of despair, pulled under by the weight of his mind? No matter how hard she tried, he felt more alone than ever.

The phone buzzed again, this time with a call from Mark. John watched it ring until it went to voicemail, the familiar sense of isolation wrapping around him tighter. Mark's attempts at reaching out, though well-intentioned, only served to remind John of the chasm that had opened between him and the rest of the world. He was a burden, a broken man who couldn't be fixed, no matter how much support he received.

John's gaze shifted to the bottle of pills on the kitchen counter, the prescription he rarely touched. It was meant to help, to take the edge off the anxiety and depression that had become his constant companions. But tonight, their presence held a different allure—a promise of escape, a way out of the unending torment. The thought of finally silencing the chaos was tempting, a seductive whisper in the back of his mind that promised peace.

He rose slowly, each step towards the counter feeling like a march towards an inevitable end. His mind raced, the voices growing louder, urging him towards the finality that the pills represented. He picked up the bottle, its heavy and liberating weight in his hand. His fingers trembled as he unscrewed the cap, the sound echoing in the oppressive silence. He poured the pills into his palm, staring at the small, white tablets that seemed to shimmer with a deadly promise. His mind was a whirl of thoughts and emotions, each vying for dominance, but amidst the chaos, one clear realization emerged: he couldn't go on like this.

He brought his hand to his mouth, the pills trembling in his grasp. As he hesitated, a single tear rolled down his cheek, a silent testament to the depth of his suffering. John closed his eyes, steeling himself for the final act. Still, in the darkness behind his eyelids, he saw something unexpected—a faint glimmer of hope, a memory of Stephanie's unwavering support, Mark's friendship, and the fleeting moments of connection that had given him a brief respite from his pain.

His hand wavered, the pills slipping from his grasp and scattering across the counter. John collapsed to the floor, his body wracked with sobs as the weight of his despair crashed over him. The darkness was still there, looming and ever-present, but for now, he had decided to endure, to fight for another day.

The phone buzzed again, Stephanie's name lighting up the screen. With trembling hands, John reached for it, his voice barely above a whisper as he answered, "Stephanie... I need help."

The words were a lifeline, a small but crucial step towards finding his way out of the abyss. And as he spoke, a flicker of hope reignited within him, fragile but tangible, a reminder that even in the darkest moments, there was still a chance for redemption.

John's cry for help did not go unanswered. Stephanie arrived at his apartment within the hour, her presence a calming force amidst the chaos of his mind. She found him on the floor, the scattered pills a stark testament to his desperation. Without a word, she knelt beside him, her hand gently resting on his shoulder.

"John, I'm here," she said softly, her voice a soothing balm to his frayed nerves. "We're going to get through this together."

Tears streamed down John's face as he looked up at her, his eyes red-rimmed and filled with a mixture of anguish and relief. "I don't know what to do, Stephanie. I feel so lost."

She nodded, her expression filled with empathy. "I know it feels overwhelming right now, but I promise you, we can find a way through this. Let's start by getting you some help, okay?"

Stephanie helped John to his feet and guided him to the couch, where he sank, exhausted. She made a quick call, arranging an emergency session at the local mental health clinic. "They're expecting us," she said, tucking her phone away. "Let's go."

The ride to the clinic was quiet, the city lights blurring past the windows. John stared out, his thoughts a tangled mess. The weight of his decision lingered heavily, but alongside it was a flicker of hope—a possibility that maybe, just maybe, things could change.

Stephanie stayed by John's side at the clinic as they navigated the labyrinth of paperwork and procedures. The sterile environment and clinical efficiency starkly contrasted with his emotional turmoil. Still, Stephanie's steady presence was a lifeline. She spoke with the intake nurse, ensuring that John's immediate needs were addressed.

"John, this is Dr. Harris," Stephanie introduced him to a kind-looking psychiatrist. "He's going to help us create a plan to get you the support you need."

Dr. Harris offered a reassuring smile. "John, I understand you're going through a very difficult time. I want you to know that you're not alone. We're here to help you."

As they talked, John felt a small measure of his burden lift. He shared, haltingly at first, the depth of his struggles—the relentless anxiety, the intrusive thoughts, and the manifestations of his Shadow Self that had grown increasingly vivid and terrifying.

Dr. Harris listened intently, nodding thoughtfully. "It's clear you've been carrying a lot on your own. The manifestations you're experiencing are a part of your mind's way of dealing with trauma. With the right support, we can work to lessen their impact and help you find some peace."

The words were a balm to John's soul, a glimmer of hope in the darkness that had consumed him. Dr. Harris prescribed a new medication regimen and arranged for a follow-up appointment to monitor his progress. Stephanie stayed with him throughout the process, her unwavering support a beacon in the storm.

Leaving the clinic, John felt a tentative sense of relief. It wasn't a cure but a start—a small step towards reclaiming his life from the shadows that had threatened to engulf it.

Stephanie drove him home, her presence a constant reminder that he wasn't alone in this fight.

"Remember, John," she said as they approached his apartment. "It's okay to reach out. You don't have to face this on your own. We're in this together."

John nodded, gratitude welling up within him. "Thank you, Stephanie. I don't know what I'd do without you."

She smiled, giving his hand a reassuring squeeze. "You're stronger than you think, John. One step at a time, we'll get through this."

As John stepped into his apartment, the shadows seemed less oppressive. The journey ahead was still daunting, but with Stephanie's support and the newfound hope that had sparked within him, he felt a flicker of determination. The darkness might be vast, but now, he had a glimmer of light to guide him.

Days turned into weeks, and John found himself slowly acclimating to the new medication. The once suffocating grip of despair loosened its hold, replaced by a cautious sense of stability. He resumed his sessions with Stephanie, their conversations weaving a delicate tapestry of vulnerability and resilience.

Stephanie's office had become a sanctuary for John, where he could untangle the knots of his mind without judgment. One afternoon, as sunlight filtered through the blinds, she gently guided him through a breathing exercise.

"Focus on your breath, John," she instructed, her voice steady and calm. "Inhale deeply, hold it for a moment, and then exhale slowly. Let each breath ground you."

John followed her lead, his breaths gradually evening out. The simple act of breathing became a lifeline, anchoring him in the present moment. After a few minutes, Stephanie spoke again. "You're doing great, John. Remember, progress isn't always a straight line. There will be good days and bad days, but each step forward is a victory."

John nodded, a small smile forming on his lips. The road to recovery was long, and the shadows of his past still lingered, but with Stephanie's support and the right help, he began to believe that he could find his way through the darkness—one step at a time.

"Can you tell me about the manifestations you've been experiencing? Are they still as frequent?"

John hesitated, his eyes flickering with a mix of fear and shame. "They're still there," he admitted. "But... they're different now. Less vivid, maybe. Or maybe I'm just getting used to them."

Stephanie nodded, her expression thoughtful. "That's progress, John. It might not feel like it, but acknowledging the changes is an important step. Can you describe what they look like now?"

He closed his eyes, trying to summon the images. "It's like... shadows in the corner of my vision. Sometimes I see faces, twisted and distorted. Other times, it's more abstract. Shapes and movements that don't make sense."

She leaned forward, her gaze intent. "And how do you feel when you see them?"

"Terrified," he said quietly. "But also... angry. Angry that they're still here, that I can't escape them."

Stephanie's eyes softened with empathy. "It's okay to feel that way, John. These manifestations are a part of your trauma, but they don't define you. We're working on understanding them, and with time, we'll find ways to reduce their power over you."

Their sessions continued to delve into the heart of John's pain, peeling back layers of trauma and fear. Stephanie encouraged him to journal his thoughts, which helped externalize the chaos within his mind. Writing became a form of release, the pages bearing the weight of his anguish.

One evening, after a particularly grueling day at work, John sat at his kitchen table, pen in hand. The apartment was quiet, the ticking of the clock the only sound. He opened his journal and began to write, his thoughts spilling onto the paper in a torrent of raw emotion.

"Today was hard. The shadows were relentless, lurking just at the edge of my vision. I tried to focus on work, but it's like they know when I'm vulnerable. Mark noticed something was off. He didn't say anything, but I could see it in his eyes. I hate that he has to see me like this."

He paused, the pen hovering over the page. The words came more slowly now, each one a struggle.

"I'm scared, Stephanie. Scared that I'll never be free of this. Scared that I'll push everyone away. But I'm also trying to hold on to the hope you've given me. It's fragile, but it's there. Thank you for believing in me, even when I can't believe in myself."

As he finished writing, a sense of calm settled over him. Putting his thoughts into words had a cathartic effect, a way to unburden his soul. He closed the journal and sat back, the shadows in the corners of his mind momentarily at bay.

The following week, Stephanie introduced a new technique during their session. "I'd like to try something called visualization," she explained. "It's a way to confront and reshape the images in your mind. Are you willing to give it a try?"

John nodded, curiosity mingling with apprehension. "I'll try anything if it helps."

Stephanie guided him through the process, her voice a steady anchor. "Close your eyes and imagine a place where you feel safe. It can be real or imaginary. Picture it in as much detail as possible."

He did as she instructed, his mind conjuring an image of a serene beach, the sound of waves crashing against the shore. Stephanie continued, "Now, imagine the shadows approaching. But this time, you have control. You can change their form, their color. You can diminish them."

John's brow furrowed as he concentrated. The shadows appeared, but instead of twisted faces, they took on the shape of wisps of smoke. With each breath, he imagined the smoke dissipating, growing fainter and fainter until it vanished.

When he opened his eyes, Stephanie was smiling. "How do you feel?"

"Lighter," he said, a hint of surprise in his voice. "It's like I took some of their power away."

Stephanie nodded her expression one of quiet pride. "That's the idea. You have more control over these manifestations than you realize. With practice, you can continue to diminish their hold on you."

For the first time in a long while, John felt a glimmer of hope that the shadows might be banished for good. It was a small victory, but in his ongoing battle with his inner demons, it felt monumental.

Despite John's progress with Stephanie's guidance, the shadows still haunted him, creeping into his life when he least expected it. His job became a battlefield, a daily struggle to maintain the semblance of normalcy. Mark Jenkins, ever vigilant, noticed the strain on John's face and the weariness in his eyes.

"Hey, John," Mark said one morning, leaning against the cubicle wall. "You doing okay? You look like you haven't slept in days."

John forced a smile, though it barely touched his eyes. "I'm hanging in there. Just… rough nights, you know?"

Mark nodded, his concern evident. "If you need to talk, you know where to find me. Don't try to handle it all on your own."

Grateful for Mark's support, John nodded. "Thanks, Mark. I appreciate it."

The brief exchange buoyed John, a small lifeline in the vast sea of his despair. But as the day wore on, the shadows grew bolder. John saw a dark figure lurking just beyond the conference room door during a meeting. He blinked, and it was gone, leaving behind a chill that settled deep in his bones.

"John?" his manager's voice cut through the haze. "Do you have the quarterly report?"

John snapped back to reality, fumbling with his notes. "Yes, uh, right here," he stammered, tremblingly handing over the report.

The rest of the meeting passed in a blur, John's focus scattered by the relentless assault of his mind. When he returned to his desk, he felt drained, his struggles pressing down on him like a physical burden.

That evening, as he prepared to leave, Mark approached him again. "John, wait up," he called, catching John by the arm. "Are you sure you're okay? You've seemed off all day."

John sighed, running a hand through his hair. "It's just… everything. The shadows, the memories. It's like they're always there, waiting to drag me down."

Mark's eyes softened with understanding. "I can't pretend to know what you're going through, but I want you to know you don't have to face it alone. There's no shame in asking for help."

"Thanks, Mark," John said, his voice barely above a whisper. "I don't know what I'd do without you."

As he walked home, John's mind replayed the conversation. Mark's words were a beacon in the darkness, a reminder that he wasn't alone in his battle. But the shadows were persistent, whispering doubts and fears that gnawed at his resolve.

Later that night, John sat on his bed, the weight of his thoughts pressing down on him. He clutched the edge of the mattress, his knuckles white with tension. The room felt stifling, the air thick with the oppressive presence of his inner demons.

He closed his eyes, trying to summon the visualization technique Stephanie had taught him. The serene beach appeared in his mind, but the shadows followed, twisting and writhing like malevolent specters. His breath quickened, panic clawing at his chest.

"No," he whispered, his voice trembling. "Not now. Not again."

But the shadows were relentless, their whispers growing louder and more insistent. They spoke of despair, hopelessness, and an end to the suffering that seemed so tantalizingly close. John's resolve wavered the urge to give in to the overwhelming darkness.

His hand shook as he reached for his phone, scrolling through his contacts until he found Stephanie's number. He hesitated, his thumb hovering over the call button. A part of him wanted to reach out, to seek the help he desperately needed. But another part, ruled by the shadows, urged him to remain silent, to let the despair consume him.

As the minutes ticked by, John fought an internal battle between the desire for relief and the will to survive. Finally, with a deep, shuddering breath, he pressed the call button, holding the phone to his ear.

"Hello, John," Stephanie's calm, reassuring voice answered. "What's going on?"

For a moment, John couldn't speak, his throat constricting with emotion. "I... I don't know what to do," he finally choked out. "The shadows, they're everywhere. I can't escape them."

"Take a deep breath, John," Stephanie said gently. "You're not alone. We're going to get through this together. Just keep breathing and stay on the line with me."

John clung to Stephanie's voice like a lifeline, the steadiness of her tone anchoring him in the storm of his thoughts. He took deep, shuddering breaths, following her guidance as best as possible.

"Focus on your breathing, John," Stephanie continued, describing a calm harbor in his turbulent sea. "Inhale slowly through your nose, hold it for a count of four, then exhale slowly through your mouth. You can do this."

John obeyed, each breath a small victory against the encroaching darkness. As he followed her instructions, he felt a slight easing of the vice gripping his chest. The shadows still lurked, but their whispers grew fainter, drowned out by the rhythm of his breathing and Stephanie's soothing words.

"Good, John," she said after a few moments. "Now, tell me what's happening. What are you feeling right now?"

"It's like... like I'm drowning," John managed to say, his

voice raw with emotion. "The shadows, they won't leave me alone. They're always there, always whispering, and I can't escape them. I feel so alone, so hopeless."

Stephanie's silence on the other end of the line was comforting, a space where he could spill his anguish without judgment. "You're not alone, John," she finally said. "I'm here with you, and we're going to get through this together. It's okay to feel what you're feeling. Your pain is real, and it's valid."

John's grip on the phone tightened her words, a balm to his frayed nerves. "I just don't know how much more I can take," he confessed, his voice breaking. "Every day feels like a battle I'm losing."

"You're stronger than you think," Stephanie reassured him. "You've made it this far, and that's a testament to your resilience. Remember, it's okay to reach out for help. You don't have to carry this burden alone."

The weight of her words sank in, a mix of comfort and a challenge to the despair that threatened to overwhelm him. John took another deep breath, his mind racing. "What if I can't do this?" he whispered, the fear evident in his voice. "What if I'm too broken?"

"None of us are beyond repair, John," Stephanie said gently. "Healing takes time, and it's not a linear process. There will be ups and downs, good days and bad days. But every step you take, no matter how small, is a step toward healing."

Her words resonated with him, a fragile hope beginning to take root amidst the desolation. John swallowed hard, fighting the tears that threatened to spill over. "Thank you, Stephanie," he said, his voice a mixture of gratitude and desperation. "I don't know what I'd do without you."

"You're not alone in this, John," Stephanie replied. "Remember that. And if you ever feel overwhelmed again, don't hesitate to reach out. We're in this together."

As they ended the call, John felt a flicker of light in the darkness. The shadows still loomed, but he felt a glimmer of hope for the first time in a long while. It was fragile and tentative, but it was there.

That night, as John lay in bed, the whispers of the shadows were quieter, the despair less consuming. He still felt their presence, but Stephanie's words provided a counterbalance, a reminder that he wasn't completely lost. As he drifted into a restless sleep, he clung to the hope that tomorrow might bring a sliver of light, a possibility of healing.

The following day, John awoke to a world bathed in muted light, the shadows that had haunted him through the night receding to the corners of his mind. He felt a sense of clarity, a newfound resolve born from the depths of his despair.

As he sat at his kitchen table, sipping a cup of coffee, John reflected on his conversation with Stephanie. Her words had struck a chord within him, a reminder that there was still hope even in his darkest moments.

With a newfound determination, John made a decision. He would seek help and reach out to those who could support him on his journey to healing. It wouldn't be easy, and there would be setbacks along the way, but he was no longer willing to let his demons consume him.

As he reached for his phone, intent on making an appointment with his therapist, a sense of calm washed over him. The road ahead would be long and complex, but he walked alone.

With each step, John felt the weight of despair lift, replaced by a glimmer of hope. The shadows still lingered, a constant reminder of his struggles, but they no longer held him captive.

The sun broke through the clouds as John stepped outside, casting a warm glow over the world. It was a new day, a chance for him to start anew. As he took his first tentative steps forward, John knew that no matter what lay ahead, he would face it with courage and determination.

For John, the healing journey had only just begun. But with each passing day, he grew stronger, his resolve unshakeable. And as he looked towards the horizon, he knew that no matter how dark the night may get, the dawn would always come, promising a brighter tomorrow.

11

Seeking Help

Despite the small glimmer of hope he felt upon receiving the notebook, John's journey remained arduous. Each night, he sat at his kitchen table, the blank pages staring back at him, challenging him to pour out his soul. At first, he could only manage a few disjointed sentences and fragmented thoughts that barely scratched the surface of his turmoil.

"Today was hard," he wrote one night. "I can't focus. The shadows are back, worse than ever. I see them at work, in the corners of my vision. I hear them whispering when it's quiet."

Writing, though difficult, began to bring a semblance of structure to his chaotic mind. He found that the words flowed more easily once he started, each entry a cathartic release. Dr. Green had been right—expressing his pain on paper felt like shedding a layer of his burden, even if only for a moment.

In their sessions, Dr. Green encouraged him to read some of his entries aloud. This exercise, though daunting, became a powerful tool. Each time John shared his written thoughts, he felt a little more of the weight lift from his shoulders. Dr. Green's insights and gentle guidance helped him see patterns, understand triggers, and develop strategies for managing his darkest moments.

One afternoon, John read an entry about an awful day at work. "I snapped at Mark today," he read, his voice shaking. "He was trying to help, but I couldn't. I feel like I'm losing control. I hate myself for pushing people away, but I can't seem to stop."

Dr. Green listened intently, her expression compassionate. "It's important to recognize these moments, John," she said. "What do you think triggered your reaction?"

John thought for a moment, struggling to articulate the jumble of emotions. "I don't know," he admitted. "I just felt overwhelmed. Like everything was closing in on me."

"Overwhelm can often lead to feelings of irritability and anger," Dr. Green explained. "It's a defense mechanism, a way for your mind to protect itself from the pain. But understanding this can help you to respond differently in the future."

Their sessions became a lifeline for John, a place where he could confront his demons in a safe and supportive environment. Dr. Green's unwavering belief in his ability to heal gave him a foundation to build his resilience.

Through their work together, John began to see a path forward. It was fraught with challenges and setbacks, but a path nonetheless. He started to find small moments of peace, fragments of joy lost to the shadows. With each step, he moved closer to a future where the light outshone the darkness.

Outside of their sessions, John began to notice small changes. The shadows that had once loomed so large seemed to recede if only a little. He found himself more aware of his triggers and better equipped to handle the moments of intense despair.

Yet, the journey was far from linear. There were setbacks and overwhelming despair, but he also experienced brief, precious instances of clarity and peace.

Dr. Green's unwavering support and the coping mechanisms she provided became John's anchor. Through their sessions, he learned not only to confront his inner demons but also to accept that healing was a gradual, often nonlinear process.

Though the shadows still loomed, they were no longer as daunting. With each passing day, John grew more assertive, resilient, and hopeful that he would emerge from the darkness into the light one day.

As the months passed, John's sessions with Dr. Green became a lifeline. He looked forward to her calm, understanding presence at each meeting. Her office, once a place of initial discomfort, had transformed into a sanctuary where he could lay bare his soul without fear of judgment.

One particular session marked a significant turning point. John sat in his usual spot with a weary but determined look. Dr. Green observed him with her characteristic empathy, ready to guide him through whatever he needed to unpack that day.

"John, I've noticed a change in you over the past few weeks," she began, her voice gentle but firm. "You seem more present, more engaged. Can you tell me what's been different?"

John took a deep breath, his thoughts swirling as he tried to articulate the subtle shift he'd felt. "I guess... I'm starting to believe that things can get better. It's not just about surviving each day anymore. It's about finding reasons to keep going, small as they might be."

Dr. Green smiled, a genuine expression of pride and encouragement. "That's a significant realization, John. Finding those reasons, however small, can be incredibly powerful. It's those moments of hope that we need to hold on to, especially when things get tough."

They spent the session delving into the positive changes John had noticed, however slight. He talked about his reconnection with Mark, the supportive atmosphere at work, and the gradual, albeit challenging, improvements in his mental health. Dr. Green helped him see the progress he often overlooked, reinforcing his efforts and resilience.

After the session, John walked home with a lighter step. The world outside felt a bit less daunting, and the shadows that had once seemed impossible were now something he could confront with the tools he'd gained. As he navigated the familiar streets, he thought about the people who had been there for him—Stephanie, Dr. Green, Mark—and felt a profound sense of gratitude.

That evening, John sat at his kitchen table, a cup of tea warming his hands. He opened his notebook, intending to capture the day's insights. Instead of recounting the struggles, he found himself writing about the moments of light, the glimmers of hope that had begun to pierce through the darkness.

"I talked to Dr. Green about the small victories," he wrote. "About how each day, I'm finding a bit more strength to face the challenges. It's not easy, and some days are still incredibly hard, but I can see a path forward now. I'm not alone in this."

As he wrote, he realized that his journey was far from over. There would be more battles, more days when the weight of his past threatened to pull him under. But there would also be days like today, where he could see the progress, however incremental, and feel a sense of accomplishment.

John closed his notebook, a sense of quiet determination settling over him. The shadows might always be a part of his life, but they no longer held the same power over him. With the support of those around him and the inner strength he was slowly rediscovering, he knew he could keep moving forward.

In the silence of his apartment, John felt a newfound peace. He knew there would be more sessions with Dr. Green, more conversations with Mark, and more moments of introspection. But for now, he allowed himself to acknowledge his progress and find solace in the knowledge that he was on a path toward healing.

As he prepared for bed, John looked out the window, the night sky a canvas of stars. For the first time in a long while, he felt a connection to the world outside, a sense of belonging that had eluded him for so long. With a deep breath, he whispered a quiet promise to himself: to keep fighting, to keep seeking help, and to never lose sight of the glimmers of hope that had begun to illuminate his path.

12

The Shadow's Grip Tightens

The once-fleeting shadows that danced at the corners of John's vision now lurked ever closer, their forms twisting and contorting into grotesque shapes. His Shadow Self, once a mere specter, had grown in strength and malignancy, its presence a constant reminder of his inner turmoil.

As John went about his daily routine, the manifestations followed, their whispers growing louder, their forms more distinct. Faces twisted in agony stared at him from the darkness of his apartment. At the same time, disembodied voices echoed through his mind, taunting and accusing.

Despite his efforts to push them away, the manifestations seeped into every aspect of his life. They tainted his interactions with others, casting a shadow of distrust and fear over his relationships. Coworkers noticed his increasingly erratic behavior and even Mark's attempts to reach out were met with distant, distracted responses.

John's mental state deteriorated rapidly. His once-ordered mind now felt like a battlefield, with the manifestations waging a relentless war against his sanity. Fear and paranoia gripped him, turning his thoughts against him. He began questioning his grip on reality, unsure of what was real and what was a twisted creation of his mind.

The weight of despair settled over John like a suffocating blanket. Each day felt like a battle for survival, and the line between his inner demons and the outside world blurred. The manifestations had taken on a life of their own, feeding off his fear and feeding his descent into darkness.

As John struggled to cope with the relentless onslaught of his inner demons, he found himself teetering on the edge of despair. The shadows that once haunted him from afar now enveloped him, their grip tightening with each passing day.

Nightmares plagued John's sleep, each one more vivid and terrifying than the last. He would wake in a cold sweat, the echoes of his screams still ringing in his ears. The line between dreams and reality blurred, leaving him exhausted and disoriented.

During the day, the manifestations grew bolder. Shadows seemed to stretch and contort, taking on grotesque forms that lurked just out of sight. Whispers followed him wherever he went, a constant reminder of his fractured mind.

Despite Stephanie's unwavering support, John found it increasingly difficult to open up about his experiences. The fear of judgment and misunderstanding weighed heavily on him, driving him further into isolation.

Dr. Green's sessions relieved some, but the medication offered only temporary respite. The shadows always returned, their presence a grim reminder of John's inner turmoil.

With each passing day, John felt himself slipping further away from reality. The world around him seemed to warp and distort, its edges fraying like a tattered tapestry.

The grip of his Shadow Self tightened, its hold unrelenting. Despair threatened to consume him whole, leaving him trapped in a nightmare from which there seemed to be no escape.

As the manifestations grew more menacing, John's grip on reality began to slip. He started to see glimpses of his Shadow Self in the reflections of windows and mirrors, a twisted version of himself that filled him with dread.

At work, his colleagues noticed his erratic behavior. He would startle at the slightest sound, his eyes darting around as if searching for unseen threats. His once-friendly demeanor was replaced by a palpable tension, driving a wedge between him and his coworkers.

Stephanie's sessions became John's lifeline, the only respite moments in his increasingly chaotic world. She patiently listened to his fears and anxieties, offering reassurance and guidance in equal measure.

Dr. Green adjusted John's medication, hoping to alleviate some of his symptoms. But the shadows persisted, their presence an ever-present reminder of John's inner turmoil.

Despite his best efforts, John's mental health continued to deteriorate. The line between reality and illusion blurred further, leaving him trapped in a waking nightmare from which there seemed no escape.

One evening, as John returned to his apartment, he was greeted by a chilling sight. The walls seemed to pulsate with dark energy, and the air was thick with an otherworldly presence. Shadows twisted and writhed, taking on grotesque forms that filled John with a primal fear.

He stumbled back, his heart pounding in his chest. The manifestations had never been this vivid, this real. He tried to rationalize it, to convince himself it was all in his mind, but the terror was too overwhelming.

In a panic, John called Stephanie, his voice trembling as he described what he was seeing. Stephanie tried to calm him down, assuring him she would come over immediately.

When she arrived, she found John huddled in a corner, his eyes wide with fear. She gently guided him out of the apartment, the manifestations fading as they left the building.

It was a turning point for John. The experience shook him to his core, forcing him to confront the reality of his condition. He knew then that he couldn't continue like this and needed help now more than ever.

As John teetered on the edge of his sanity, Stephanie decided that it was time to call in additional support. She contacted Maria, a fellow therapist and a close friend known for her work with trauma patients.

Maria arrived at Stephanie's request, calming into John's turbulent life. Her approach was compassionate yet firm, and she quickly assessed the severity of John's situation.

"John, my name is Maria," she said gently, kneeling beside him. "Stephanie called me because she's concerned about you, and I want to help."

John looked at Maria, a glimmer of hope in his eyes. "I don't know how to make it stop," he whispered. "The shadows… they're everywhere."

Maria nodded, understanding the depth of his pain. "I know it feels overwhelming, but we're going to work through this together. First, we need to get you to a safe place."

Under Maria's guidance, John was admitted to a specialized trauma center where he could receive intensive care and supervision. The environment was designed to be soothing, with natural light, calming colors, and spaces for reflection and healing.

During his stay, Maria worked closely with John, helping him navigate his mind's labyrinth. They engaged in various therapies, from cognitive-behavioral therapy to mindfulness and relaxation techniques. Maria's methods were holistic, addressing the mind and body to restore balance.

"Tell me about the shadows, John," Maria said in one session. "What do they say to you?"

John hesitated, but Maria's calm demeanor encouraged him to open up. "They tell me I'm worthless," he said. "That I'll never be free from my past."

Maria listened, her expression thoughtful. "Those shadows are manifestations of your trauma. They feed on your fear and self-doubt. But you are not defined by them. We will work to diminish their power over you."

With Maria's help, John began confronting the deep-seated fears that fueled his shadows. They explored his past, delving into the roots of his trauma. Maria helped John reframe his experiences, turning his pain into a source of strength.

"Your past has shaped you, but it does not have to define you," Maria told him. "You have the power to rewrite your story."

Gradually, John's condition improved. The shadows that had once dominated his life began to recede, replaced by a growing sense of self-awareness and resilience. Maria's unwavering support and innovative techniques gave John the tools to reclaim his life.

John was ready to return home after several weeks at the trauma center. The journey ahead was still daunting, but he felt more equipped to face his challenges. Maria and

165

Stephanie remained integral parts of his support system, offering guidance and encouragement every step of the way.

As John settled back into his apartment, he felt renewed hope. The shadows were still there, but they no longer held the same power over him. He had learned to confront them, to understand their origins, and to reclaim his life from their grasp.

In the following weeks and months, John continued his therapy with Maria and Stephanie, steadily building a foundation of resilience. His relationship with his coworkers, particularly with Mark, improved as he became more open about his struggles and progress.

Maria's presence in John's life was transformative. Her expertise and compassion helped him navigate his darkest moments, guiding him toward the light. With her support, John discovered a strength within himself he never knew existed.

As the sun set on another day, John sat at his kitchen table, writing in his notebook. The words flowed easily now, a testament to his journey and his progress. He no longer wrote solely about his struggles but also his victories, no matter how small.

"I faced my shadows today," he wrote. "They whispered their lies, but I didn't listen. I am not defined by my past. I am stronger than I ever believed."

John looked out the window at the night sky, a canvas of stars. For the first time in a long while, he felt at peace. With Stephanie, Maria's support, and his newfound resilience, he knew he could face whatever challenges lay ahead.

The shadows of his past would always be a part of him, but they no longer held him captive. John had reclaimed his life, one step at a time, and he was determined to keep moving forward, guided by the light of hope and the strength of his spirit.

13

Reaching Out

Sarah Walker had been working as a social worker for over a decade, specializing in helping individuals facing housing and financial difficulties. When she first met John, she could see the world's weight on his shoulders. His eyes were sunken, and his demeanor was that of someone who had been through hell and back.

Despite John's initial reluctance to accept help, Sarah was determined to make a difference. Building trust would be crucial, so she listened to John's story. She learned about his struggles with PTSD, his financial woes, and his ongoing battle with his inner demons.

Sarah's approach was gentle yet firm. She offered practical solutions to John's immediate problems, such as connecting him with local resources for housing assistance and financial support. She also checked in with him regularly, providing a listening ear and a shoulder to lean on.

Despite Sarah's efforts, John remained guarded. He was used to dealing with his problems independently, and accepting help from someone else was foreign to him. But Sarah was patient. Building trust took time, and she was willing to wait for John to come around.

As the days turned into weeks, Sarah noticed a subtle change in John. He seemed more open and more willing to accept help. She knew there was still a long road ahead, but she was hopeful that John could overcome his challenges and build a better life with her support.

Sarah's persistence began to pay off as John slowly started to open up to her. He shared more about his past traumas, his struggles with mental health, and the daily challenges he faced. Sarah listened intently, offering empathy and understanding without judgment.

One of the biggest hurdles for John was his housing situation. He was on the verge of being evicted and had nowhere else to go. Sarah knew that finding stable housing was crucial for John's well-being, so she worked tirelessly to find him a solution.

After weeks of searching, Sarah finally found a small apartment that fit within John's budget. It wasn't much, but it was a roof over his head. John initially hesitated, but Sarah reassured him that it was only temporary and that they would continue working towards a more permanent solution.

With housing secured, Sarah turned her attention to John's financial struggles. She helped him create a budget, prioritize his expenses, and find ways to increase his income. It was a slow process, but John was determined to turn his life around, and Sarah was there every step of the way to support him.

As their relationship grew, Sarah became not just a social worker but a friend to John. She was someone he could rely on, someone who believed in him when he didn't believe in himself. For the first time in a long time, John felt a glimmer of hope for the future.

Despite the progress John made with Sarah's help, his inner demons continued to haunt him. The manifestations of his Shadow Self grew more frequent and intense, tormenting him day and night. No amount of support or guidance seemed to alleviate his suffering.

Sarah noticed the toll that these manifestations were taking on John. She could see the fear and desperation in his eyes, which pained her to see him in such distress. She encouraged him to continue with his therapy and medication, but John's faith in his recovery was beginning to wane.

One evening, as John sat alone in his apartment, the shadows around him seemed alive. The twisted forms of his inner demons danced in the darkness, mocking him and taunting him. John felt himself slipping into despair, his grip on reality becoming more tenuous by the day.

Sarah sensed that John was reaching a breaking point. She knew that she needed to intervene before it was too late. She arranged for an emergency therapy session, hoping that it would provide John with the support and guidance he so desperately needed. But she also knew that, ultimately, John's recovery depended on his willingness to confront his inner demons and find the strength to overcome them.

The emergency therapy session with Stephanie was John's last lifeline. As he sat across from her, the weight of his struggles felt heavier than ever. Stephanie's gentle presence offered a sliver of comfort. Still, John's mind was consumed by the darkness lurking around every corner of his consciousness.

Stephanie sensed the urgency of the situation. She knew that John was teetering on the edge and needed to reach him before he slipped away. She guided him through grounding exercises, encouraging him to focus on breathing and the present moment.

As John's breathing slowed, his mind began to clear. For the first time in weeks, he felt a glimmer of hope. Stephanie seized this moment of clarity, gently probing John's thoughts and feelings. She encouraged him to confront his inner demons, acknowledge them, and, ultimately, let them go.

John hesitated at first, his fear and despair threatening to overwhelm him. But with Stephanie's unwavering support, he found the strength to face his demons head-on. He spoke of his trauma, his fears, and his struggles, laying bare his innermost thoughts and feelings.

Stephanie listened intently, offering words of encouragement and understanding. She helped John reframe his thoughts, guiding him towards a more positive and hopeful outlook. By the end of the session, John felt lighter, as if a weight had been lifted from his shoulders.

But Stephanie knew this was just the beginning of John's journey towards healing. The road ahead would be long and challenging. Still, with the proper support and guidance, she was confident that John could overcome his inner demons and reclaim his life.

In the following days, John's sessions with Stephanie became his lifeline. Each session brought new insights and revelations, helping John to untangle the web of trauma and pain that had consumed him for so long. Stephanie's patient and empathetic approach gave John the courage to confront his past and embrace his future.

As John's mental health improved, so too did his relationships with those around him. He found solace in the support of his co-workers, who had noticed a change in him and rallied around him with words of encouragement and acts of kindness. Even Dave Richardson, his landlord, seemed to soften towards him, offering him an extension on his rent payments and a sympathetic ear.

However, the most significant change was in John himself. He began to see a future for himself, free from the shadows of his past. He enrolled in therapy, taking proactive steps towards healing and growth. And as he did, the grip of his Shadow Self began to loosen, its power fading in the light of John's newfound resilience.

Stephanie watched with pride as John blossomed before her eyes. She knew his journey was far from over, but she was confident he was on the right path. With her guidance and support, John had found the strength to confront his demons and emerge victorious. And as he stepped into the light, Stephanie knew his future was bright.

One evening, as John sat alone in his apartment, he felt a sense of peace. The shadows that had haunted him for so long seemed to fade into the background, their voices growing fainter with each passing moment. In that moment of clarity, John realized that he was not alone. He had a support system of people who cared about him and were there to help him through the darkest times.

With a newfound sense of hope and determination, John made a decision. His past or the shadows within him would no longer define him. Instead, he would embrace the light, stepping boldly into a future filled with promise and possibility.

As John looked towards the future, he knew challenges would be ahead. But he also knew he was strong enough to face them with Stephanie, Sarah, and his co-workers. As he took that first step towards healing, John felt a weight lift off his shoulders, knowing that he was finally free from the shadows that had once consumed him.

And so, John's journey continued as a testament to the power of resilience, hope, and the unwavering support of those who believed in him. As he walked towards the light, John knew that no matter what lay ahead, he would face it with courage and determination, ready to embrace whatever the future held.

14

Distorted Reality

As the weeks turned into months, John's hard work and the unwavering support of those around him started to yield positive changes. Though still present, the manifestations of his inner demons had lost their grip on his daily life. Shadows still danced at the corners of his vision, but they were no longer overwhelming. John could now acknowledge them without succumbing to fear.

John's progress was evident in his interactions at work and with his support network. Mark and Maria were instrumental in this transformation, offering consistent encouragement and practical support. Mark often checked in on John as a colleague and friend, helping him manage the workload and ensuring he didn't feel overwhelmed. With her nurturing presence, Maria brought a sense of calm and stability to John's life. Her home-cooked meals and regular visits became a source of comfort and normalcy.

Dr. Green's therapy sessions became a cornerstone of John's recovery. She introduced John to various techniques to manage his PTSD and anxiety. One technique that resonated with John was Cognitive Behavioral Therapy (CBT), which helped him identify and challenge negative thought patterns. Dr. Green also guided him through mindfulness exercises, which proved invaluable in grounding him during moments of intense anxiety.

In a particularly poignant session, Dr. Green asked John to visualize a safe place—a sanctuary where he could retreat when the world felt too overwhelming. John chose a serene beach, where the rhythmic sound of waves provided a soothing backdrop. This visualization became a powerful tool for John, helping him find calm amidst the chaos.

John also began to see the value in sharing his experiences. He joined a local support group for individuals dealing with PTSD, where he found solace in the shared stories of struggle and resilience. It wasn't long before he became a mentor to newer members, using his journey to offer hope and practical advice. He spoke candidly about his darkest moments and the techniques that had helped him, such as grounding exercises and the importance of a supportive network.

One evening, during a group session, John noticed a young man named Alex who reminded him of his earlier self—withdrawn and haunted by his inner demons. After the meeting, John approached Alex, offering a friendly ear and sharing his story. Over time, John became Alex's mentor, guiding him through his recovery. This mentorship helped Alex and reinforced John's progress, giving him a sense of purpose and fulfillment.

John's relationships with his colleagues improved as well. He no longer viewed them suspiciously but saw them as allies in his journey. He rekindled friendships strained by his illness, finding joy in simple interactions and shared experiences.

John's woodworking hobby became another avenue for healing and growth. He transformed his garage into a workshop, where he spent hours crafting intricate pieces of furniture. Creating something tangible gave him a sense of accomplishment and control. His creations, each a testament to his resilience, were displayed proudly in his home and given as gifts to friends and family.

Seeing John's passion for woodworking, Maria suggested they organize a small exhibition at a local community center. The event was a resounding success, with many attendees admiring John's craftsmanship and buying his pieces. The exhibition boosted John's confidence and solidified his place within the community.

Despite the progress, John's journey was not without setbacks. There were days when the shadows seemed to return, threatening to pull him back into the abyss. But unlike before, John now had the tools and support to face these challenges head-on. He reached out to his support network, practiced his grounding exercises, and reminded himself of his progress.

In a challenging moment, John found solace in a letter he wrote to himself, an idea suggested by Stephanie. The letter, filled with encouragement and reminders of his strength, became a source of inspiration during tough times. Reading it reminded him of how far he had come and the resilience that had brought him through his darkest days.

The bonds John had formed with Mark, Maria, and his support group became his pillars of strength. They celebrated his victories, no matter how small, and supported him through the setbacks. These relationships were a testament to the power of community and the importance of not facing challenges alone.

One day, as John sat in his workshop, he reflected on his journey. The scars of his past were still there, but they no longer defined him. He had faced his inner demons, rebuilt his life, and found a sense of peace he once thought unattainable.

As John looked to the future, he did so with optimism and hope. He knew there would be challenges ahead, but he also knew he had the strength and resilience to face them. His journey was far from over, but he was now prepared to embrace it fully.

With each passing day, John embraced the new beginning he had worked so hard to create. His story became one of hope, resilience, and the power of community. As he looked toward the horizon, he knew that no matter what the future held, he would face it with courage, determination, and a heart full of gratitude.

15

Strained Relationships

John awoke to a sense of clarity he hadn't felt in years. The nightmares that once dominated his nights were now infrequent visitors, and the shadows that haunted his waking hours had receded. His journey of recovery had been long and arduous, but the hard work and support from his loved ones were beginning to pay off.

John's life began to show significant positive changes. He returned to work with a renewed sense of purpose and found solace in helping others who faced similar struggles. His own experiences with mental health became a source of strength and empathy, allowing him to connect with and support his colleagues in ways he never thought possible.

John's renewed dedication to his job was noticed. Mark, his boss, observed the transformation and was genuinely impressed. John's performance improved dramatically, and he became a reliable and valued team member again. Once wary and distant, his colleagues now saw a man who had faced his demons and emerged stronger.

Outside of work, John immersed himself in volunteer activities. He joined a local mental health advocacy group, sharing his story to inspire and support others on their journeys. He also began mentoring young adults struggling with their mental health, offering guidance and understanding that only someone who had walked a similar path could provide.

John's experiences gave him a unique perspective and a profound ability to connect with others. He often spoke at community events and support groups, where he shared his journey of overcoming trauma and mental illness. His honesty and vulnerability resonated with many, and his words offered hope to those who felt lost in their struggles.

At one of these events, John met Maria Sanchez, a young woman battling severe depression and anxiety. Maria attended the support group for a few weeks but mainly remained silent. However, John's story struck a chord with her, and she found the courage to approach him after the meeting.

"Your story really spoke to me," Maria said, trembling. "I've been struggling for so long, and it's hard to see a way out. But hearing you talk about your recovery gives me hope."

John smiled warmly, remembering his feelings of hopelessness. "Thank you, Maria. It means a lot to hear that. Recovery is a journey, and it's not easy. But with the right support and a lot of determination, it's possible."

Maria's eyes filled with tears, but she nodded. "I want to try. I want to get better."

John's relationships with those closest to him continued to flourish. His bond with Stephanie grew more robust, and their friendship became a source of joy and comfort. They often met for coffee, sharing updates on their lives and reflecting on John's progress. Stephanie's unwavering support had been a cornerstone of John's recovery, and he was endlessly grateful for her presence in his life.

Sarah, the social worker who had helped John secure stable housing and financial support, remained a close friend and ally. They often collaborated on community projects to provide resources and support for those in need.

Elena Rodriguez, John's co-worker who had reached out to him during his darkest days, became a dear friend. They shared lunch breaks and often stayed after work to chat about their lives. Elena's kindness had been a lifeline for John, and he cherished their friendship deeply.

As John reflected on his journey, he felt a profound sense of closure. He had faced his darkest fears, confronted his inner demons, and emerged stronger. The shadows that once held him captive were now just whispers of the past, reminders of the strength he had found within himself.

Yet, John knew that his journey was far from over. Recovery was an ongoing process, and he was committed to continuing his therapy, taking his medication, and staying connected with his support system. He also knew his purpose was to use his experiences to help others find their way out of the darkness.

One evening, as John sat in his apartment, he felt a sense of peace. The walls, once oppressive and suffocating, now felt like a sanctuary. He looked out the window, the city lights twinkling in the distance, and smiled. The future was filled with promise, and he was ready to embrace whatever came his way.

John's story was a testament to the power of resilience, hope, and the unwavering support of those who believed in him. As he walked toward the light, he knew that no matter what lay ahead, he would face it with courage and determination, ready to embrace the future with an open heart and a renewed sense of self.

With a deep breath, John whispered a quiet promise to himself: to keep fighting, to keep seeking help, and to never lose sight of the glimmers of hope that had begun to illuminate his path. The journey ahead might still be challenging, but he was no longer alone, which made all the difference.

Part 3

The Abyss

III

Part Three

16

The Awakening of the Eldritch

John nodded, though reliving the night's terrifying events filled him with dread. "I will," he promised, his voice barely a whisper. "I just... I don't know how to explain it."

Elena's eyes were filled with sympathy and determination. "You don't have to go through this alone, John. We'll figure it out together. But you need to be honest with Dr. Green. She can't help you if she doesn't know the whole story."

John swallowed hard, feeling a lump in his throat. "Okay," he repeated, a bit more firmly this time. "I'll tell her everything."

John sat in Dr. Green's office the next day, feeling fear and relief. Elena had insisted on accompanying him, waiting in the reception area while he met with the psychiatrist. He took a deep breath as Dr. Green regarded him with a calm, understanding gaze.

"John, it's good to see you," she began. "Elena called me last night and mentioned that you've been experiencing some intense hallucinations. Can you tell me more about what's been happening?"

John's hands trembled slightly as he recounted the events—

the shadows, the whispers, the nightmarish creatures that seemed to stalk him. He spoke of the oppressive presence that filled his apartment and the terrifying encounter with the entity in his kitchen. Dr. Green listened without interruption, expressing deep concern and empathy.

"It sounds like you've been through a very difficult and frightening experience," she said gently. "Hallucinations like the ones you've described can be a symptom of severe stress, anxiety, or even a manifestation of deeper psychological trauma. We need to address this head-on."

John nodded, feeling a flicker of hope amidst his fear. "I just want it to stop," he admitted. "I feel like I'm losing my mind."

Dr. Green offered a reassuring smile. "You're not losing your mind, John. What you're experiencing is very real to you, and it's important that we find a way to help you manage these symptoms. I'd like to adjust your medication and increase the frequency of our sessions. Additionally, I think it would be beneficial for you to work with a therapist who specializes in trauma."

John agreed, feeling relieved that a plan was in place. He knew the road to recovery would be long and challenging, but for the first time, he felt like he had the support he needed to face his demons.

Over the following weeks, John adhered to his new treatment regimen with renewed determination. Dr. Green's adjustments to his medication helped to reduce the frequency and intensity of his hallucinations. Regular therapy sessions allowed him to explore the underlying trauma that had triggered his psychological distress.

Elena remained a constant source of support, her presence grounding in his life. She accompanied him to his appointments, encouraged him to stay active, and ensured he cared for himself. Gradually, John began to notice subtle improvements. The hallucinations, while still present, were less overwhelming. The whispers that had once filled his mind with terror grew fainter, more straightforward to ignore.

In therapy, John confronted painful memories that had long been buried. He spoke about his past traumas, the events that had shaped his fears and anxieties. With the guidance of his therapist, he learned coping mechanisms to manage his stress and anxiety. Techniques like grounding exercises and mindfulness helped him stay anchored in reality, reducing the power of his hallucinations.

One evening, as John sat on his couch with Elena, he reflected on his journey. "I feel like I'm finally starting to see a way out," he said, his voice filled with cautious optimism. "It's still hard, and I know I have a long way to go, but I'm not as scared as I used to be."

Elena smiled, her eyes shining with pride. "You've come so far, John. I'm so proud of you. And no matter what, I'm here for you. We'll get through this together."

John took her hand, feeling a warmth and connection that had eluded him for so long. "Thank you, Elena," he said softly. "I couldn't have done this without you."

As the days turned into weeks, John continued to make steady progress. The entities that had once haunted him became less and less a part of his daily life. He learned to recognize the signs of stress and anxiety that triggered his hallucinations and took proactive steps to manage his mental health.

One afternoon, during a particularly reflective therapy

session, John's therapist asked him to describe his journey in his own words. "It's like I was living in a nightmare," John began, "but now, I'm starting to wake up. The shadows are still there, but they're not as powerful. I know they can't hurt me because I have the tools and the support to keep them at bay."

His therapist nodded, a pleased expression on her face. "That's a powerful realization, John. Your resilience and determination have brought you a long way. Remember, healing is a journey, not a destination. You'll have good days and bad days, but each step forward is a victory."

John left the session feeling a profound sense of accomplishment. He knew there would be challenges ahead, but he also knew he had the strength to face them. With Elena, Dr. Green, and his therapist, he felt equipped to navigate whatever came his way.

As John stood on the balcony of his apartment, looking out at the city below, he took a deep breath and felt a sense of peace. The journey had been long and arduous, but it had also been transformative. He had faced his inner demons and emerged more assertive, a testament to the power of resilience and the human spirit.

With the sun setting on the horizon, John embraced the promise of a new beginning. He was ready to face the future with courage and hope, knowing he was never alone. And as he stepped back into the warmth of his home, he carried with him the lessons he had learned and the strength he had gained, ready to embrace whatever the future held.

17

The Neighbor's Concern

John's breath came in ragged gasps as he clung to Gregory's arm, his eyes darting around the room as if expecting something to leap from the shadows.

"They... the shadows... the voices," he stammered, his grip tightening. "I can't... they're everywhere."

Gregory guided him to the couch, speaking calmly and soothingly. "John, listen to me. You're safe here. There's nothing here that can hurt you. Take a deep breath."

John tried to follow Gregory's instructions, but his breaths remained shallow and rapid. Gregory sat beside him, his mind racing through the possible explanations for John's state. He had seen PTSD, schizophrenia, and severe anxiety in his career. Still, John's terror seemed to come from something deeper, something more insidious.

"Tell me about the shadows, John," Gregory said gently. "What do they look like?"

John's eyes filled with tears as he struggled to form the words. "They... they don't have a shape. They're like smoke, but darker. They move and whisper... they tell me things, horrible things."

Gregory listened intently, his detective instincts kicking in. "When did this start, John? When did you first notice the shadows?"

John wiped his eyes, his body trembling. "After the accident. It was like something followed me home from the hospital. At first, it was just whispers, but then I started seeing them… everywhere."

Gregory nodded, piecing together the puzzle. "And the voices? What do they say?"

John hesitated, the fear in his eyes intensifying. "They tell me I'm worthless, that I should give up. They say… they say they're going to take me, that I'll never escape."

Gregory felt a surge of protectiveness for the broken man beside him. "John, I believe you. We're going to get through this together. You're not alone, and I won't let anything happen to you."

John looked at Gregory, a flicker of hope in his eyes. "You really believe me?"

"I do," Gregory said firmly. "But we need to get you some help. Have you ever talked to a therapist about this?"

John shook his head. "I was too scared. What if they locked me up?"

Gregory placed a reassuring hand on John's shoulder. "That's not going to happen. I know a good psychiatrist—Dr. Green. She's helped a lot of people dealing with trauma. Will you let me set up an appointment for you?"

John hesitated, then nodded. "Okay. I'll try."

Gregory smiled, feeling a slight sense of victory. "That's all I ask. One step at a time."

The following day, Gregory called Dr. Green to explain

John's situation. Dr. Green agreed to see John as soon as possible, understanding the urgency of his condition. Gregory accompanied John to the appointment, providing a steady presence as they navigated the unfamiliar terrain of mental health care.

Dr. Green was a warm, empathetic woman who immediately put John at ease. She listened carefully as John described his experiences, nodding thoughtfully and asking gentle questions to draw out more details. Gregory watched as John slowly began to open up, the weight of his secrets lifting slightly with each word.

"John," Dr. Green said after a long pause, "it sounds like you're dealing with a severe form of PTSD, possibly complicated by other factors. The shadows and voices you're experiencing are your mind's way of coping with the trauma you've been through. We're going to work together to find a way to help you manage these symptoms."

John nodded, a mixture of relief and apprehension in his eyes. "Will it ever go away?"

"With time and the right treatment, many people see significant improvements," Dr. Green assured him. "But it's important to be patient with yourself. This is a journey, and it won't happen overnight."

As they left Dr. Green's office, Gregory felt a renewed sense of hope. John had taken the first step towards healing, and Gregory knew there was a real chance for recovery with continued support. He vowed to stand by John's side, no matter how long it took until the shadows that haunted him were banished for good.

In the following weeks, John's treatment plan began to take shape. Dr. Green prescribed medication to help manage his anxiety and hallucinations, and John started attending regular therapy sessions. Gregory checked in on him daily, offering encouragement and support.

Slowly but surely, John began to show signs of improvement. The shadows that had once seemed so menacing started to fade, and the voices grew quieter. He reconnected with Elena, who was overjoyed to see him making progress. Together, they formed a network of support that helped John navigate the challenges of his recovery.

Gregory watched with pride as John reclaimed his life step by step. The road ahead was still long and fraught with obstacles, but John had hope for the first time in a long while. And with Gregory, Elena, and Dr. Green by his side, he knew he could face whatever came next.

As the days turned into months, John's progress continued. He began volunteering at a local community center, helping others struggling with mental health issues. It gave him a sense of purpose and reminded him that he was not alone in his fight.

One evening, as John and Gregory sat on the porch, enjoying the cool night air, John turned to his friend and mentor. "Greg, I don't know how to thank you. You saved my life."

Gregory smiled, shaking his head. "You did all the hard work, John. I just gave you a little push. I'm proud of you."

John nodded, a sense of peace settling over him. The shadows that had once dominated his life were now just a distant memory. He knew they might never disappear altogether, but with the support of his friends and the tools he had learned, he was confident that he could keep them at bay.

As they sat in comfortable silence, the night sky filled with stars, John felt a sense of hope and possibility for the future. He had faced his inner demons and emerged more robust, a testament to the power of resilience and the human spirit. With the love and support of those around him, he knew he could face whatever challenges lay ahead, ready to embrace the light and leave the darkness behind.

Gregory approached John with the idea that afternoon, finding him sitting listlessly at the kitchen table, staring at a half-eaten piece of toast.

"John, I've found a support group that meets nearby," Gregory said gently, trying to gauge his friend's reaction. "They're people who've been through similar experiences, dealing with PTSD and trauma. It might help to talk to others who understand what you're going through."

John looked up, his eyes shadowed with fatigue and fear. "A support group?" he echoed, his voice skeptical. "I don't know, Greg. I can barely keep it together on my own. How can I talk to strangers about this?"

"I understand it's daunting," Gregory replied, sitting across from him. "But sometimes, sharing your burdens can make them a little lighter. You don't have to speak if you don't want to. Just being there and listening might help."

John sighed, running a hand through his messy hair. "I'll think about it," he said finally, though he sounded unconvinced.

Gregory nodded, accepting the small victory. "That's all I ask. Just think about it."

The next few days were passed in a blur of routine and anxiety. Gregory continued to watch John closely, supporting him through the worst of his episodes. John's therapy sessions with Dr. Green provided some relief, but the shadows and whispers still haunted him relentlessly.

The night before the support group meeting, John finally agreed to try it. "I'll go," he said, his voice weary but determined. But only because you believe it might help."

Gregory felt a surge of hope. "That's all I need, John. We'll go together."

The following evening, Gregory and John went to the community center. The building was a modest structure, its walls adorned with posters advocating mental health awareness and support. They were greeted by a friendly woman named Susan, who introduced herself as the group facilitator.

"Welcome," Susan said warmly, shaking their hands. "We're glad to have you here. There's no pressure to share. You can just listen if that's what you're comfortable with."

John nodded, his expression guarded but appreciative. They took seats in a circle of chairs. As the meeting began, Gregory watched as John slowly relaxed, his tension easing as he listened to others recount their experiences.

The stories shared were raw and powerful—tales of loss, fear, and resilience. Each person's journey was unique, yet there was a common thread of struggle and hope. As the session progressed, Gregory noticed a shift in John's demeanor. The haunted look in his eyes softened, replaced by a tentative sense of connection.

When it was John's turn to speak, he hesitated, glancing at Gregory for reassurance. Gregory nodded encouragingly, and John took a deep breath, his voice trembling as he began to share.

"I... I've been seeing things," he said, his eyes darting nervously around the room. "Shadows, whispers... they won't leave me alone. I've tried everything, but they just keep coming back."

The group listened with empathy and understanding, offering nods and murmurs of support. John continued, his words spilling out in a rush. "I thought I was losing my mind. But hearing all of you... it makes me feel like maybe I'm not alone in this."

Susan smiled gently. "You're definitely not alone, John. We're all here for each other. It's a long road, but having support makes all the difference."

After the meeting, Gregory and John walked home silently, the weight of the evening's revelations settling over them. As they reached their building, John turned to Gregory, his eyes reflecting a mixture of exhaustion and hope.

"Thank you," he said quietly. "For not giving up on me."

Gregory smiled, clapping him on the shoulder. "We're in this together, John. One step at a time."

The support group became a regular part of John's routine. Each week, he found strength in the shared experiences and collective support, slowly rebuilding his sense of self. Gregory continued to stand by his side, offering unwavering encouragement.

Dr. Green adjusted John's treatment plan, incorporating the support group's benefits into their sessions. With the combination of therapy, medication, and the camaraderie of the group, John began to make tangible progress.

The shadows and whispers, though still present, lost some of their power. John learned techniques to manage his anxiety and ground himself in reality. He reconnected with Elena, who had remained a steadfast friend despite his struggles, and they began to rebuild their bond.

Months passed, and John's transformation became evident. He volunteered at the community center, helping others battling their demons. His experiences became a source of strength, and he found purpose in supporting those in need.

One evening, as Gregory and John sat on the porch, watching the sunset over the horizon, John turned to his friend with a smile.

"I never thought I'd get here," he said, his voice filled with gratitude. "But you never gave up on me. Thank you, Greg."

Gregory nodded, feeling a profound sense of fulfillment. "You did the hard work, John. I'm just glad I could be here to see it."

As the last rays of sunlight faded, John felt a sense of peace that had eluded him for so long. The road ahead was still uncertain, but he knew he had the strength and support to face whatever challenges came his way. With Gregory, Elena, and the support group, he was ready to embrace the future, leaving the shadows of his past behind.

18

The Final Descent

John sat in the dim light of his apartment, the weight of his despair pressing down on him like a suffocating shroud. The eldritch manifestations had grown bolder and more tangible, and the line between reality and nightmare had blurred beyond recognition. He could no longer distinguish his waking hours from the torment of his dreams. His mind, once a battleground, was now a war-torn wasteland where the horrors reigned supreme.

In the oppressive silence, John reflected on his life. The trauma of war, the relentless shadows of his past, and the ceaseless whisper of his inner demons had all led him to this moment. He felt trapped in an endless cycle of pain and fear, and no amount of therapy or medication had been able to silence the cacophony within his mind. The support from Stephanie, Dr. Green, and even Gregory had been a lifeline. Still, it now seemed like a distant memory, swallowed by the darkness.

John's thoughts turned to the idea of release. Death, he reasoned, was the only escape from this relentless torment.

The eldritch entities, those grotesque figments of his fractured psyche, would finally be silenced. He would find peace in the oblivion of nonexistence.

As the hours dragged on, John made his decision. He wrote a letter, his hands shaking, the words blurring on the page as tears streamed down his face. It was a farewell, an attempt to explain the inexplicable to those he was leaving behind. He hoped it would provide some semblance of closure for them, a fragile bridge over the chasm of grief his death would leave.

With a final glance around his apartment, the shadows dancing mockingly in the corners of his vision, John steeled himself. He reached for the bottle of pills on his nightstand, the one he'd been prescribed to numb his pain but had never fully trusted. Tonight, they would serve a different purpose. He swallowed them, his thoughts a turbulent storm of regret and resignation.

As the darkness closed in, John lay down, feeling the pull of oblivion. He hoped, prayed even, that this would be the end. That the horrors would not follow him into whatever lay beyond. His last conscious thought was a whispered plea for peace, a final, desperate hope that his suffering would cease.

The dawn broke with an eerie stillness, the first light of day filtering through the half-drawn blinds of John's apartment. The silence was deafening, the usual morning sounds of the neighborhood conspicuously absent, as if the world held its breath in mourning.

Gregory Thompson, the ever-watchful neighbor, had grown increasingly concerned over the past weeks. John's erratic behavior had taken a severe turn for the worse. Gregory couldn't shake the feeling that something terrible was about to happen. Today, that feeling is more vital than ever. He found himself standing at John's door, his hand hovering uncertainly before he knocked, the echoes of his knuckles on the wood like a funeral drumbeat.

"John?" Gregory called out, his voice tinged with anxiety. "It's Gregory. Are you alright?"

There was no response. The silence stretched on, heavy and foreboding. Gregory tried the door handle, and to his surprise, it turned quickly. The door creaked open, revealing the dim interior of John's apartment. The air inside was stale, imbued with an unsettling sense of abandonment.

"John?" Gregory called again, stepping cautiously into the apartment. His eyes scanned the room, taking in the disarray, the signs of a life unraveling. Books and papers were strewn across the floor, the remnants of meals left untouched, and the oppressive weight of despair hung in the air.

As Gregory ventured further in, his gaze fell upon the sight that made his heart clench with dread. Unnaturally still, John lay on the bed, a collection of empty pill bottles scattered across the nightstand. Gregory rushed to his side, shaking John's shoulder, desperately trying to rouse him.

"John! Wake up! Please, wake up!"

But John's body remained lifeless, his skin cold to the touch. Gregory's mind raced, a torrent of panic and helplessness washing over him. He fumbled for his phone, his fingers trembling as he dialed emergency services. The operator's calm, detached voice contrasted with the chaos in his mind.

"Please, send help! My neighbor... he... he's taken something, and he's not responding. Please, hurry!"

Gregory's voice cracked with emotion as he provided the necessary details, his eyes never leaving John's still form. The following minutes felt like an eternity, the sound of sirens in the distance a cruel reminder of the reality unfolding before him.

The paramedics arrived swiftly, their professionalism a stark contrast to the chaos that had taken hold in Gregory's mind. They moved with practiced precision, assessing John's condition, and their faces were grave. Gregory watched, helpless, as they worked to revive him, the cold reality of the situation sinking in deeper with each passing second.

"Clear," one of the paramedics called out as they applied the defibrillator pads to John's chest. The jolt caused John's body to twitch, but he remained unresponsive. They repeated the process, their efforts increasingly desperate. Gregory could hardly breathe, his heart pounding in his chest.

Finally, one of the paramedics shook his head, his expression grim. "I'm sorry," he said softly, turning to Gregory. "There's nothing more we can do. He's gone."

The words hit Gregory like a sledgehammer, knocking the breath from his lungs. He stumbled back, his hand covering his mouth as he tried to process the enormity of the loss. John was gone. The realization was too much to bear, and he sank to the floor, tears streaming down his face.

The paramedics began to pack up their equipment, their movements respectful and subdued. They spoke in hushed tones, their voices a distant murmur as Gregory's mind spiraled with grief and guilt. He had tried to help John, but it hadn't been enough. The weight of that failure crushed him, leaving him feeling utterly powerless.

In the following hours, the police arrived to take statements and assess the scene. Gregory recounted the events as best he could, his voice hollow and detached. The officers were kind, their questions gentle, but it all felt like a terrible dream, one he couldn't wake from.

As the day wore on, word of John's death spread through the building, the news sending shockwaves through the community. Neighbors who had once greeted John with friendly smiles now spoke in hushed whispers, their faces etched with sorrow and disbelief. John had been a familiar presence, his quiet demeanor masking the torment that had ultimately consumed him.

Elena, too, was devastated by the news. She arrived at the scene, her eyes red-rimmed and swollen from crying. She and Gregory shared a long, grief-stricken embrace, the weight of their shared loss pulling them together in a moment of profound sorrow.

"Why didn't he let us help him?" Elena whispered, her voice breaking. "Why did he have to do this alone?"

Gregory shook his head, his tears flowing freely. "I don't know," he admitted. "I wish I had the answer."

In the following days, the community came together to mourn John's passing. A small memorial was set up in the lobby of the building, where residents could leave flowers, notes, and mementos in their memory. The sense of loss was palpable, a stark reminder of the fragility of life and the silent battles that so many fought behind closed doors.

Stephanie was deeply affected by the news of John's death. She had worked tirelessly to help him, offering him compassion and support in his darkest moments. The news of his suicide shook her to the core, leaving her grappling with feelings of sadness and regret.

She had seen the signs of John's distress and had tried to reach out to him, but ultimately, she had been unable to save him from his demons. She wondered if there was more she could have done if she had missed any signs.

In her office, surrounded by the tools of her trade, Stephanie sat alone with her thoughts. She replayed her sessions with John in her mind, searching for clues for any indication of the turmoil that lay beneath the surface. She recalled his guarded demeanor and reluctance to open up, and she wondered if she could have done more to break through his defenses.

But the truth was, John's struggles ran deep, far beyond what Stephanie could have imagined. His mind was a battlefield, his inner demons relentless in their pursuit. Despite her best efforts, she could not save him from himself.

As the days passed, Stephanie found herself haunted by John's memory. She thought of him often, wondering what could have been done differently, what might have saved him from his tragic fate. She attended his memorial, laying a single white rose at the foot of his picture, a silent tribute to a life lost too soon.

In the following weeks, Stephanie threw herself into her work, determined to honor John's memory by helping others in need. She worked with renewed purpose, and her compassion and empathy shone through in client interactions. She knew that she couldn't save everyone, but she was determined to make a difference where she could.

And so, life went on. The memory of John lingered in the lives of those who had known him. His death served as a stark reminder of the fragility of life and the importance of reaching out to those in need. And though he was gone, his spirit lived on in the hearts of those who had known him, a testament to the impact that one life can have on those around them.

Meanwhile, the eldritch entities that had been bound to

John's tortured psyche were set free upon his death. His demise shattered the fragile barrier between their realm and ours, unleashing them upon the unsuspecting world.

At first, their presence was subtle—mere whispers on the edge of perception, strange noises in the dead of night. But as time passed, their influence grew, and their manifestations became more pronounced and unsettling.

Reports began to surface of strange happenings, of things that defied explanation. People spoke of shadowy figures lurking in the darkness, of voices whispering in forgotten tongues. The air itself seemed to thicken with dread as if the very fabric of reality was beginning to unravel.

As the manifestations grew more frequent, so did the fear and uncertainty gripping the world. Governments struggled to maintain order to reassure their citizens that everything was under control. But deep down, everyone knew something had been unleashed that could not be contained.

And so, the world descended into chaos, the once-familiar streets now teeming with eldritch horrors. The entities, now free from prison, reveled in their newfound freedom, wreaking havoc wherever they went.

But amidst the chaos and destruction, there were whispers of hope, of a prophecy that spoke of a chosen one who would rise to challenge the eldritch entities and restore balance to the world. Whether this prophecy would come to pass remained to be seen, but one thing was sure—the world would never be the same again.

In the aftermath of John's death, Stephanie, Gregory, and Sarah were left grappling with the loss of someone they had tried so hard to help. Each of them wondered if there was more they could have done if they could have somehow prevented this tragedy.

Stephanie, in particular, was haunted by John's final moments, by the knowledge that despite her best efforts, she had been unable to save him. She questioned her abilities as a therapist, wondering if she had failed him somehow.

Gregory struggled with guilt, wondering if he had missed signs that could have alerted him to John's intentions. He couldn't shake the feeling that he could have done more and should have reached out to John sooner.

Sarah, too, was wracked with guilt, wondering if there was something she could have said or done to make a difference. She couldn't help but feel she had let John down when he needed her most.

As they mourned John's passing, they were left to grapple with the harsh reality of mental illness and its devastating effects. They vowed to do better, to be more vigilant in recognizing the signs of distress in others, and to offer support and understanding to those who needed it most.

Stephanie, Gregory, and Sarah found solace in each other's company, drawing strength from their shared grief. They decided to channel their sorrow into action, forming a support group for those struggling with mental illness and trauma. They named it "John's Light," a tribute to the man they had lost and a beacon of hope for those still fighting their battles.

Through their efforts, they hoped to create a community where people could find understanding and compassion. In this place, no one would feel alone in their struggles. They organized workshops, therapy sessions, and awareness campaigns, determined to break the stigma surrounding mental health and ensure that John's death was not in vain.

In time, "John's Light" grew, silently touching the lives of many suffering. Stephanie, Gregory, and Sarah became pillars of support, their dedication and empathy inspiring others to seek help and share their stories. They knew that they couldn't save everyone, but they were determined to make a difference where they could.

As the world grappled with the eldritch horrors unleashed by John's death, the members of "John's Light" remained steadfast in their mission. They faced the darkness with courage and resilience, guided by the memory of a man who had fought bravely against his demons.

And though the battle against the eldritch entities raged on, there was a glimmer of hope—a reminder that the human spirit could endure and overcome even in the face of unimaginable horror.

Stephanie, Gregory, and Sarah stood together, united by their loss and determination to make a difference. They knew the road ahead would be long and complex, but they were ready to face it together, one step at a time.

As they looked to the future, they carried the lessons they had learned from John's struggle. They knew that compassion, understanding, and support could make all the difference in the world, and they vowed to be a source of light for those lost in the darkness.

In the end, John's legacy was not despair but hope. Through the efforts of those who had loved and cared for him, his memory lived on as a beacon of resilience and strength, a testament to the enduring power of the human spirit.

19

Reflections on a Life Lost

The office was quieter than usual, the air heavy with a palpable sense of loss. Liam Carter sat at his desk, his usually sharp mind clouded with thoughts of John. He remembered him as a diligent employee, always willing to go the extra mile. As Liam reflected on John's life, he couldn't help but feel a deep pang of regret for not recognizing the missed deadlines, uncharacteristic absences, and subtle changes in behavior that now took on a new significance. He blamed himself for not reaching out when he had the chance, but he knew he couldn't change the past.

Determined to do better, Liam made a vow. He promised to create a more supportive environment where mental health was openly discussed and addressed. This vow was not just for John but for everyone in the workplace. He understood now that mental health was just as important as physical health and that ignoring it could have devastating consequences.

As Liam sat in his office, surrounded by the trappings of corporate success, he saw the profound impact of John's death on the entire office. People were more aware and more willing to talk about mental health. The stigma surrounding the topic began to fade, replaced by a sense of openness and understanding. John's death sparked a long overdue conversation, forcing people to confront their attitudes toward mental illness and the importance of seeking help.

In the following weeks and months, Liam remained true to his vow. He implemented mental health awareness programs, encouraged open dialogue, and provided resources for needy people. He brought in experts to educate employees about the signs of mental illness and the support available. These changes transformed the workplace culture, creating a safer and more compassionate environment.

Though Liam would never forget John or his death's impact on the office, he found solace in knowing that his legacy lived on. John's death had not been in vain; it had sparked a movement towards greater understanding, compassion, and support for those struggling with mental illness. As Liam looked out at the office, now filled with renewed hope and purpose, he knew this was the beginning of a long journey toward healing and awareness.

The impact was immediate. Employees began to open up about their mental health issues, sharing their stories and seeking support. What was once a stigmatized topic became a regular part of office conversations, and the culture shifted towards greater understanding and acceptance. Liam knew there was still work to be done. Still, he vowed to continue advocating for mental health awareness and support in the workplace to ensure that no one else suffered in silence like John had.

John's death sent shockwaves through the office, prompting a wave of introspection among his colleagues. They began to question their attitudes towards mental illness, realizing they had overlooked signs of suffering in others. Sharing stories and memories of John, they saw him in a new light—a man who struggled silently and faced his demons alone. His death served as a stark reminder of the importance of seeking help and the devastating consequences of untreated mental illness.

For many, John's death was a wake-up call, forcing them to confront their mental health issues, seek help, and support each other. The office became more compassionate and understanding, where employees felt safe sharing their feelings and seeking support. The ripple effects of John's death extended beyond the office, reaching into the community and sparking a conversation about mental health. People began to realize that mental illness was not something to be ashamed of but something that needed to be addressed openly and honestly.

Determined to make a difference, Liam took this message to heart and began to advocate for change. He implemented mental health initiatives in the workplace, ensuring employees had access to necessary resources. He partnered with local organizations to raise awareness about mental health and provide community support. Though change wouldn't happen overnight, Liam was committed to making a difference.

The ripple effects of John's death prompted others to reflect on their attitudes towards mental illness. People began to realize that mental health was as important as physical health and that seeking help was okay. As the months passed, the culture around mental health shifted. The stigma faded, replaced by understanding and acceptance. People felt more comfortable discussing their mental health issues, knowing they would be met with compassion and support.

John's death was a tragedy, but it was also a catalyst for change. It sparked a long-overdue conversation about mental health, leading to greater awareness and understanding. As Liam looked back on John's life, he knew his legacy would live on. John's death prompted a wave of change that would benefit countless others. Though he would never forget John, he took comfort in knowing his death had not been in vain.

In the end, John's death served as a poignant reminder of the fragility of life and the importance of mental health awareness and support. It sparked a movement towards greater understanding and compassion in the workplace and the community. As Liam reflected on John's impact, he felt a sense of peace. He knew he couldn't change the past but could make a difference in the future. He could honor John's memory by advocating for mental health awareness and support, creating a more compassionate workplace, and being there for those who needed help.

And so, as he looked out at the world beyond his office window, Liam made a silent vow. He vowed never to forget John and the lessons his death had taught him. He promised to continue fighting for mental health awareness and support to ensure no one else suffered in silence like John had. As the sun set, casting long shadows across the office, Liam felt a renewed sense of purpose. John's death had been a tragedy, but it had also been a catalyst for change. Though he would never forget the man who inspired it all, he knew John would have been proud of the legacy he left behind.

20

The Shadow's Revelation

The office was quieter than usual, the air heavy with a palpable sense of loss. Liam Carter sat at his desk, his usually sharp mind clouded with thoughts of John. He remembered him as a diligent employee, always willing to go the extra mile. As Liam reflected on John's life, he couldn't help but feel a deep pang of regret for not recognizing the missed deadlines, uncharacteristic absences, and subtle changes in behavior that now took on a new significance. He blamed himself for not reaching out when he had the chance, but he knew he couldn't change the past.

Determined to do better, Liam made a vow. He promised to create a more supportive environment where mental health was openly discussed and addressed. This vow was not just for John but for everyone in the workplace. He understood now that mental health was just as important as physical health and that ignoring it could have devastating consequences.

As Liam sat in his office, surrounded by the trappings of corporate success, he saw the profound impact of John's death on the entire office. People were more aware and more willing to talk about mental health. The stigma surrounding the topic began to fade, replaced by a sense of openness and understanding. John's death sparked a long overdue conversation, forcing people to confront their attitudes toward mental illness and the importance of seeking help.

In the following weeks and months, Liam remained true to his vow. He implemented mental health awareness programs, encouraged open dialogue, and provided resources for needy people. He brought in experts to educate employees about the signs of mental illness and the support available. These changes transformed the workplace culture, creating a safer and more compassionate environment.

Though Liam would never forget John or his death's impact on the office, he found solace in knowing that his legacy lived on. John's death had not been in vain; it had sparked a movement towards greater understanding, compassion, and support for those struggling with mental illness. As Liam looked out at the office, now filled with renewed hope and purpose, he knew this was the beginning of a long journey toward healing and awareness.

The impact was immediate. Employees began to open up about their mental health issues, sharing their stories and seeking support. What was once a stigmatized topic became a regular part of office conversations, and the culture shifted towards greater understanding and acceptance. Liam knew there was still work to be done. Still, he vowed to continue advocating for mental health awareness and support in the workplace to ensure that no one else suffered in silence like John had.

John's death sent shockwaves through the office, prompting a wave of introspection among his colleagues. They began to question their attitudes towards mental illness, realizing they had overlooked signs of suffering in others. Sharing stories and memories of John, they saw him in a new light—a man who struggled silently and faced his demons alone. His death served as a stark reminder of the importance of seeking help and the devastating consequences of untreated mental illness.

For many, John's death was a wake-up call, forcing them to confront their mental health issues, seek help, and support each other. The office became more compassionate and understanding, where employees felt safe sharing their feelings and seeking support. The ripple effects of John's death extended beyond the office, reaching into the community and sparking a conversation about mental health. People began to realize that mental illness was not something to be ashamed of but something that needed to be addressed openly and honestly.

Determined to make a difference, Liam took this message to heart and began to advocate for change. He implemented mental health initiatives in the workplace, ensuring employees had access to necessary resources. He partnered with local organizations to raise awareness about mental health and provide community support. Though change wouldn't happen overnight, Liam was committed to making a difference.

The ripple effects of John's death prompted others to reflect on their attitudes towards mental illness. People began to realize that mental health was as important as physical health and that seeking help was okay. As the months passed, the culture around mental health shifted. The stigma faded, replaced by understanding and acceptance. People felt more comfortable discussing their mental health issues, knowing they would be met with compassion and support.

John's death was a tragedy, but it was also a catalyst for change. It sparked a long-overdue conversation about mental health, leading to greater awareness and understanding. As Liam looked back on John's life, he knew his legacy would live on. John's death prompted a wave of change that would benefit countless others. Though he would never forget John, he took comfort in knowing his death had not been in vain.

In the end, John's death served as a poignant reminder of the fragility of life and the importance of mental health awareness and support. It sparked a movement towards greater understanding and compassion in the workplace and the community. As Liam reflected on John's impact, he felt a sense of peace. He knew he couldn't change the past but could make a difference in the future. He could honor John's memory by advocating for mental health awareness and support, creating a more compassionate workplace, and being there for those who needed help.

And so, as he looked out at the world beyond his office window, Liam made a silent vow. He vowed never to forget John and the lessons his death had taught him. He promised to continue fighting for mental health awareness and support to ensure no one else suffered in silence like John had. As the sun set, casting long shadows across the office, Liam felt a renewed sense of purpose. John's death had been a tragedy, but it had also been a catalyst for change. Though he would never forget the man who inspired it all, he knew John would have been proud of the legacy he left behind.

John's final moments were a blur of despair and resignation. The pain and confusion that had plagued him for so long seemed to reach a crescendo, drowning out any remaining hope. He lay there, his life ebbing away, and felt a chilling presence creeping into the periphery of his awareness.

In the oppressive silence, John's thoughts fragmented. The room around him seemed to pulse with an eerie, unnatural energy. The Shadow Self, a dark figure lurking in his mind's corners, stepped forward. Its form was an unsettling reflection of John, twisted and distorted, with eyes that gleamed with an evil intelligence.

"You never understood, did you?" The Shadow's voice was a cold whisper filled with sinister delight. "This was always the plan."

John's vision blurred, but the Shadow's words cut through the haze like a knife. He had always felt haunted by his inner demons, but he had never realized the full extent of their influence. The Shadow began to reveal its true intentions. This narrative had been unfolding behind the scenes, manipulating every aspect of John's life.

"You thought you were losing your mind, but I orchestrated it all," the Shadow continued, widening grin. "Every failure, every moment of despair, I was there, guiding you to this very end."

Memories flashed through John's mind, moments he had attributed to his own weakness and mental instability. The Shadow had been whispering doubts, feeding his paranoia, and amplifying his fears. It had preyed on his vulnerabilities, pushing him further into isolation and despair.

"You see, John," the Shadow said, its tone almost affectionate, "you were never meant to survive. Your suffering, your downfall, was all part of the plan. And now, as you fade away, I will take over. Your life, your identity, will be mine."

John's heart pounded in his chest, terror and anger surging

through him. But it was too late. His strength was gone, his will broken. The Shadow had won, and he could do nothing to stop it.

As darkness closed in, John felt a deep sense of betrayal, not just by his mind but by the very fabric of his existence. The Shadow's revelation was a final, cruel twist, a reminder of the insidious nature of untreated mental illness and the devastating consequences it could bring.

John slipped into oblivion with a final, shuddering breath, leaving the Shadow to claim its prize. The room grew still, the air thick with an oppressive silence, as the extent of the Shadow's influence became evident.

As John's consciousness faded, the Shadow Self began to form, stepping out of the recesses of John's mind and into the physical world. The room, once a silent witness to John's suffering, now seemed to pulse with an evil energy. The air grew heavy and thick with the weight of the Shadow's presence.

It moved with a grace that belied its sinister nature, each step echoing with a sense of finality. The Shadow glanced around the room, a mocking smile on its lips. It was no longer confined to the abstract corners of John's psyche; it was free, ready to inhabit the life it had meticulously dismantled.

The Shadow paused by the mirror, gazing at its reflection. It was a twisted parody of John, bearing his likeness but with an eerie, otherworldly quality. The eyes, dark and void-like, held a gleam of triumph.

"I am free," it whispered, relishing the sound of its voice in the room's stillness. "Free to live, to continue where you failed."

As the Shadow began to explore its new reality, it reveled

in the physical sensations it had only ever observed from the depths of John's mind. It flexed its fingers, feeling the stretch of skin and muscle, the subtle creak of bones. The experience was intoxicating, starkly contrasting to the abstract existence it had known.

The Shadow's thoughts turned to the world outside, a realm it had influenced but never fully interacted with. It remembered the people John had known, the relationships it had strained and severed. There was a dark satisfaction in the knowledge that it could now manipulate them directly, continuing its insidious work on a grander scale.

In the days leading up to John's final act, the Shadow had woven itself into his interactions, subtly steering conversations and amplifying conflicts. It pushed John to the brink, ensuring his sense of isolation was absolute. With John gone, the Shadow could continue its manipulations without resistance.

It thought of Elena, whose concern for John had grown into desperation. The Shadow could feel her presence, her lingering worry like a thread it could pull at any moment. There was Gregory, the neighbor, who had tried to offer support, unaware of the true nature of John's torment. And then there was Sarah, the social worker, whose compassion had been another avenue for the Shadow's influence.

As the Shadow stood there, surveying the remnants of John's life, it felt an almost giddy anticipation. It had been patient, biding its time, and finally, it emerged victorious. The plan had come to fruition, and the world lay before it, a canvas for its dark designs.

With a final glance around the room, the Shadow entered the hallway, leaving behind John Miller's physical shell. It moved with a newfound confidence, ready to embrace its role in the world beyond. The Shadow was no longer a mere figment of John's fractured mind; it was a living entity, poised to continue its work with chilling precision.

The Shadow moved through the apartment, transforming the familiar surroundings into a landscape of ominous potential. It paused by the bookshelf, running a hand over the dusty spines of neglected books. Each title reminded John's once vibrant curiosity, now reduced to mere relics of a life overshadowed by despair.

As it continued its exploration, the Shadow felt a surge of satisfaction. John's memories were now its own, a rich tapestry of experiences it could draw upon and manipulate. The Shadow knew the intimate details of John's relationships, fears, and deepest regrets. It was equipped with all it needed to navigate and exploit the world John had left behind.

The first task was to visit Elena. She had been the closest to John in his final days, and her concern became a relentless pursuit of understanding. The Shadow relished the thought of their reunion, anticipating her shock and confusion. It would be easy to play on her emotions, to twist her empathy into something more sinister.

Elena's apartment was just a few blocks away, a familiar path in John's mind. As the Shadow approached her building, observing its new surroundings through John's eyes took a moment. The world seemed more prosperous, more vibrant, each detail imbued with an unsettling clarity.

When it reached Elena's door, the Shadow hesitated briefly, savoring the moment. Then, raising a hand, it knocked a sound that echoed with the weight of its newfound reality.

Elena answered, her face a mix of surprise and relief. "John? I thought—"

"Yes, it's me," the Shadow replied, mimicking John's voice with eerie precision. "I'm sorry for worrying you. I just needed some time to think."

She stepped aside, allowing the Shadow to enter. The apartment was warm and inviting, starkly contrasting John's home's cold, oppressive atmosphere. The Shadow took a seat, noting the familiar scent of Elena's perfume mingling with the faint aroma of coffee.

"I've been so worried," Elena said, trembling. "You just disappeared. What happened?"

The Shadow crafted its response carefully, drawing on John's memories to weave a convincing tale. "I've been struggling more than I let on. The pressure, the… demons, they got the best of me. But I'm here now, trying to make sense of it all."

Elena's eyes softened with sympathy. "I'm here for you, John. Whatever you need."

The Shadow nodded, its expression mirroring John's familiar look of gratitude. Inside, it relished the ease with which it had gained her trust. This was only the beginning, a first step in a larger plan to entangle itself deeper into the lives of those around John.

As they talked, the Shadow fed on Elena's concern, using it to strengthen its hold. Each word and each gesture was calculated to deepen her sense of connection and dependency. The Shadow knew controlling Elen could further isolate her from others, ensuring her focus remained entirely on its fabricated struggles.

Their conversation stretched late into the evening, and the Shadow masterfully deflected any probing questions about its sudden reappearance. When it left, Elena was convinced of its sincerity, and her relief was palpable.

Stepping back into the night, the Shadow felt a surge of triumph. It had successfully infiltrated the first of John's relationships, laying the groundwork for future manipulations. The path ahead was clear, and the Shadow was ready to continue its insidious work, spreading its influence further into John's world.

As it walked, the Shadow reveled in the freedom of its new existence. No longer confined to the abstract confines of John's mind, it was free to shape reality to its will, to extend its reach and deepen its control. The night seemed to embrace it, the darkness a fitting cloak for its evil intentions.

The following day, the Shadow stood before John's former workplace, an old warehouse converted into a small tech firm. John's presence here had always been understated, a diligent worker who preferred the background to the limelight. The Shadow's intent, however, was different. It was not content to linger unnoticed. It wanted to infiltrate, to unsettle.

As it approached the entrance, it could feel the familiar twinge of anxiety that John had often experienced. But unlike John, the Shadow thrived on this energy, twisting it into a weapon of manipulation. It entered the building, greeted by the sterile hum of fluorescent lights and the soft murmur of office chatter.

Liam Carter, the manager, spotted it almost immediately. "John! Good to see you. We've been worried sick."

The Shadow offered a strained smile, John's memories of Liam's kindness guiding its expression. "Sorry for disappearing like that. I needed some time to get my head straight."

Liam's concern was palpable. "No need to apologize. We were just worried about you. Is everything okay?"

The Shadow nodded, letting a hint of vulnerability seep into its voice. "I'm trying to work through some things. It's been tough, but I'm getting there."

Liam's expression softened. "Take all the time you need. Your job will be here when you're ready. If there's anything we can do to help, just say the word."

As they spoke, the Shadow noted the subtle dynamics within the office—the hushed conversations and the wary glances from colleagues who had once been friendly but now seemed unsure. It knew that exploiting these minor fractures could deepen its influence.

"I appreciate that, Liam," the Shadow replied, its tone carefully measured. "Actually, I was hoping to talk to a few people. Maybe share a bit of what I've been going through. I think it might help to be open about it."

Liam's face lit up with approval. "That's a great idea, John. I think it would be good for everyone to hear your story. It might help others who are struggling, too."

The Shadow nodded, already planning how it would twist John's narrative into a tale of continued despair and confusion designed to seed doubt and discomfort among his colleagues. It knew that by presenting itself as a cautionary example, it could subtly undermine the sense of security and solidarity within the office.

Later that day, a small gathering was arranged in the break room. The Shadow stood before a group of familiar faces, John's former coworkers who had once shared camaraderie and support. It began to speak, drawing on the raw emotions of John's final days but twisting them into a portrayal of relentless, consuming darkness.

"I've been fighting a battle in my mind," it said, voice

trembling with feigned vulnerability. "Every day feels like a struggle, and some days, it's hard to see a way out."

The room was silent, the weight of the Shadow's words pressing down on the assembled group. It could see the discomfort in their eyes, the way they shifted uneasily in their seats. This was what it wanted—to plant the seeds of doubt and fear, to erode the foundation of support that John had once leaned on.

As the Shadow continued, it wove a narrative of relentless torment, of inner demons that refused to be exorcised. It spoke of sleepless nights and days filled with an unshakeable dread. It described the suffocating feeling of isolation, the belief that no one could truly understand the depths of its suffering.

When it finished, the room was heavy with silence. Liam was the first to speak, his voice thick with emotion. "John, I had no idea it was this bad. We're here for you. Whatever you need."

The Shadow nodded, its expression one of grateful exhaustion. "Thank you, Liam. Just knowing that helps more than you can imagine."

But inside, it reveled in the unease it had sown. Each worried glance, each whispered conversation that followed, was a victory. The Shadow knew that by maintaining this façade of vulnerability, it could continue to manipulate and control, deepening its influence with each passing day.

As it left the office that evening, the Shadow felt renewed purpose. John's life was now its own, a canvas on which it could paint a narrative of control and domination. It relished the thought of the chaos it would bring, the lives it would disrupt, all in the name of its twisted existence.

221

The days that followed were a blur of manipulation and deceit. The Shadow, masquerading as John, continued to exploit his colleagues' sympathy and concern, weaving a web of lies and half-truths that only deepened their unease. It played the part of the tormented soul with practiced ease, drawing others into its dark and twisted narrative.

Elena, John's former girlfriend, was one of the few who remained unconvinced. She had sensed something off about John's behavior, even before his death, and now, as she watched the Shadow manipulate those around her, her suspicions grew.

One evening, as the Shadow sat alone in John's apartment, reveling in the chaos it had created, there was a knock at the door. It opened to reveal Elena, her expression a mixture of concern and determination.

"John, we need to talk," she said, stepping into the apartment without waiting for an invitation.

The Shadow tensed, its facade slipping momentarily before it regained control. "Elena, what are you doing here?"

"I've been watching you, John," Elena said, her voice firm. "Something isn't right. You're not acting like yourself."

The Shadow laughed, a cold, mocking sound. "And how would you know what I'm supposed to act like? You think you know me, but you don't. You never did."

Elena's gaze was steady. "I know you're hurting, John. I know you're struggling. But this…this isn't you. This isn't the man I fell in love with."

The Shadow's facade cracked momentarily, revealing a glimpse of the darkness beneath. "You don't know anything about me," it said, voice low and dangerous. "You never did."

Elena took a step forward, undeterred. "I know enough to

see when someone is in pain. I know enough to see when someone is being manipulated. And right now, John, it's clear to me that you're not in control. Something else is."

The Shadow's eyes narrowed, a flicker of fear crossing its face before it masked it with a sneer. "And what if something else is in control? What does it matter to you?"

Elena reached out, taking the Shadow's hand in hers. "Because I care about you, John. Because I don't want to see you consumed by this darkness. Please, let me help you."

For a moment, the Shadow wavered, the facade slipping further as John's memories of Elena's kindness and compassion fought against its grip. But then, with a snarl, it pulled away, retreating into the darkness that lurked within.

"You can't help me, Elena," it said, voice cold and final. "No one can."

With that, it turned and fled, leaving Elena standing alone in the empty apartment, the weight of what she had just witnessed settling heavily upon her shoulders. She knew then that John was truly gone, consumed by the darkness that had taken hold of him.

As the days turned into weeks, the Shadow's grip on John's life tightened, its influence spreading like poison through his former workplace and beyond. It reveled in the chaos it had created, the lives it had disrupted, all in the name of its twisted existence.

But Elena wasn't the only one who sensed something amiss. John's confidante, Stephanie, had quietly observed the Shadow's actions, piecing together the truth behind its facade. She had seen the toll it had taken on John's life, the pain and suffering it had caused in its quest for control.

Stephanie confronted it one night as the Shadow reveled

223

in its power. Her voice was filled with a quiet resolve. "You don't belong here," she said, her words cutting through the darkness surrounding them. "You're not John, and you never will be."

The Shadow laughed, a hollow, mocking sound. "And who are you to challenge me? I am the true master of this world, the puppeteer pulling the strings."

Stephanie shook her head, her gaze steady. "No, you're not. You're just a shadow, a twisted reflection of the man John once was. But he's gone now, consumed by your darkness. And it's time for you to leave as well."

With that, Stephanie touched the Shadow's hand gently but firmly. There was a flash of light, blinding in its intensity. The Shadow screamed, a sound of pure rage and anguish, as it was torn from the physical world and banished back to the darkness from whence it came.

As the light faded, Stephanie stood alone in the empty room, the weight of what she had just accomplished settling upon her shoulders. John was lost to the darkness that had consumed him, but she had saved others from the same fate.

And as she looked at the world, she knew the battle was far from over. The shadows would always linger, waiting for a chance to return. But for now, the light had triumphed, and hope had prevailed.

21

Reflections on a Lost Soul

Dr. Michael Chang sat in his office, the soft glow of the desk lamp casting a warm light over the room. He had just finished reviewing John's case file, and a lingering sadness hung in the air. John's story was a tragic one, a life lost to the shadows of untreated mental illness.

As Dr. Chang reflected on John's case, he felt a deep sense of frustration. Treating complex mental health issues stemming from childhood trauma was never easy, but John's case had been particularly challenging. The intricacies of Complex Post-Traumatic Stress Disorder (CPTSD) make effective treatment complicated. Despite his best efforts, Dr. Chang could not reach John in time.

He thought about their sessions, the moments of breakthrough followed by setbacks. He had seen glimpses of hope in John's eyes, only to watch them fade as the darkness closed in again. It was a heartbreaking cycle that often left Dr. Chang feeling powerless.

Yet, amidst the sadness and frustration, Dr. Chang felt a surge of determination. John's story was a sobering reminder of the importance of mental health awareness and support. It highlighted the need for better education and resources for those struggling with mental illness, especially those stemming from childhood trauma.

As Dr. Chang considered the broader implications of John's case, he realized that his story was not unique. There were countless others like John battling their demons in silence. This was a stark reminder of the limitations of the current mental health care system and the urgent need for continued advocacy and support.

He leaned back in his chair, memories of John's haunted eyes flashing through his mind. John had walked into his office with a look of profound pain, a pain that therapy alone had struggled to heal. Despite moments of progress, the deep wounds of John's past had resisted treatment, leaving Dr. Chang feeling helpless.

The challenges of treating CPTSD were immense. Traditional therapy methods often fell short, unable to fully address the deep-seated traumas that individuals like John carried. It required a delicate balance of patience, understanding, and empathy—qualities that Dr. Chang prided himself on, yet sometimes felt inadequate against such profound pain.

Reflecting on John's case, Dr. Chang felt an overwhelming sadness for the life lost and the potential unrealized. But amidst the sadness, he also felt a renewed sense of purpose. John's story reminded him why he had chosen to become a therapist: to help those in need, to be a beacon of light in their darkest hours.

As he sat in his office, surrounded by the quiet of the evening, Dr. Chang made a silent vow. He vowed to continue fighting for those who couldn't fight for themselves and to advocate for better mental health care and support. He knew it wouldn't be easy, but he also knew it was necessary. John's story had left a mark on him that would stay with him for the rest of his life.

Dr. Chang's reflections led him to contemplate the broader implications of his work. John's story was not isolated but a reflection of a more significant societal issue. The prevalence of untreated mental illness stemming from childhood trauma affected countless individuals, yet it often went unnoticed or ignored.

As a therapist, Dr. Chang understood the complexities of mental health care. Treating conditions like CPTSD requires a multi-faceted approach, encompassing therapy, support networks, education, and awareness. Yet, he knew these resources were often lacking, especially for those who needed them most.

John's case opened Dr. Chang's eyes to the need for improved mental health awareness and support. Society as a whole needed to change its attitudes towards mental illness. It was not enough to treat the symptoms; the root causes must also be addressed.

He thought about the stigma that still surrounded mental illness, the misconceptions and stereotypes that prevented many from seeking help. To make a real difference, these barriers needed to be broken down, and people needed to be educated about the realities of mental health.

As he sat in his office, Dr. Chang made a silent vow. He vowed to continue advocating for improved mental health awareness and support within his practice and the wider community. He knew it wouldn't be easy, but he also knew it was necessary. John's story had taught him that much.

Dr. Chang felt renewed purpose as he prepared to close up for the night. John's story had left a mark on him, guiding him in his work and reminding him of the importance of his role as a therapist. Though he couldn't change the past, he was determined to make a difference in the future.

Walking through the empty streets, Dr. Chang's thoughts turned to the countless others silently suffering. He thought about the limitations of the current mental health care system and the need for continued advocacy and support. He knew the task ahead was daunting, and the road to progress was long and uncertain.

But amidst the uncertainty, Dr. Chang felt a sense of resolve. John's story reminded him of the importance of his work and the need to keep fighting for those who couldn't fight for themselves. He knew change wouldn't happen overnight but was determined to do his part.

Dr. Chang felt a sense of peace wash over him as he reached his home. He knew that John's story would stay with him for the rest of his life, guiding him in his work and reminding him of the importance of compassion and understanding in treating mental illness.

As he settled into bed, the weight of the day's events lingered in his thoughts. John's story stirred something profound: a sense of purpose and determination to make a difference in mental health care.

Dr. Chang thought about the challenges ahead as he lay in the darkness, the faint glow of streetlights casting shadows on the walls. He knew the road to improving mental health care would be long and arduous, but he was prepared to face it head-on.

He envisioned a world where mental health was treated

with the same importance as physical health, where those in need could access the support and resources they deserved. He knew achieving this vision would require perseverance and dedication, challenging the stigma surrounding mental illness, and advocating for better education and resources.

However, Dr. Chang felt renewed determination as he thought about John and the countless others suffering. He couldn't change the past but could work towards a better future.

As he closed his eyes and let sleep take him, Dr. Chang made a silent promise to himself: to never give up, to continue fighting for those who couldn't fight for themselves, to be a voice for the voiceless and a beacon of hope in the darkness of mental illness.

And as he drifted into dreams, Dr. Chang felt a sense of peace. The road ahead would be difficult, but he knew he was not alone. With John's spirit guiding him, he was ready to face whatever challenges lay ahead to improve mental health care for all.

Part 4
The Unleashing

IV

Part Four

22

The Unleashing

The sky darkened unnaturally over the city, casting an eerie twilight despite it being midday. The air felt heavy, charged with an unseen energy that prickled the skin and set nerves on edge. Birds fell silent, their songs replaced by an oppressive, unnatural quiet as people went about their daily routines; an uneasy feeling crept over them like a shadow just out of sight.

In the heart of John's old apartment, the point of his final despair, something ancient and evil stirred. Invisible to the naked eye, the eldritch entities began to seep through the thin veil separating their realm from the human world. Their forms were nebulous, shifting masses of darkness and light, defying any logical shape or structure.

The first to notice were the animals. Dogs howled, and cats hissed at seemingly empty spaces. Birds took to the sky in frantic flocks, their instinctive fear sensing the unnatural presence before it fully manifested. Humans, less attuned to these subtle shifts, merely felt an inexplicable sense of dread.

As the entities gained strength, they began to take form. A shimmering distortion appeared in a quiet suburban neighborhood, bending light and casting strange shadows. It merged into a vaguely humanoid shape but wrong in proportions, with limbs too long and joints bent at impossible angles. It moved with a fluid, almost liquid grace, leaving a trail of frost on the ground where it passed.

A passerby, an elderly man walking his dog, was the first to see it. His dog, a usually calm Labrador, whimpered and crouched behind him. The man's breath caught in his throat as he stared at the entity, his mind struggling to comprehend what he saw. The entity turned its head—if it could be called that—toward him, and the man felt a cold, invasive presence probe at the edges of his sanity. He stumbled backward, the leash slipping from his hand as the dog bolted.

Across town, another entity emerged, a writhing mass of tentacles and eyes, each orb reflecting a different reality and nightmare. It materialized in the middle of a busy street, causing cars to screech to a halt. Drivers and passengers gaped in horror as the entity slithered and pulsed, its eyes locking onto each person, filling their minds with unspeakable visions.

Panic spread rapidly. Emergency services were overwhelmed with calls describing impossible creatures and unnatural phenomena. Police and first responders, unprepared for the eldritch horrors, found themselves paralyzed by fear and confusion. In the chaos, societal norms began to fray. People barricaded themselves in their homes, seeking refuge from the incomprehensible terror stalking their streets.

As the entities spread, their influence grew, warping reality around them. Plants withered and died, their life force drained by the unnatural cold. Buildings groaned as if under extraordinary weight, glass windows shattering without

234

cause. The very air seemed to thicken, making each breath a struggle.

A young mother clutched her children in a remote farmhouse as the temperature plummeted. Frost crept up the walls and outside; shadows twisted and writhed in the failing light. She whispered prayers to any deity that might listen, but deep down, she knew no divine intervention was coming. The world was changing, and not for the better.

Through it all, a sense of foreboding and dread permeated every corner of the city, spreading outward like a dark stain. The eldritch entities, once bound by the fragile mind of a broken man, were now free to roam, their malevolence unleashed upon an unsuspecting world. Their presence disrupted the natural order, bending reality to their will and instilling fear wherever they went.

And so began the reign of the eldritch entities, a time of chaos and confusion where the boundaries between the known and the unknown were irrevocably shattered.

As the eldritch entities spread their influence, chaos unfolded with terrifying momentum. In the city center, a group of office workers huddled in their building's lobby, peering out at the streets now cloaked in unnatural shadows. The air outside seemed to ripple as if the presence of the entities was warping reality itself. Those brave enough to venture outside were lost in a disorienting labyrinth of shifting streets and twisted buildings.

The media needed help understanding the phenomenon. News anchors stammered through reports, their faces pale and eyes wide with fear. Broadcasts showed footage of the creatures, but the camera lenses distorted their proper forms, making them appear as writhing masses of darkness and light, defying any coherent description. Experts were brought on to speculate, but their theories were drowned out by the sheer, inexplicable horror of what was happening.

A woman stood at her kitchen window in one neighborhood, staring in numb disbelief as a shadowy figure moved through her garden. It had no clear outline, just a shifting, smoky presence that seemed to absorb the light around it. Playing in the next room, her children were blissfully unaware of the terror just outside. She wanted to scream, to warn them, but her voice caught in her throat, choked by an overwhelming sense of dread.

The eldritch entities did not merely wander; they seemed to seek places where fear and despair were most potent. Hospitals became focal points of their venom. Patients already suffering from illness and injury found their conditions exacerbated by the presence of these beings. Doctors and nurses, trained to handle crises, found themselves powerless against the creeping madness that spread through their wards.

One nurse, Maria, struggled to maintain her composure while checking on her patients. She moved from room to room, her steps faltering as shadows seemed to stretch and reach for her. In the ICU, she saw a patient thrashing in his bed, eyes wide with terror as he screamed about the things he could see. Maria tried to comfort him, but her sanity was slipping, frayed by the whispers coming from everywhere and nowhere.

Elsewhere, in a small apartment, a young artist named Alex huddled under a blanket, sketchpad clutched to his chest. He had been drawing furiously since the entities first appeared, compelled to capture their forms on paper. His sketches, once lifelike and detailed, had devolved into chaotic, nightmarish scribbles. The entities visited him frequently, their shapes twisting and merging in his mind's eye, leaving him unable to distinguish between his art and reality. Each stroke of his pencil seemed to pull them closer as if his drawings were a gateway they could step through.

The city was becoming a landscape of fear. Schools closed, their halls empty, echoing the cries of children who had seen too much. Shops were abandoned, shelves still stocked with goods no one dared to claim. Once bustling with life, the streets were deserted, except for the occasional figure darting from one hiding place to another. Each step was fraught with the terror of encountering one of the eldritch entities.

In a high-rise building, a businessman named Richard watched the chaos unfold from his office window. He had always prided himself on his rational mind and unshakeable composure. But now, as he watched shadows dance and warp across the skyline, his confidence crumbled. He saw his colleagues, normally stoic and collected, break down into sobs or lash out in irrational anger. Richard himself felt a cold, creeping dread that gnawed at his sanity. He picked up the phone to call his family, but the line was dead, replaced by a whispering static that seemed to speak directly to his darkest fears.

The world was unraveling, and with each passing moment, the eldritch entities tightened their grip. They thrived on the chaos and confusion, drawing strength from the fear they instilled. The boundaries between reality and nightmare blurred, leaving humanity in terror. The once-stable world was now a realm of shadows and whispers, where the eldritch entities reigned supreme, their presence a constant, haunting reminder of the fragility of sanity.

As the eldritch entities spread their influence, more and more people fell victim to their power. Some succumbed to madness, their minds unable to comprehend the horrors they witnessed. Others were consumed by fear, unable to find solace in a world irrevocably changed.

In the city's heart, a makeshift shelter had been set up for those seeking refuge from the chaos outside. Volunteers worked tirelessly to provide food and comfort, but their efforts could have been more successful. The entities' influence seeped into the shelter, manifesting as shadows that twisted and stretched along the walls. People whispered of seeing things in the dark, their voices tinged with hysteria.

A young woman named Lily clutched her infant son to her chest, her eyes wide with fear. She had fled her home after an entity appeared in her living room, its presence warping reality around it. Now, in the shelter, she felt no safer. The whispers followed her, filling her mind with doubts and fears. She glanced around at the other refugees, seeing the same haunted look in their eyes.

An elderly man, James, sat in a corner, his hands trembling as he muttered to himself. He had been a respected professor before the entities arrived, known for his rational mind and sharp intellect. But now, he was a shadow of his former self, his mind fractured by the horrors he had witnessed. He spoke of ancient beings and forgotten realms, his words a jumble of fear and madness.

The volunteers, too, struggled to maintain their composure. Sarah, a nurse, had worked in the shelter since the entities first appeared. She had seen the toll it took on people, the way it broke them down, leaving them hollow and terrified. She tried to stay strong, to offer comfort and hope, but she felt the darkness closing in on her as well. The whispers were always there, gnawing at her sanity, making her question her reality.

Outside the shelter, the city continued to fall apart. Buildings crumbled as the entities moved through them, their presence warping the very fabric of reality. Streets twisted and turned in impossible ways, leading people in circles or trapping them in dead ends. The sky, once a comforting blue, was now a churning mass of dark clouds, the sun obscured by the eldritch presence.

In the chaos, a small group of survivors banded together, determined to find a way to fight back. Led by a former soldier named Mark, they cautiously moved through the city, avoiding the entities as best they could. Mark had seen combat, but nothing had prepared him for this. He had lost friends and comrades to the entities, their minds shattered by what they had seen.

Mark's group included people from all walks of life. There was Jenny, a schoolteacher who had lost her entire class when an entity appeared in their classroom. Tom, a mechanic, had watched his garage twist and collapse as an entity passed through it. And Rachel, a scientist who had been studying the entities since they first appeared, was desperate to find a way to stop them.

As they moved through the city, the group encountered others like them, people who had not yet succumbed to the madness. They shared stories and supplies, offering what little comfort they could in the face of such overwhelming terror. But even among the survivors, there was a sense of hopelessness, a fear that no matter what they did, the entities would eventually consume them all.

The eldritch entities thrived on this fear, drawing strength from the chaos and confusion they caused. Their influence spread like a dark stain, warping reality and breaking the barriers between the known and the unknown. The world was no longer a place of order and reason but a realm of shadows and whispers where the eldritch entities reigned supreme.

Among the survivors, a sense of desperation grew. They knew they were facing a threat unlike anything they had ever encountered, a danger that defied explanation or reason. But still, they fought on, driven by a flicker of hope that burned within them, a hope that they could push back the darkness.

Amid this turmoil, Stephanie remained a beacon of light for those around her. Her infectious optimism and unwavering courage inspired others to fight despite overwhelming odds. She refused to give in to despair, instead choosing to focus on the task at hand, on finding a way to defeat the eldritch entities once and for all.

Meanwhile, John's Shadow Self reveled in the chaos it had unleashed. It delighted in the suffering of others, feeding off their fear and despair. It knew that its power was growing and that soon, it would be able to reshape the world according to its twisted desires.

But even as the Shadow Self plotted and schemed, a glimmer of hope remained. Deep within the hearts of the survivors, a spark of defiance burned brightly, a determination to not let the darkness win. They knew the road ahead would be long and complex. Still, they were willing to face it together, united in their resolve to protect their world from the horrors that threatened to consume it.

The city lay in ruins, a twisted landscape of destruction and despair. Buildings crumbled, streets lay empty and silent, and the once vibrant cityscape was now a shadow of its former self.

But amidst the devastation, a faint glimmer of hope remained. The survivors had not given up or surrendered to the darkness that threatened to consume them. They banded together, united in their determination to fight back against the eldritch entities that had brought them to destruction.

Stephanie emerged as a leader among them, her unwavering resolve inspiring others to join the fight. She knew that they faced an uphill battle, that the odds were stacked against them. But she refused to back down, to let fear dictate their actions. She rallied her fellow survivors, urging them to stand firm, to hold fast against the encroaching darkness.

As the eldritch entities continued their onslaught, the survivors fought back with everything they had. They used whatever weapons they could find and improvised barricades to defend their positions. They stood together against the horrors that assailed them.

But even as they fought, a sense of dread lingered. They knew that the eldritch entities were unlike anything they had ever faced and that their power was vast and incomprehensible. And yet, they refused to give in, to let despair take hold.

And so, as the night wore on and the battle raged around them, the survivors stood their ground, their spirits unbroken, their will unyielding. They knew that the coming days would be filled with hardship and danger. Still, they were ready to face whatever challenges lay ahead, to fight for their survival and the survival of their world.

As the sun rose on the shattered city, quiet determination

settled over the survivors. They had weathered the storm, had faced unimaginable horrors, and emerged victorious, if only for now.

But as they surveyed the destruction around them, they knew their fight was far from over. The eldritch entities still lurked in the shadows, their presence a constant reminder of the fragility of their world.

Stephanie stood among her fellow survivors, her gaze steady, her resolve unwavering. She knew the road ahead would be long and complicated, and they would face many more challenges and hardships. But she also knew they were not alone and had each other to lean on, support, and encourage them in the coming days.

And so, as they began to rebuild, to pick up the pieces of their shattered lives, the survivors did so with a renewed sense of purpose. They knew that they could not undo the damage that had been done, that they could not erase the memories of the horrors they had faced. But they also knew they could choose how to move forward and shape their future after such devastation.

As they worked together, side by side, they began to see signs of hope amidst the ruins. New life sprouted from the scorched earth, a testament to the resilience of the human spirit. Though the scars of the past would always remain, they served as a reminder of the strength and courage it took to survive, endure, and emerge from the darkness into the light once more.

23

The Aftermath

Rachel Hayes sat in the quiet of her small apartment, the evening light casting long shadows across the room. The day's events weighed heavily on her mind, a constant, pressing reminder of the fragility of human existence. John Miller's tragic story had been a harrowing journey that she could not quickly shake off.

She remembered the first time she had met John, a man haunted by the invisible scars of his past. His eyes, dark and brooding, held a depth of pain that she had seldom seen in her years as a nurse. He had been a patient in the psychiatric ward, a place that often felt more like a prison than a haven for healing.

As she sipped her tea, Rachel's thoughts drifted to the last days of John's life. His descent into madness had been swift and unrelenting, a testament to the devastating impact of untreated mental illness. She had watched, helpless, as he spiraled further into the abyss, his cries for help going unheard by a system ill-equipped to offer the support he so desperately needed.

Rachel's heart ached for John and all those who suffered in silence; their voices lost in the din of a world too busy to listen. She knew that his story was not unique, that countless others like him were struggling to navigate the treacherous waters of their minds. The thought filled her with a profound sense of urgency, a need to do more and improve.

She realized the medical system was failing those who needed it the most. This stark and sobering truth left her feeling both angry and determined. She thought of the many times John had reached out for help only to be met with indifference or inadequacy. His death was a tragic reminder of the consequences of neglect, a poignant call to action for those in her profession.

Rachel's reflections were interrupted by a knock on the door. She set her cup down and rose to answer it, her mind still occupied by the weight of her thoughts. Opening the door, she found herself face-to-face with her colleague, Dr. Michael Chang, his expression somber and contemplative. They had shared many conversations about John's case, and she knew he was grappling with the same questions and doubts.

"Rachel," he said quietly, stepping inside. "I wanted to talk to you about John."

She nodded, closing the door behind him. "I've been thinking about him a lot," she admitted, her voice tinged with sadness. "We need to find a way to prevent this from happening again."

Dr. Chang sighed, his eyes reflecting the same sense of frustration and determination. "You're right. We need to do more, for John and for everyone else out there who is suffering. We owe it to them to be better."

Rachel and Dr. Chang's conversation stretched into the night, their shared sense of purpose deepening with each passing hour. Rachel's apartment, usually a place of solitude, now hummed with the energy of their commitment to making a difference.

"We need to start with awareness," Dr. Chang said, his tone resolute. "So many people still don't understand the gravity of mental health issues. They don't see the signs or they dismiss them as minor problems that will resolve on their own."

Rachel nodded. "Education is crucial. We should implement more comprehensive training for healthcare professionals, teachers, even employers. Everyone needs to know what to look for and how to respond."

Dr. Chang leaned forward, his eyes intense. "And we need to create a support network that doesn't fail people like John. More resources, more accessibility, better follow-up care. It's not enough to just treat the symptoms; we need to address the root causes and provide continuous support."

Rachel's mind raced with ideas. "We could start a community outreach program, hold workshops and seminars. We can partner with schools and workplaces to ensure that mental health is a priority everywhere, not just in medical settings."

"Yes," Dr. Chang agreed. "And we need to advocate for policy changes. Increased funding for mental health services, insurance coverage for therapy and medication without the bureaucratic red tape that keeps people from getting the help they need."

Rachel's heart swelled with a mix of determination and sorrow. "John's death has to mean something. If we can prevent even one person from suffering as he did, it will be worth it."

They fell into a contemplative silence, the enormity of their task settling around them. Rachel's thoughts drifted back to the countless faces she had seen over the years, each one a testament to the pervasive and often invisible struggle with mental illness. John's face, in particular, haunted her— the hollow eyes, the desperate pleas for help that had gone unanswered.

"We need to do better," she whispered, more to herself than Dr. Chang. "We can't let this continue."

Dr. Chang placed a reassuring hand on her shoulder. "We won't. We'll make sure John's story isn't just another statistic. It will be a catalyst for change."

Rachel looked up, meeting his gaze. She saw the same fire burning in his eyes, the same resolve to fight for those who couldn't fight for themselves. It was a small comfort in the face of such an overwhelming loss, but it was enough to keep her going.

Rachel felt a renewed sense of purpose as they continued planning and strategizing. John's death was a tragedy, but it could also be the spark that ignited a movement. She could almost hear his voice urging her on, a reminder that their work was far from over.

By the time Dr. Chang left, the first light of dawn was creeping through the windows. Rachel watched him walk away, his silhouette blending into the early morning mist. She felt a sense of calm settle over her, a quiet assurance that they were on the right path.

Turning back to her apartment, Rachel took a deep breath. There was much to do, but she felt hopeful for the first time in a long while. John's story would not end in darkness. It would be a beacon, guiding them toward a better future for all those who struggled in silence.

As the weeks passed, Rachel and Dr. Chang's commitment to honoring John's memory grew stronger. They held their first community outreach event in the local library, inviting mental health professionals, patients, and families to share their stories and experiences.

Rachel stood before a small crowd, her heart pounding with nerves and determination. Although she had never been much of a public speaker, her voice carried the weight of John's story tonight.

"Good evening, everyone," she began, her voice steadying as she continued. "My name is Rachel Hayes, and I'm a nurse. But more importantly, I'm here because of a man named John Miller. John was a patient of mine, but he was more than that—he was a reminder of how much we need to change the way we approach mental health."

She paused, scanning the faces in the audience. Some were tearful, others stoic, but all were attentive.

"John struggled with complex post-traumatic stress disorder, or CPTSD. He battled his demons alone for far too long, and despite our best efforts, he felt like there was no way out. His story didn't have to end the way it did, and that's why we're here tonight. To make sure that no one else has to feel that same sense of hopelessness."

Dr. Chang stepped up next, his presence commanding and calm. "Mental health is just as important as physical health. Yet, it's often neglected, misunderstood, or stigmatized. We need to change that narrative. We need to provide better support systems, not just within healthcare, but within our communities."

Rachel listened as he spoke, feeling a surge of pride. Together, they were turning John's tragedy into a force for good.

The event continued with personal testimonies from individuals who had experienced their mental health struggles. A young woman named Emily shared her journey with depression, detailing how she had felt isolated and ashamed until she found a support group that changed her life. An older man, Mr. Thompson, spoke about his battle with anxiety and the relief he found in therapy.

As the night drew close, Rachel felt a profound sense of accomplishment. They had taken the first step towards creating a more compassionate and understanding community.

After the event, as Rachel and Dr. Chang packed up, a middle-aged woman approached them. She introduced herself as Sarah and explained that she had lost her brother to suicide a few years ago. "What you're doing here is so important," she said, tears glistening. "Thank you for giving people like my brother and John a voice."

The conversation with Sarah was a poignant reminder of why Rachel and Dr. Chang had embarked on this journey. It was a testament to the impact they could have, not just on those struggling with mental illness but also on their families and communities.

As the weeks turned into months, their efforts began to bear fruit. Awareness grew, and more people sought help. The stigma surrounding mental illness slowly began to erode, replaced by a growing sense of empathy and understanding.

Rachel knew that there was still much work to be done. The road ahead would be long and fraught with challenges. But she also knew they were on the right path, guided by the memory of John Miller and the countless others whose stories had yet to be told.

As she stood with Dr. Chang, looking at the faces of those they had helped, Rachel felt a renewed hope. Together, they were making a difference, one person at a time. In doing so, they were honoring the memory of a man who had been lost to the darkness but whose story would continue to inspire and guide them toward a brighter future.

Rachel hugged Sarah, feeling the weight of their shared grief. "We're all in this together," she replied. "And we'll keep fighting for better support and understanding."

As Rachel lay in bed that night, she reflected on the evening's events. She thought about John, imagining him somewhere, finally at peace. The work ahead was daunting, but it was necessary. They were making a difference, one step at a time.

The following morning, Rachel met with Dr. Chang to discuss their next steps. They planned more community events, petitioned for better mental health resources, and contacted local schools and businesses to offer workshops.

Each day brought new challenges and triumphs. There were moments of frustration when progress seemed slow, but there were also moments of joy when they saw the impact of their efforts.

Rachel knew they couldn't change the past but could shape the future. With every step forward, she felt John's presence guiding her and reminding her of the importance of their mission.

As they continued their work, Rachel felt a renewed sense of purpose. John's story was no longer just a tale of tragedy—it was a beacon of hope, a call to action, and a testament to the power of community and compassion.

Rachel and Dr. Chang's dedication to mental health

advocacy soon caught the attention of the local media. A small article about their community outreach event appeared in the local newspaper, drawing interest from the public and potential allies. Calls and emails began to flood in from individuals and organizations wanting to collaborate.

One sunny afternoon, Rachel received a call from a local high school principal, Mrs. Watson, who expressed interest in implementing mental health awareness programs in her school. "We need to educate our students early," Mrs. Watson said, her voice filled with conviction. "If they learn to recognize and talk about these issues now, it could change their lives."

Rachel and Dr. Chang met with Mrs. Watson and her staff to discuss potential programs. They developed a series of workshops and seminars aimed at students, teachers, and parents. These programs would focus on understanding mental health, recognizing signs of distress, and knowing where to seek help.

The first seminar was held in the school's auditorium, with curious students and concerned parents present. Rachel felt a familiar mix of nerves and determination as she stood before the audience. She began with a simple question: "How many of you know someone who has struggled with their mental health?" Nearly every hand went up.

Rachel shared John's story, emphasizing the importance of seeking help and supporting one another. She watched as the students listened intently, some with tears in their eyes. The parents, too, seemed deeply moved, many of them nodding in agreement or wiping away tears.

Dr. Chang followed, offering practical advice and resources for those in need. "Mental health is not something to be ashamed of," he said firmly. "It's a part of all our lives, and we need to treat it with the same care and attention we would any other health issue."

The seminar ended with a Q&A session, where students and parents asked questions ranging from how to support a friend in crisis to understanding the difference between sadness and depression. Rachel and Dr. Chang answered each question with compassion and expertise, reinforcing their commitment to creating a supportive community.

In the weeks that followed, the impact of their work became evident. The school counselor reported an increased number of students seeking help, and several parents thanked Rachel and Dr. Chang for their efforts. Rachel felt a deep sense of fulfillment, knowing they were making a tangible difference.

As their outreach expanded, Rachel and Dr. Chang began collaborating with local businesses to implement mental health support programs in the workplace. They held workshops for managers and employees, educating them on creating a supportive environment and recognizing signs of mental distress.

One of the businesses they worked with was a manufacturing company where John had once been employed. The company's HR manager, Mr. Smith, admitted that they had not been equipped to support John during his struggles. "We want to do better," he said, his voice heavy with regret. "We don't want to lose anyone else like we lost John."

Rachel and Dr. Chang developed a comprehensive mental health program for the company, including regular workshops, access to counseling services, and a peer support network. The employees responded positively, grateful for the new resources and the company's commitment to their well-being.

Rachel often reflected on how far they had come since John's death. She remembered her helplessness when she couldn't save him and the determination that had driven her to make a difference. Now, she saw the fruits of their labor in the lives they were touching and the changes they were making.

Their journey was far from over, but each step forward felt like a victory. Rachel and Dr. Chang's dedication sparked a ripple effect, spreading awareness and compassion throughout the community. John's story had become a catalyst for change, transforming a tale of tragedy into one of hope and resilience.

Rachel knew challenges would always be, but she also knew they were making a difference. As they continued their work, she felt a deep sense of purpose and fulfillment, knowing they were honoring John's memory by helping others find the support and understanding he needed.

Rachel's tireless efforts, alongside Dr. Chang, began to garner attention beyond their local community. They were invited to speak at regional conferences and seminars on mental health, sharing their insights and experiences. Each time they recounted John's story, it resonated deeply with their audiences, fostering a sense of urgency and empathy.

One evening, Rachel received an unexpected email from a national mental health advocacy organization. They had heard about her and Dr. Chang's work and were interested in collaborating on a larger scale. The prospect of extending their reach excited Rachel and brought a new wave of responsibility.

The national organization invited Rachel and Dr. Chang

to its headquarters to discuss potential partnerships. As they prepared for the meeting, Rachel felt excitement and nervousness. This was an opportunity to make a significant impact and bring their message to a broader audience.

They presented their work at the meeting and shared John's story again. The organization's leaders were impressed by their dedication and the tangible results they had achieved. They proposed a national campaign to raise awareness about mental health, with Rachel and Dr. Chang as critical spokespersons.

Rachel agreed, feeling both honored and determined. This was a chance to honor John's memory on a grand scale, to ensure that his story reached as many people as possible. They planned to create educational materials, public service announcements, and nationwide events.

As they left the meeting, Rachel turned to Dr. Chang, her eyes shining with determination. "We're going to make a real difference, Michael. John's story will help save lives."

Dr. Chang nodded, sharing her resolve. "Together, we can change the narrative around mental health. We'll make sure no one has to suffer in silence."

Rachel and Dr. Chang worked tirelessly on the national campaign in the following months. They traveled nationwide, speaking at schools, businesses, and community centers. They appeared on television and radio, sharing their message with a broad audience. The campaign gained momentum, attracting support from mental health professionals, advocates, and celebrities.

Rachel often thought of John, feeling his presence guiding her. His story had transformed from a personal tragedy into a powerful movement for change. She knew that their work was making a difference, that they were reaching people who needed to hear their message.

As the campaign grew, Rachel and Dr. Chang saw tangible results. More people sought help for their mental health issues, schools and businesses implemented support programs, and the stigma around mental illness began to erode. Their work's impact was profound, filling Rachel with a deep sense of fulfillment.

Rachel knew that the fight for mental health awareness and support would never indeed be over. There will always be new challenges and obstacles to overcome. But she also knew they were making a lasting difference, one step at a time.

And as they continued their journey, Rachel felt a renewed sense of purpose and hope. John's story had become a beacon of light, guiding them toward a brighter future for all those who struggled with mental illness. Together, they created a world where everyone had access to the support and understanding they needed, ensuring that no one else would face their demons alone.

24

The Ripple Effect

The news of John's death sent shockwaves through the community, with the repercussions of his untreated mental illness rippling far beyond his immediate circle. Neighbors, friends, family, and coworkers were left reeling, struggling to come to terms with the tragic end of his story.

Neighbors remembered seeing John in passing, noting his increasing isolation and haunted expression. They regretted not reaching out and reflecting on the missed opportunities to offer support.

Friends were reminded of their shared good times, laughter, and camaraderie. They also recognized the signs they had missed, wishing they had offered more support during his struggles.

Family members were devastated, remembering the happy, carefree boy John had once been. They mourned the loss of that innocence and wondered if there was something more they could have done.

Coworkers recalled John as a dedicated, hardworking employee who was always willing to help. They, too, wondered if they had missed signs and regretted not offering more support.

As the community grappled with their grief, they committed to do better, be more aware, and reach out to those suffering. They knew they couldn't change the past. Still, they were determined to shape a future where mental health was taken seriously, and support was readily available.

Discussions about mental health awareness became more prevalent. People opened up about their struggles, finding solace and understanding in shared experiences. These conversations extended to community meetings, where residents gathered to discuss how to support those in need better.

Local organizations and support groups saw increased participation as people sought to educate themselves about mental health issues. Workshops and seminars were held to break down stigma and encourage those needing help.

The impact of John's story on the broader community was profound. It served as a sobering reminder of the importance of mental health awareness and the devastating consequences of untreated mental illness. It sparked a movement towards greater understanding and compassion.

Local leaders and advocates began to push for change, calling for increased funding for mental health services and improved access to care. They pointed to John's story as an example of what could happen when mental illness went untreated and vowed to do everything in their power to prevent another tragedy.

Fundraisers and awareness campaigns were organized to support mental health initiatives. New programs and resources were implemented aimed at providing support for those struggling with mental illness.

Support groups flourished, offering a safe space for people to share their experiences and seek advice. Mental health professionals reported an increase in people seeking therapy, a sign that the stigma surrounding mental illness was slowly being eroded.

Schools and workplaces implemented new mental health initiatives, recognizing the importance of supporting mental well-being from an early age. They offered counseling services and mental health days, acknowledging that mental health was as important as physical health.

The ripple effect of John's death extended far beyond what anyone could have imagined. His story touched many hearts, inspiring action and change in the world of mental health.

As the community healed from the loss of John, they did so with a renewed sense of purpose. They knew that his memory would live on in the changes they were making, in the lives they were touching. Though they could never forget the man who had sparked this movement, they were grateful for the legacy he had left behind.

And as they moved forward, they carried John's memory with them, a constant reminder of the impact one person can have on the world. They knew that his story was not just a tale of tragedy—it was a beacon of hope, a call to action, and a testament to the power of community and compassion.

25

The Legacy of John Miller

The news spread like wildfire through the small town, igniting whispers and hushed conversations in every corner. John Miller, the man who had been a quiet fixture in their lives, was now lying in a hospital bed, his fate hanging by a thread. The initial shock was palpable, a collective gasp that echoed through the community. John suddenly became the center of everyone's thoughts, always there but never fully present.

The town's usual rhythm was disrupted in the days following the incident. People gathered in small groups, their voices low and filled with concern. The local diner, usually a place of casual chatter and laughter, had become somber. Diners shared worried glances over their coffee cups, their thoughts drifting inevitably to the man fighting for his life just a few miles away.

At the grocery store, neighbors exchanged updates, each piece of news a small token of hope or despair. Mrs. Henderson, who had known John since he was a boy, clutched her shopping basket tightly as she recounted the latest from the hospital. "They say he's stable," she whispered to anyone who would listen, her eyes glistening with unshed tears. "But you know how these things go. It could change any moment."

The high school held a special assembly, the principal addressing the students with a gravity usually reserved for graduation speeches. He spoke of John's contributions to the community, his quiet strength, and the hope that everyone held for his recovery. The students, many of whom only knew John as the man who fixed things around town, listened intently, a new respect for him taking root in their hearts.

Even the local church saw an increase in attendance, the pews filled with parishioners seeking solace and strength. Prayers for John became a familiar refrain, a chorus of hope rising to the heavens. Father Thomas, the town's pastor, dedicated his Sunday sermon to John's fight, urging the congregation to keep their faith and support one another during this uncertain time.

As the days turned into a week, the initial shock gave way to a deeper, more profound sense of unity. The community, which was always interconnected but often distant in their daily routines, was drawn together by John's plight. Each person, in their way, contributed to a collective vigil, their thoughts and prayers converging on the small hospital room where John lay in a coma.

Amidst this, Stephanie Thompson was at the heart of the town's emotional turmoil. As John's therapist and close confidante, she was inundated with questions and concerns. People looked to her for reassurance, hoping she could offer some insight into John's condition and his chances of recovery. Stephanie did her best to provide comfort, her heart heavy with her fears and hopes. She reflected on their therapy sessions, the breakthroughs and setbacks, and the quiet moments of understanding that had defined their relationship. One particular memory stood out: a session where John had spoken about his hopes for the future. "I want to find peace," he had said, his voice filled with quiet determination. "I just want to feel whole again."

As the community grappled with the uncertainty of John's condition, personal stories and memories began to surface, weaving a tapestry of his life that many had never seen before. Each recollection, shared in whispers and quiet conversations, painted a picture of a man whose impact had been far more significant than anyone had realized.

Long-time residents exchanged tales of John's quiet acts of kindness in the quiet corners of the local diner. Mr. Peterson, the retired postman, recounted how John had fixed his mailbox without being asked, simply noticing it was broken and taking the time to repair it. "He never said a word about it," Mr. Peterson recalled, his eyes misty. "Just did it because it needed doing. That's the kind of man John is."

At the high school, teachers and students shared stories revealing a different side of John. Mrs. Collins, the art teacher, remembered how John had volunteered to help set up the annual art fair, his hands deftly handling fragile sculptures and paintings. "He had an eye for detail," she said, her voice filled with admiration. "And he always made sure everything was perfect. The kids loved him for it."

Family members spoke of John's resilience and strength in living rooms and kitchens across the town. His sister, Anne, visited the hospital daily, her presence a steadfast beacon of hope. She told stories of their childhood, John's unwavering support during their parents' difficult divorce, and his determination to keep their small family together.

"He's always been a fighter," Anne said softly, her hand resting gently on his. "I just hope he has enough fight left in him now."

These shared and cherished stories became a source of strength for the community. Each memory, whether of a grand gesture or a small act of kindness, added to the collective hope that John would pull through. They spoke of a man who, despite his struggles, had touched many lives in meaningful ways.

As days turned into nights and the waiting continued, the town's initial anxiety began to mix with a deep sense of hope. They clung to their memories of John, finding comfort in the stories that showcased his character and resilience. The hospital waiting room became a gathering place for those who wanted to be close to John, to offer their support and share in the hope for his recovery.

Outside the hospital, a community garden began to take shape, initiated by a group of John's friends. They planted flowers and herbs, each representing a wish for John's healing. The garden quickly symbolizes the town's unity and collective desire to see John return to them.

The community's reaction to John's critical condition had evolved from shock to deep, abiding hope. They drew strength from each other and the memories of John they held dear. In their stories, they found solace and a renewed determination to support John in his fight. As they waited for any sign of improvement, their shared hope became a powerful testament to the impact one man could have on so many lives.

In the town square, the usual bustle was tempered with a subdued energy. Market days, usually vibrant with chatter and laughter, were quieter. Vendors spoke in hushed tones, their minds half on their wares and half on the latest news from the hospital. It was as if the whole town held its breath, waiting for any sign that John was improving.

At home, families grappled with the implications of John's condition. Parents tried to explain the situation to their children, who struggled to understand why the friendly man who always fixed their bikes and helped with school projects was now lying in a hospital bed. The children asked innocent questions, their eyes wide with confusion and concern. "Will Mr. Miller be okay?" they would ask, their voices small and uncertain. The adults, unsure of how to answer, offered reassurances that felt fragile and incomplete.

The impact of John's coma rippled through workplaces as well. His absence was keenly felt at the local repair shop where John had worked part-time. Tools lay untouched, and projects were delayed as his colleagues found it hard to focus, their thoughts constantly drifting to their missing friend. Bill, the shop owner, found himself staring at John's empty workspace, the silence a stark reminder of his friend's condition. "He was always so reliable," Bill told a customer one day, his voice tinged with sadness. "It's hard to keep going without him."

In this collective uncertainty, the community's spirit remained unbroken. They organized candlelight vigils and prayer circles, drawing strength from each other's presence. The town's social media pages were flooded with messages of support and hope, a digital echo of the solidarity felt in every corner of the community.

Stephanie Thompson felt the weight of the town's hopes and fears more than anyone. She spent hours at the hospital, speaking with doctors and comforting John's family. Her role as a therapist had always been to offer support and guidance, but now she found herself leaning on the community just as much as they leaned on her. Each day, she shared updates with the town, her voice a steady anchor in the storm of uncertainty.

One evening, as she stood in the community garden, Anne joined Stephanie. The two women walked among the flowers, their silence speaking volumes. "He's always been strong," Anne finally said, her voice barely above a whisper. "But this... this is different."

Stephanie nodded, her heart heavy with shared grief. "We have to believe he can pull through. The whole town is behind him."

The two women stood together as the sun set, casting a warm glow over the garden. They drew strength from the earth beneath their feet and their community. They knew the road ahead was uncertain but weren't walking it alone.

The impact of John's condition reached far beyond the hospital walls, touching every aspect of life in the small town. It brought people together in ways they had never anticipated, forging new connections and strengthening old ones. Through the uncertainty and fear, a sense of unity and hope emerged, a testament to the enduring strength of the community.

Church services became gatherings of hope and prayer. Father Thomas led special prayer sessions, during which the congregation lit candles and prayed for John's recovery. The customarily composed priest moved to tears more than once, his faith tested by the weight of his congregation's hopes and fears. "We must trust in the power of our prayers," he would say, his voice thick with emotion. John needs our strength now more than ever."

Even the local school felt the impact. Teachers incorporated lessons about hope, resilience, and the power of community into their classes, using John's situation as a poignant example. Students, many of whom had interacted with John through various school events, wrote letters and made cards wishing him well. These were delivered to the hospital, where they lined the walls of John's room, a colorful testament to the town's collective hope.

As the days dragged on, the weight of the uncertainty began to take its toll. People found themselves growing more anxious, their patience wearing thin. Small arguments flared up more efficiently, and the overall mood was one of tension. Yet, despite the strain, there was also a remarkable sense of solidarity. The community leaned on each other, drawing strength from their shared experience.

Stephanie, more than anyone, felt the acute pressure of John's condition. Her role as both therapist and friend placed her at the heart of the emotional storm. She spent countless hours at the hospital, balancing her professional responsibilities with her personal need to be close to John. Her reflections during this time were a mix of professional analysis and deep personal anguish. She knew the medical facts and understood the prognosis. Still, she also clung to the personal hope that John would wake up and continue the journey they had started together.

In the quiet moments when she was alone by John's bedside, Stephanie allowed herself to feel the total weight of her emotions. She thought about their sessions, the breakthroughs they had made, and the future John had spoken of with such quiet determination. Her hopes for his recovery were intertwined with her belief in his strength, a belief that she now held onto with everything she had.

The community's reaction to John's condition was a testament to the interconnectedness of their lives. The uncertainty of his coma was a shared burden, one that brought them closer even as it tested their limits. They grappled with the potential outcomes, each person processing the situation in their way, yet all united by their hope for John's recovery. In this waiting period, the town's true strength was revealed in their collective hope and unwavering support for one another.

As the days turned into weeks, the community continued to hold onto hope, each member contributing to the collective strength needed to support John. Once sterile and impersonal, the hospital room had transformed into a sanctuary filled with tokens of love and encouragement. Cards from schoolchildren, flowers from neighbors, and photographs of happy times adorned the walls, a testament to the lives John had touched.

Stephanie often found herself reflecting on the deeper meaning of legacy. What did it mean to leave a mark on the world? John had always questioned his worth and doubted his existence's significance. Yet, here he was, lying in a hospital bed, surrounded by the tangible proof of his impact. It was a poignant reminder that sometimes, the most minor acts of kindness could ripple outwards, touching lives in ways one could never anticipate.

The town's newspaper ran a unique feature on John, recounting his quiet heroism and how he had enriched the community. Stories poured in from all corners of the town— of broken fences mended without a word, of groceries delivered to the elderly during winter storms, of children taught to ride bikes. Each story, trim in its own right, painted a picture of a man who had dedicated himself to the well-being of others, even as he battled his demons.

In the feature, Stephanie was interviewed about her experiences with John. She spoke of his resilience, his capacity for growth, and the courage it took for him to seek help. "John's journey is a testament to the strength of the human spirit," she told the reporter, her voice filled with conviction. "He has faced unimaginable pain and yet found a way to give to others. His fight isn't over, and neither is the impact he's had on all of us."

As time passed, the community began to heal from the shock of John's condition. Their initial fear had given way to a steady, enduring hope. They found strength in their shared experiences, in the knowledge that they were not alone in their concern for John. Each person, in their way, contributed to the collective effort to support him.

In those moments of shared vulnerability, the community discovered profound resilience. They learned that it was okay to feel scared and acknowledge their fears but also to find hope in their shared connections. Their varied and complex emotional responses were a testament to the depth of their care for John and each other.

For Stephanie, these days were a journey of self-discovery. She realized that her strength came from within and the community around her. Their hope and resilience became her anchor, guiding her through the emotions that threatened to overwhelm her. And in supporting others, she found a renewed sense of purpose, a commitment to seeing John through his fight.

In the end, the community's emotional responses reflected

their collective heart. They faced each day with fear and hope, their spirits buoyed by the belief that John would wake up and return to them. And in that belief, they found the courage to keep going and fighting for John and each other.

Stephanie Thompson has always been a pillar of strength for the community. This role now carried even greater weight as John lay in a coma. As a therapist, she was used to helping others navigate their emotional landscapes. Still, this situation tested her in ways she had never anticipated. Her dual role as a professional and a close friend of John demanded a delicate balance of personal vulnerability and professional composure.

Stephanie became an integral part of the support network when John was hospitalized. She spent countless hours at the hospital, coordinating with medical staff and updating the anxious community. Her background in trauma therapy gave her a unique insight into John's condition. Still, it also made her acutely aware of the precariousness of his situation. Each medical update was a rollercoaster of emotions as she oscillated between hope and fear, sharing each development with a mix of professional detachment and personal investment.

Stephanie's days were long and emotionally draining. She juggled her regular therapy sessions, where she supported others through their struggles, with her vigil at John's bedside. Her office became a sanctuary for those seeking solace, and her empathetic ear comforted many. She encouraged people to talk about their feelings, helping them process their anxiety and fears. "It's okay to be scared," she would tell them, her voice steady. "What's important is that we face this together."

The community looked to Stephanie for guidance and reassurance, and she rose to the occasion with a quiet strength.

She organized support groups where people could share their stories and offer mutual support. These gatherings became lifelines for many, providing a space to express their worries and find comfort in the shared experience. Stephanie's ability to create a safe, supportive environment helped the community cope with the uncertainty and stress of John's condition.

In her quieter moments, Stephanie reflected deeply on her feelings. The sight of John lying motionless, hooked up to machines, was a constant reminder of the fragility of life. She struggled with her helplessness, the fear that she might lose someone who had come to mean so much to her. Yet, she drew strength from the very hope she inspired in others. Her belief in John's resilience and the power of community support kept her going through the darkest days.

Stephanie's reflections were often intense and introspective. She thought about her journey with John, the progress they had made, and the setbacks they had faced together. She recalled his breakthroughs, the moments of clarity and hope that had marked his path to healing. These memories fueled her determination to see him through this crisis. She spoke to him often, her words a blend of encouragement and personal reflection. "You've come so far, John," she would say, her voice soft but firm. "You have so much to live for. Keep fighting. We're all here for you."

One tough evening, as the hospital quieted down and the world outside seemed distant, Stephanie allowed herself a rare moment of vulnerability. She sat by John's bedside, holding his hand, and let the tears flow. "You mean so much to so many people," she whispered. "And you mean so much to me. Please, don't give up. We need you. I need you." Her words

268

hung in the air, a testament to her deep connection.

Stephanie's role extended beyond the hospital walls. She became a mediator for the community, helping coordinate efforts and ensuring everyone's contributions were meaningful and effective. She worked with local organizations to organize fundraisers and support events, leveraging her connections to maximize their impact. Her leadership helped channel the community's energy into positive action, providing a sense of purpose and direction during uncertainty.

In many ways, Stephanie's role mirrored that of a lighthouse, guiding the community through the storm with her unwavering light. Her ability to balance professional responsibilities with personal commitment was a testament to her strength and dedication. She was a source of comfort and hope for many, and her presence reminded them they were not alone in their struggle.

Through it all, Stephanie found a more profound sense of purpose. Her work with John had always been about more than just therapy; it was about helping him find his way to a better life. Now, that purpose has expanded to include the entire community. She saw firsthand the impact of collective hope and support, reinforcing her belief in the power of connection.

Stephanie's reflections and actions during this time were powerful testaments to the impact one person could have on a community. Her role in supporting John's recovery, both emotionally and practically, highlighted the importance of compassion, resilience, and the strength found in unity. As she continued fighting for John, she knew she was not alone. The community stood with her, their collective hope and determination a beacon of light in the darkest times.

The community's support for John and his family grew stronger each day. What began as a spontaneous outpouring of concern had evolved into a well-coordinated network of care and action. Every corner of the town buzzed with activity aimed at supporting John's recovery and providing comfort to his loved ones.

The local diner became a hub for organizing these efforts. Each morning, a group of volunteers would gather around a large table, planning the day's activities. They coordinated meal deliveries to the hospital, ensuring Anne and the others were vigilant and never worried about where their next meal would come from. The diner's owner, Sally, ensured that no one left without a hot meal and a kind word. "We're all in this together," she would say, her smile a constant source of warmth and reassurance.

Fundraising efforts took off with remarkable energy. Local businesses donated goods and services for auctions and raffles, with all proceeds supporting John's medical expenses. The town hall hosted a charity concert featuring performances by local musicians who dedicated their songs to John. The event was a huge success, bringing together people from all walks of life united by a common cause. The sense of community was palpable, each note and melody a testament to their collective hope and solidarity.

The high school played a significant role in these efforts as well. Students organized car washes, bake sales, and sporting events to raise funds. They created a large banner with messages of hope and encouragement for John, which they hung outside the hospital. Each day, students added new messages, their words a vibrant display of their support and belief in his recovery.

Social media became another powerful tool for mobilizing support. A page dedicated to John's recovery quickly gained followers, providing updates on his condition and information about upcoming events. The page was filled with messages of encouragement from near and far, turning John's fight into a global cause. People shared their stories of hope and resilience, creating a virtual community of supporters who believed in John's strength and the power of collective hope.

Prayer chains and vigils became regular events. Father Thomas continued to lead nightly prayers at the church, but the spirit of these gatherings extended beyond its walls. People lit candles in their homes, joined hands, and prayed for John's recovery. The sight of flickering candles in windows throughout the town was a moving testament to the unity and hope that had taken hold.

In addition to the emotional and financial support, practical help was organized. Volunteers took on tasks such as mowing the lawn at John's house, caring for his pets, and ensuring his bills were managed during his hospitalization. These acts of service, though small individually, collectively alleviated the burdens on John's family, allowing them to focus on his recovery.

For Stephanie, the community's response was both heartening and humbling. She saw firsthand the impact of their collective efforts, each act of kindness a thread in the fabric of support woven around John and his family. She worked closely with the volunteers, offering guidance and ensuring their efforts were coordinated and effective. Her background in community organization proved invaluable, helping to channel the outpouring of support into meaningful actions.

One particularly moving initiative was the creation of a community garden in the park across from the hospital. Volunteers planted flowers, herbs, and vegetables, each plant symbolizing a wish for John's recovery. The garden quickly became a place of reflection and hope, a living testament to the community's commitment to supporting John. People visited the garden daily, tending to the plants and finding solace in nurturing something new.

As the garden grew, so did the community's unity and purpose. Coming together to create something beautiful amid uncertainty was a powerful reminder of their collective strength. The garden was not just a symbol of hope for John's recovery; it was a testament to the resilience and compassion of the community itself.

For Anne, the community's support was a lifeline. The constant presence of friends and neighbors, the meals and messages, and the practical help all provided a much-needed sense of stability and hope. She often felt overwhelmed by their kindness, tears of gratitude mingling with her fears for John. "I don't know how we would get through this without all of you," she would say, her voice thick with emotion. "Thank you from the bottom of my heart."

As the weeks turned into months, the community's support did not waver. They continued to rally around John and his family, their collective hope a beacon of light in the darkest times. The bonds strengthened during this crisis would endure, a lasting testament to the power of unity and compassion.

Stephanie often reflected on the incredible spirit of the community. Their unwavering support and dedication were a powerful reminder of the impact that one person's life could have. John's fight had brought them all closer, reinforcing the idea that they were stronger together in the face of adversity. As they continued to support John, they also supported each other, creating a web of care and connection that would sustain them through whatever came next.

The community's support for John was a living, breathing legacy of his impact on their lives. Each act of kindness, each message of hope, each moment of shared vulnerability added to the tapestry of resilience and compassion that defined them. As they faced each new day, they did so with the knowledge that they were not alone, their hearts united in the fight for John's recovery.

As the weeks stretched into months, the community settled into a new rhythm defined by hope, resilience, and an unyielding commitment to John's recovery. The initial frenzy of activity had given way to a steady, enduring support network surrounding John and his family. Once uncertain, the future now held a sense of cautious optimism. They had created a foundation of care and support to carry them through the long journey.

One morning, Stephanie received a call from the hospital with news that John had shown signs of regaining consciousness. His fingers had twitched, and his eyelids fluttered. It was a small sign but enough to reignite the hope that had kept the community going.

Stephanie immediately shared the news with Anne and the rest of the community. The response was overwhelming. People gathered outside the hospital, holding candles and singing softly. It was a spontaneous celebration and solidarity, a testament to the hope they had nurtured.

Days later, John finally opened his eyes. The road to

recovery was still long, but this moment was a victory. Anne was by his side, her tears of joy mingling with those of the nurses and doctors who had cared for him so diligently. Stephanie arrived shortly after, her heart swelling with gratitude and relief.

As John began his rehabilitation, the community's support continued unabated. Volunteers helped with his physical therapy exercises, brought nutritious meals to aid his recovery, and maintained the garden, symbolizing their collective hope.

The high school students organized a welcome home event for John, decorating the hospital entrance with banners and flowers. They performed songs they had written, shared poems, and presented him with a scrapbook filled with their art and messages of encouragement.

The diner hosted a celebratory dinner, free for all who had contributed to John's recovery. It was an evening of laughter, tears, and heartfelt speeches. Sally, the diner's owner, spoke of the power of community while Anne expressed her most profound gratitude. John, still weak but determined, thanked everyone for their unwavering support.

Father Thomas held an exceptional service at the church, focusing on resilience, hope, and gratitude themes. He praised the community for its unity and compassion, highlighting how it had turned a moment of crisis into a testament to its strength and humanity.

Throughout John's recovery, Stephanie continued to play a vital role. She supported him through his emotional ups and downs, helping him navigate the psychological impact of his experience. Their sessions were filled with tears and breakthroughs, each a step towards healing.

As John grew stronger, he began to participate in community activities again. He worked in the garden, attended school events, and joined the nightly vigils, which had transformed into gatherings of gratitude and celebration. His presence was a powerful reminder of what the community had achieved together.

John's journey was not just about his recovery; it had brought the community closer, teaching them the importance of compassion, resilience, and unity. His story became a source of inspiration, showing that even in the darkest times, light can be found in the connections we share.

In the months that followed, the community continued to thrive. Drawing from their experiences with John, they initiated new projects to support mental health. They organized regular health and wellness workshops, created support groups, and established a fund to help others in need. John's legacy was now woven into the very fabric of the town, a constant reminder of the power of collective hope and action.

For Stephanie, the experience was transformative. She had seen firsthand the profound impact one person could have on a community and vice versa. Her reflections on compassion, resilience, and the strength found in unity deepened her commitment to her work and the people she served. She knew their journey was far from over, but she faced the future with renewed purpose and hope.

As the towns supported each other, they held onto the lessons they had learned. They knew they were stronger together, that their collective hope and determination could overcome even the most significant challenges. As they looked to the future, they did so with a deep sense of gratitude, knowing they were part of something greater—a community united by love, resilience, and the unbreakable bonds they had forged in the face of adversity.

Stephanie's role remained central to this ongoing effort. She balanced her professional responsibilities with her commitment to John by setting clear boundaries and delegating tasks to trusted colleagues. Her reflections during this time were profound, touching on themes of healing, community, and the enduring impact of love and support. She knew that whatever happened, the community's response to John's crisis had created lasting bonds that would continue to shape their collective future.

The community garden across from the hospital had flourished, its vibrant colors and fragrant blooms a testament to the care and hope of those who tended it. It became a place where people could find solace and reflect on their journey. Community planting days were held regularly, where families and friends gathered to plant new flowers and share stories about John. Each plant and flower symbolized the future they hoped for, John—a future filled with life, growth, and renewal.

At the hospital, the steady stream of visitors continued. The waiting room remained a gathering place for those who wanted to be close to John, their presence a constant reminder of the support he had. Anne spent her days there, her strength unwavering, buoyed by the love and support of the community. She often looked out the window at the garden, drawing comfort from seeing it. Friends and neighbors brought meals, shared updates, and participated in small rituals of hope and encouragement, creating a supportive and nurturing environment.

The high school students, who had once seen John as the friendly handyman, now viewed him as a symbol of resilience.

They organized regular visits to the garden, where they shared updates and continued to add messages of hope to the banner outside the hospital. They also created a mural in the garden, each brushstroke expressing their collective support. Their actions were a powerful reminder of John's lasting impact on their lives.

Local businesses continued their support, ensuring the Miller family never had to worry about financial burdens. The fundraisers and charity events had not only provided much-needed funds but had also strengthened the sense of community. The diner hosted monthly charity markets, the grocery store organized a mentorship program for local youth, and the repair shop provided free services to needy people. Each contribution forged deeper connections among the townspeople, reinforcing their collective strength.

Father Thomas's nightly vigils became a tradition for the community to unite and find strength in their shared faith and hope. The flickering candles in the church and homes throughout the town were a poignant symbol of the light they held for John. The sound of collective prayers, the sight of candles lighting the night, and the personal testimonies shared during these vigils highlighted their emotional and spiritual impact. These collective prayer and reflection moments were a cornerstone of their support network, providing a sense of continuity and hope.

For Stephanie, the future held hope and a renewed sense of purpose. She had witnessed firsthand the profound impact of collective support and the strength that came from unity. Her reflections on John's journey and the community's response deepened her understanding of resilience and healing. She knew that whatever the outcome, the legacy of this time

277

would endure.

One late afternoon, as the sun began to set, casting a golden glow over the hospital and the garden, Stephanie sat by John's bedside with Anne. The room was quiet; the only sound was the gentle hum of the machines that monitored John's vital signs. Anne reached out and took Stephanie's hand, her grip firm and steady. "Thank you for everything," she said softly, her eyes shining with gratitude. "I don't know what we would have done without you."

Stephanie squeezed her hand in return, her heart full. "We're all in this together," she replied. "And we'll keep fighting for John, no matter what."

The future felt less daunting as the two women watched over John silently. The journey ahead was still uncertain, but they were not alone. The community's support had created a foundation of hope and resilience, a legacy that would carry them forward.

John Miller's legacy chapter was still written, adding new lines of hope, strength, and unity each day. The community's response to his crisis revealed the best of humanity—their capacity for compassion, willingness to support one another, and unyielding belief in the power of collective hope.

As the sun dipped below the horizon, casting long shadows over the hospital and the vibrant garden, the future remained an open book. But in those quiet moments, surrounded by the symbols of their collective journey, Stephanie, Anne, and the entire community held onto the belief that they could face whatever came next together. Their hearts were united in the fight for John's recovery; in that unity, they found the strength to keep moving forward.

And so, with the sun setting and a new day on the horizon,

the community continued to hold John in their thoughts and prayers, their hopes and dreams intertwined with his fight. John Miller's legacy was not just in the past but in the present and future; they were building together—a legacy of love, resilience, and unbreakable bonds.

26

The Turning Point

Stephanie's role remained central to this ongoing effort. She balanced her professional responsibilities with her commitment to John by setting clear boundaries and delegating tasks to trusted colleagues. Her reflections during this time were profound, touching on themes of healing, community, and the enduring impact of love and support. She knew that whatever happened, the community's response to John's crisis had created lasting bonds that would continue to shape their collective future.

The community garden across from the hospital flourished, and its vibrant colors and fragrant blooms were a testament to the care and hope of those who tended it. Community planting days were held regularly, where families and friends gathered to plant new flowers and share stories about John. It became a place where people could find solace and reflect on their journey. Each plant and flower symbolized the future they hoped for, John—a future filled with life, growth, and renewal.

At the hospital, the steady stream of visitors continued.

The waiting room remained a gathering place for those who wanted to be close to John, their presence a constant reminder of the support he had. Anne spent her days there, her strength unwavering, buoyed by the love and support of the community. She often looked out the window at the garden, drawing comfort from seeing it. Friends and neighbors brought meals, shared updates, and participated in small rituals of hope and encouragement, creating a supportive and nurturing environment.

The high school students, who had once seen John as the friendly handyman, now viewed him as a symbol of resilience. They organized regular visits to the garden, where they shared updates and continued to add messages of hope to the banner outside the hospital. They also created a mural in the garden, each brushstroke expressing their collective support. Their actions were a powerful reminder of John's lasting impact on their lives.

Local businesses continued their support, ensuring the Miller family never had to worry about financial burdens. The fundraisers and charity events had not only provided much-needed funds but had also strengthened the sense of community. The diner hosted monthly charity markets, the grocery store organized a mentorship program for local youth, and the repair shop provided free services to needy people. Each contribution forged deeper connections among the townspeople, reinforcing their collective strength.

Father Thomas's nightly vigils became a tradition for the community to unite and find strength in their shared faith and hope. The flickering candles in the church and homes throughout the town were a poignant symbol of the light they held for John. The sound of collective prayers, the sight

281

of candles lighting the night, and the personal testimonies shared during these vigils highlighted their emotional and spiritual impact. These collective prayer and reflection moments were a cornerstone of their support network, providing a sense of continuity and hope.

For Stephanie, the future held hope and a renewed sense of purpose. She had witnessed firsthand the profound impact of collective support and the strength that came from unity. Her reflections on John's journey and the community's response deepened her understanding of resilience and healing. She knew that whatever the outcome, the legacy of this time would endure.

One late afternoon, as the sun began to set, casting a golden glow over the hospital and the garden, Stephanie sat by John's bedside with Anne. The room was quiet; the only sound was the gentle hum of the machines that monitored John's vital signs. Anne reached out and took Stephanie's hand, her grip firm and steady. "Thank you for everything," she said softly, her eyes shining with gratitude. "I don't know what we would have done without you."

Stephanie squeezed her hand in return, her heart full. "We're all in this together," she replied. "And we'll keep fighting for John, no matter what."

The future felt less daunting as the two women watched over John silently. The journey ahead was still uncertain, but they were not alone. The community's support had created a foundation of hope and resilience, a legacy that would carry them forward.

John Miller's legacy chapter was still written, adding new lines of hope, strength, and unity each day. The community's response to his crisis revealed the best of humanity—their capacity for compassion, willingness to support one another, and unyielding belief in the power of collective hope.

As the sun dipped below the horizon, casting long shadows over the hospital and the vibrant garden, the future remained an open book. But in those quiet moments, surrounded by the symbols of their collective journey, Stephanie, Anne, and the entire community held onto the belief that they could face whatever came next together. Their hearts were united in the fight for John's recovery; in that unity, they found the strength to keep moving forward.

And so, with the sun setting and a new day on the horizon, the community continued to hold John in their thoughts and prayers, their hopes and dreams intertwined with his fight. John Miller's legacy was not just in the past but in the present and future; they were building together—a legacy of love, resilience, and unbreakable bonds.

In the waiting area, Stephanie finally paused, leaning against the wall for support. The weight of the day's events pressed down on her, but she refused to give in to despair. She pulled out her phone and began to make calls, notifying John's closest friends and family members about his condition.

The first call she made was to Anne, John's sister. Her voice shook as she explained what had happened, but she managed to convey the urgency and the hope that still lingered. "He's in a coma, but he's stable," Stephanie said, her voice cracking. "The doctors are doing everything they can. You should come as soon as you can."

Anne's response was immediate, her voice filled with fear and determination. "I'm on my way," she said. "I'll be there as soon as I can."

Next, Stephanie called Father Thomas, the town's pastor,

who had always provided comfort and strength for the community. He listened quietly as she explained the situation, his voice calm and reassuring when he finally spoke. "I'll start a prayer chain," he said. "And I'll come to the hospital to be with you. John needs all the support he can get."

Word spread quickly, and soon, the hospital was filled with familiar faces. Friends and family members arrived, their expressions a mix of hope and fear. They gathered in the waiting room, sharing stories about John and offering each other comfort. The atmosphere was solidarity and support, each contributing to the collective hope for John's recovery.

Stephanie returned to the ICU room, where John had been brought back from the CT scan. The doctors had explained that the results would take some time, but the initial assessment was cautiously optimistic. "He's stable for now," one of the doctors said, his voice professional but compassionate. We'll know more once we have the results, but he's in good hands."

As the hours passed, the hospital room became a place of quiet vigil. Stephanie sat by John's bedside, her hand holding his, her thoughts a mixture of memories and prayers. Anne arrived, her face pale but determined, and she took her place on the other side of the bed, her eyes fixed on her brother.

The initial wave of visitors eventually gave way to a more manageable number, with close friends and family members taking turns sitting with John. The waiting room was always full, though; as people came and went, their concern for John was constant. Father Thomas arrived, offering prayers and words of comfort, his presence a balm for the weary hearts gathered there.

Stephanie and Anne worked together to coordinate the

influx of support. They ensured that everyone had a chance to spend time with John and to speak words of encouragement and hope. The medical staff was understanding, accommodating the visitors as much as possible while maintaining the necessary protocols.

As night fell, the room was bathed in the soft glow of the monitors. Stephanie and Anne sat silently, their thoughts focused on John's still form. The hum of the machines and the rhythmic beeping of the heart monitor were the only sounds, a steady reminder of the fragile balance between life and death.

In those quiet moments, Stephanie felt a renewed sense of resolve. She thought about the community outside, those who cared about John, and prayed for his recovery. She knew they were not alone in this fight, and that knowledge gave her strength.

"You're not alone, John," she whispered, her voice steady despite the tears that filled her eyes. "We're all here for you. Keep fighting."

As the night wore on, the waiting room remained a place of hope and solidarity. The community rallied around John, and their collective support was a testament to his impact on their lives. They faced the uncertainty of the future together, united in their belief that John would wake up and return to them.

And in the ICU room, bathed in the soft glow of the monitors, Stephanie and Anne held onto hope, their hearts filled with determination. The road ahead was long and uncertain, but they were ready to face it with their friends, family, and community support.

The news of John's condition spread through the community like wildfire, igniting a wave of concern and support. As friends and family gathered at the hospital, their faces reflected hope and fear. Each person brought a story, a memory, a connection to John that added to the tapestry of love and care surrounding him.

Anne Miller sat by her brother's bedside, her hand clutching his as if her grip alone could keep him tethered to life. She had always been the strong caretaker in their family, but seeing John like this tested the limits of her strength. She whispered words of encouragement, her voice steady even as her heart broke. "You've got to fight, John. We're all here, waiting for you. Don't give up."

Stephanie watched the interactions with a heavy heart, seeing the toll it took on those who loved John. She moved between the ICU room and the waiting area, offering comfort and updates. Her professional training gave her the tools to help others cope, but it did little to ease her pain. Every moment spent away from John felt like an eternity. Yet, she knew her role was to bridge the gap between the medical staff and John's anxious loved ones.

In the waiting room, emotions ran high. Friends who had known John for years shared their memories, each story a reminder of the man they were fighting for. David, John's best friend since childhood, spoke of their adventures and mischief, his voice choked with emotion. "He's always been there for me," David said, tears glistening. "I can't imagine life without him. He's got to pull through this."

The group nodded in agreement, their collective hope a fragile but vital lifeline. Father Thomas led them in a prayer, his words a soothing balm for their troubled hearts. "We must have faith," he said softly. "John is a fighter, and with our prayers and support, he will find his way back to us."

The hospital staff noticed the steady stream of visitors and the outpouring of love and support and made accommodations to ensure everyone had a chance to spend a few moments with John. The ICU nurses, seasoned veterans of many crises, handled the situation gracefully and compassionately, allowing family and friends to rotate in and out of the room while maintaining the necessary medical protocols.

John's colleagues from the repair shop also went to the hospital. Bill, the shop owner, stood by John's bed, his rugged exterior masking a heart full of concern. "You're a tough guy, John," he said gruffly, his voice cracking. "I need you back at the shop, fixing things like you always do. Don't let me down now."

Students from the high school where John had volunteered his time and skills sent handmade cards and letters. These tokens of affection filled the room, a colorful testament to John's impact on young lives. The messages of hope and encouragement were taped to the walls, creating a mosaic of support that was impossible to ignore.

In quieter moments, when the room was still, and the only sound was the rhythmic beeping of the heart monitor, Stephanie and Anne found solace in each other's presence. They spoke in hushed tones, sharing their fears and hopes and drawing strength from their determination to see John through this crisis.

"Do you remember the camping trip we took when we were kids?" Anne asked one evening, her voice filled with nostalgia. "John got lost trying to find firewood, and we were all so scared. But he found his way back, just like he always does."

Stephanie smiled, the memory a brief respite from the

weight of the present. "He's always had a knack for finding his way," she agreed. "And he's going to find his way back to us now. I know he will."

The days were blurred together, marked by a routine of medical updates, visitors, and quiet vigils. The community continued to rally around John, their support unwavering. Fundraisers and prayer groups were organized, each event a testament to the collective hope that John would recover.

Anne coordinated with the hospital staff, ensuring that John received the best possible care. She spoke with doctors and nurses, her questions pointed and informed, and her resolve was unshakeable. She was determined to leave no stone unturned and explore every possible avenue for John's recovery.

Stephanie, too, played a vital role, and her presence was a source of comfort for John's family and friends. She balanced her professional responsibilities with her connection to John, finding strength in the community's support. Her conversations with John, though one-sided, were filled with hope and determination. "You're not alone, John," she would whisper. We're all here, waiting for you to wake up."

The initial shock gave way to a more profound, enduring hope as the days turned into weeks. The community's support did not waver; instead, it grew stronger, each act of kindness and solidarity reinforcing their collective belief in John's recovery.

The ICU room, once a place of sterile efficiency, had become a sanctuary filled with love and hope. The walls were lined with cards and letters, the air filled with the quiet hum of machines and the soft murmur of prayers and conversations. It was a place where the power of human connection was on full display, where the lines between patient and community blurred in the face of a shared struggle.

And in the midst of it all, John lay still, his fate uncertain but his presence a beacon of hope for those who loved him. The road ahead was long and fraught with challenges. Still, the community was ready to face it together, united in their determination to see John wake up and return to the life he had touched so deeply.

The fight was far from over for Stephanie, Anne, and the entire community. But as they looked around at the faces filled with love and resolve, they knew they were not alone. They were stronger together and would continue to fight for John, one day at a time.

Stephanie's world had narrowed to the space around John's hospital bed, and the days bled into nights, marked by the steady rhythm of machines that kept John tethered to life. The hospital room had become a sanctuary where time seemed to stand still, each moment suspended in a fragile balance between hope and fear.

As a therapist, Stephanie was no stranger to trauma and crisis, but this was different. This was personal. The sight of John, so still and vulnerable, pierced her professional armor, leaving her feeling exposed and helpless. She had always been the one to offer strength and guidance, but now, she found herself clinging to the very hope she tried to instill in others.

In the quiet hours, Stephanie allowed herself to reflect on the journey that had brought John to this point. She remembered their first meeting, how guarded he had been, his eyes shadowed by past pain. Over time, he had opened up, sharing his struggles and fears. She had watched him fight back from the brink, each small victory a testament to his resilience. She willed him to find that strength again as she sat by his bedside.

Stephanie's reflections were often interrupted by the flurry of medical staff performing their duties. She watched intently as they checked his vitals, adjusted his medications, and updated his charts. She asked questions, seeking to understand every aspect of his care. The doctors and nurses were patient and kind, recognizing her need for information as part of coping.

Dr. Patel, John's primary physician, spoke privately with Stephanie one afternoon. His face was severe but compassionate, the weight of his words evident in his eyes. "John is stable for now, but his condition is critical," he explained. "The next few days will be crucial in determining his recovery. We're doing everything possible, but it's a waiting game now."

Stephanie nodded, her throat tight with emotion. "Thank you, Dr. Patel," she said softly. "I just need to know that there's hope."

Dr. Patel placed a reassuring hand on her shoulder. "There is always hope," he replied. "John is a fighter, and he has a lot of people rooting for him. That support makes a difference, even if it's not something we can measure."

His words were a balm to her soul, offering a glimmer of light in the darkness. Stephanie returned to John's side, and her resolve strengthened. She spoke to him often, her voice steady and filled with encouragement. "You're not alone, John," she would whisper. "We're all here, fighting with you. You have so much to live for, so many people who need you."

Stephanie coordinated closely with Anne, ensuring that John's care was seamless and that his visitors were managed in a way that provided comfort without overwhelming him.

They became a formidable team, their shared goal forging a deep bond. They leaned on each other, drawing strength from their mutual determination to see John through this crisis.

Despite her professional training, Stephanie found herself grappling with her own emotions. The trauma of finding John unconscious had left a deep scar, and she often replayed that moment in her mind, questioning if she could have done more if she had missed any signs. The guilt was a constant companion, a shadow that darkened even the brightest moments of hope.

Stephanie turned to her colleagues and friends in those dark moments for support. She confided in Father Thomas, who offered spiritual guidance, a listening ear, and a shoulder to lean on. "You've done everything you could, Stephanie," he would say gently. "Sometimes, despite our best efforts, things are beyond our control. Trust in the strength of the community and the power of prayer."

The waiting area outside the ICU was a testament to the power of community support. It was filled with John's friends, family, and colleagues, all united in their concern for him. The walls were covered with cards and letters from high school students, their colorful drawings and heartfelt messages creating a mosaic of hope. Each note was a reminder of the lives John had touched and the impact he had made.

Stephanie and Anne found solace in each other's presence in quiet moments. They shared stories, laughed, and cried together, drawing strength from their determination to see John through this crisis. "Do you remember the camping trip we took as kids?" Anne asked one evening, her voice filled with nostalgia. "John got lost trying to find firewood, and we were all so scared. But he found his way back, just like he always does."

Stephanie smiled, the memory a brief respite from the weight of the present. "He's always had a knack for finding his way," she agreed. "And he's going to find his way back to us now. I know he will."

The initial shock gave way to a more profound, enduring hope as the days turned into weeks. The community's support did not waver; instead, it grew stronger, each act of kindness and solidarity reinforcing their collective belief in John's recovery. Fundraisers and prayer groups were organized, each event a testament to the collective hope that John would recover.

The ICU room, once a place of sterile efficiency, had become a sanctuary filled with love and hope. The walls were lined with cards and letters, the air filled with the quiet hum of machines and the soft murmur of prayers and conversations. It was a place where the power of human connection was on full display, where the lines between patient and community blurred in the face of a shared struggle.

And in the midst of it all, John lay still, his fate uncertain but his presence a beacon of hope for those who loved him. The road ahead was long and fraught with challenges. Still, the community was ready to face it together, united in their determination to see John wake up and return to the life he had touched so deeply.

The fight was far from over for Stephanie, Anne, and the entire community. But as they looked around at the faces filled with love and resolve, they knew they were not alone. They were stronger together and would continue to fight for John, one day at a time.

The news of John's condition spread through the community like wildfire, igniting a wave of concern and support. As friends and family gathered at the hospital, their faces reflected hope and fear. Each person brought a story, a memory, a connection to John that added to the tapestry of love and care surrounding him.

Anne Miller sat by her brother's bedside, her hand clutching his as if her grip alone could keep him tethered to life. She had always been the strong caretaker in their family, but seeing John like this tested the limits of her strength. She whispered words of encouragement, her voice steady even as her heart broke. "You've got to fight, John. We're all here, waiting for you. Don't give up."

Stephanie watched the interactions with a heavy heart, seeing the toll it took on those who loved John. She moved between the ICU room and the waiting area, offering comfort and updates. Her professional training gave her the tools to help others cope, but it did little to ease her pain. Every moment spent away from John felt like an eternity. Yet, she knew her role was to bridge the gap between the medical staff and John's anxious loved ones.

In the waiting room, emotions ran high. Friends who had known John for years shared their memories, each story a reminder of the man they were fighting for. David, John's best friend since childhood, spoke of their adventures and mischief, his voice choked with emotion. "He's always been there for me," David said, tears glistening. "I can't imagine life without him. He's got to pull through this."

The group nodded in agreement, their collective hope a fragile but vital lifeline. Father Thomas led them in a prayer, his words a soothing balm for their troubled hearts. "We must have faith," he said softly. "John is a fighter, and with our prayers and support, he will find his way back to us."

The hospital staff noticed the steady stream of visitors and the outpouring of love and support and made accommodations to ensure everyone had a chance to spend a few moments with John. The ICU nurses, seasoned veterans of many crises, handled the situation gracefully and compassionately, allowing family and friends to rotate in and out of the room while maintaining the necessary medical protocols.

John's colleagues from the repair shop also went to the hospital. Bill, the shop owner, stood by John's bed, his rugged exterior masking a heart full of concern. "You're a tough guy, John," he said gruffly, his voice cracking. "I need you back at the shop, fixing things like you always do. Don't let me down now."

Students from the high school where John had volunteered his time and skills sent handmade cards and letters. These tokens of affection filled the room, a colorful testament to John's impact on young lives. The messages of hope and encouragement were taped to the walls, creating a mosaic of support that was impossible to ignore.

In quieter moments, when the room was still, and the only sound was the rhythmic beeping of the heart monitor, Stephanie and Anne found solace in each other's presence. They spoke in hushed tones, sharing their fears and hopes and drawing strength from their determination to see John through this crisis.

"Do you remember the camping trip we took when we were kids?" Anne asked one evening, her voice filled with nostalgia. "John got lost trying to find firewood, and we were all so scared. But he found his way back, just like he always does."

Stephanie smiled, the memory a brief respite from the weight of the present. "He's always had a knack for finding his way," she agreed. "And he's going to find his way back to us now. I know he will."

The days were blurred together, marked by a routine of medical updates, visitors, and quiet vigils. The community continued to rally around John, their support unwavering. Fundraisers and prayer groups were organized, each event a testament to the collective hope that John would recover.

Anne coordinated with the hospital staff, ensuring that John received the best possible care. She spoke with doctors and nurses, her questions pointed and informed, and her resolve was unshakeable. She was determined to leave no stone unturned and explore every possible avenue for John's recovery.

Stephanie, too, played a vital role, and her presence was a source of comfort for John's family and friends. She balanced her professional responsibilities with her connection to John, finding strength in the community's support. Her conversations with John, though one-sided, were filled with hope and determination. "You're not alone, John," she would whisper. "We're all here, waiting for you to wake up."

The initial shock gave way to a more profound, enduring hope as the days turned into weeks. The community's support did not waver; instead, it grew stronger, each act of kindness and solidarity reinforcing their collective belief in John's recovery.

The ICU room, once a place of sterile efficiency, had become a sanctuary filled with love and hope. The walls were lined with cards and letters, the air filled with the quiet hum of machines and the soft murmur of prayers and conversations.

295

It was a place where the power of human connection was on full display, where the lines between patient and community blurred in the face of a shared struggle.

And in the midst of it all, John lay still, his fate uncertain but his presence a beacon of hope for those who loved him. The road ahead was long and fraught with challenges. Still, the community was ready to face it together, united in their determination to see John wake up and return to the life he had touched so deeply.

The fight was far from over for Stephanie, Anne, and the entire community. But as they looked around at the faces filled with love and resolve, they knew they were not alone. They were stronger together and would continue to fight for John, one day at a time.

27

The Unknown Future

The sun barely rose when the first wave of townspeople arrived at County General Hospital. News of John's coma had spread through the small community like wildfire; each whispered conversation and urgent phone call added to the collective shock. By mid-morning, the hospital waiting room was filled with familiar faces, their expressions a mix of fear, hope, and bewilderment.

Stephanie Thompson stood by the large window, her eyes scanning the horizon as she tried to process the events of the past 24 hours. The image of John lying unresponsive on his apartment floor was seared into her mind, a haunting reminder of the fragility of life. As she watched friends and family gather, she felt a profound responsibility to support them through this crisis.

Anne Miller, John's sister, was one of the first to arrive. She rushed into the hospital, her face pale but resolute, and made her way to the ICU where John was being treated. The sight of her brother, surrounded by machines and monitors, brought tears to her eyes, but she quickly composed herself.

There was no time for breakdowns; John needed her to be strong.

As the morning progressed, more people arrived. David, John's best friend, appeared at the entrance, his usual carefree demeanor replaced with a grave seriousness. He joined the growing group in the waiting room, offering hugs and quiet words of comfort. Each new arrival was greeted with the same hope and anxiety, the unspoken question hanging in the air: Would John wake up?

The hospital staff did their best to accommodate the influx of visitors, setting up extra chairs and providing updates whenever possible. Dr. Patel, John's primary physician, frequently visited the waiting room, and his presence was reassuring and a stark reminder of the gravity of the situation. "We're doing everything we can," he would say, his voice calm and steady. "John's condition is critical but stable. The next few days will be crucial."

Throughout the day, Stephanie moved between the waiting room and John's bedside, her role shifting seamlessly between professional caregiver and personal friend. She offered words of comfort to those who needed them, her own emotions carefully controlled. Inside, she felt a storm of fear and hope but knew she had to stay vital for everyone else.

At one point, she found herself alone in the hallway, the weight of the situation pressing down on her. She took a deep breath, trying to steady her racing heart. The waiting room was filled with people who loved John and needed her to anchor. She couldn't afford to fall apart now.

Returning to the waiting room, Stephanie noticed small groups forming, people huddled together in whispered conversations. There was a palpable sense of community, a collective strength from shared concern and love for John. The initial shock led to determined solidarity, each person contributing to the support network forming around John and his family.

As evening approached, the atmosphere in the hospital shifted. The initial flurry of activity began to calm, replaced by a quieter, more reflective mood. People settled into their roles, finding ways to help and support each other. Some took over meal duties, ensuring that everyone had something to eat. Others coordinated with the hospital staff, offering to help with anything they could.

Outside, the sun dipped below the horizon, casting long shadows over the hospital grounds. Inside, the waiting room was a mosaic of emotions, each person grappling with their fears and hopes. Yet, despite the uncertainty, there was a sense of unity, a collective determination to see John through this crisis.

Stephanie glanced around the room, her heart swelling with pride and sorrow. These people had always been there for John, who had shared in his joys and sorrows. Now, they were united in their hope for his recovery, their love and support a powerful testament to the bonds they shared.

As the night fell and the hospital settled into a quieter rhythm, the community's resolve grew more assertive. They knew the uncertain road ahead but were ready to face it together. And as they waited for news, their thoughts and prayers were with John, each person holding onto the hope that he would wake up and return to them.

The waiting room was filled with a heavy silence, punctuated only by the occasional whisper or the rustling of paper as someone flipped through a magazine without reading it.

The tension was palpable, the air thick with unspoken fears and fragile hopes. Each person dealt with their emotions in their way. Still, the collective anxiety and hope formed an invisible thread connecting them all.

David sat in a corner, his head bowed, and his hands clasped tightly together. Known for his easy-going nature, he now wore an expression of deep concern. He replayed the moments he had spent with John over the years, shared laughter and quiet talks about life's uncertainties. He couldn't bear the thought of losing his best friend. "Come on, John," he whispered under his breath. "You've got to pull through."

Nearby, a group of John's colleagues from the repair shop huddled together, their faces drawn and serious. Bill, the shop owner, was among them, his gruff exterior masking a heart full of worry. "He's a tough guy," Bill said, his voice gruff but tinged with emotion. "If anyone can make it through this, it's John." The others nodded in agreement, drawing comfort from the shared sentiment.

Anne moved around the room, offering quiet encouragement and hugs to those who needed it. She felt the weight of her role as John's sister, the responsibility to stay vital for everyone else. But inside, she was battling a storm of emotions—fear, hope, despair, and a fierce determination not to lose her brother. She repeatedly checked on John, needing to see him, to remind herself that he was still there, still fighting.

Stephanie observed the range of emotions swirling around her, each person grappling with their fears and hopes. She deeply empathized with them all, knowing how hard it was to balance on the knife-edge of uncertainty. As a therapist, she had always been the one to help others navigate their emotional landscapes. Now, she needed to do the same for this community she cared so deeply about.

Throughout the day, there were moments of quiet conversation where friends and family shared memories of John, their voices filled with sorrow and hope. "Remember the time John fixed Mrs. Henderson's fence after that storm?" one person said a soft smile on their face. "He didn't even ask for anything in return. Just did it because it needed doing."

"He's always been that way," another replied. "Always looking out for everyone else, never thinking about himself."

These conversations were a lifeline, a way to hold onto the essence of John's character even as they faced the uncertainty of his condition. They spoke of his kindness, resilience, and quiet strength, drawing on these memories to fuel their hope for his recovery.

As the hours passed, Stephanie noticed the toll the situation took on everyone. The initial shock was wearing off, replaced by a deep, gnawing anxiety. People were exhausted, emotionally and physically, but they refused to leave. They wanted to be there for John, to be ready for any news, good or bad.

Amid this, Stephanie was slipping into her professional role, offering support to those who needed it most. She sat with David, who was struggling to hold back tears. "It's okay to be scared," she told him gently. "We're all scared. But we're in this together, and that makes us stronger."

David nodded, his eyes glistening. "I just don't know what I'd do without him," he admitted, his voice breaking.

Stephanie placed a reassuring hand on his shoulder. "He's a fighter, David. And he's not alone. We're all here, fighting with him."

She moved to sit with Bill and the others from the repair

shop, listening as they shared their worries and hopes. Her presence was a calming influence, her quiet strength a source of comfort. She encouraged them to talk about their feelings and share their fears and hopes, knowing that these conversations were vital to the healing process.

Stephanie also cared for herself, knowing she couldn't support others if she didn't look after her emotional well-being. She took short breaks, stepping outside for fresh air, allowing herself moments of quiet reflection. She leaned on Anne and the others, drawing strength from their determination to see John through this crisis.

The hospital took on a quieter, more contemplative atmosphere as evening approached. The initial flurry of activity had subsided, replaced by a steady, enduring hope. People found small ways to comfort each other, sharing food, blankets, and stories. The bonds of friendship and community were strengthened, each drawing on the collective strength to keep their spirits up.

In the quiet moments, Stephanie allowed herself to hope. She thought about John, the progress they had made together, and the strength he had shown. She believed in him and felt he could return to them. And as she looked around at the faces filled with love and concern, she knew that they would all be there to support him every step of the way.

The waiting room, once a place of anxiety and uncertainty, had become a sanctuary of shared hope and determination. The community was united in its love for John; its hearts and minds focused on his recovery. As it faced each new day, it did so with the knowledge that it was not alone, its collective strength a beacon of light in the darkness.

The days following John's hospitalization saw Stephanie

taking on multiple roles, each one demanding her total emotional and mental capacity. As a therapist, she was well-versed in guiding others through their darkest hours, but this situation was intensely personal. She balanced the thin line between professional detachment and personal anguish, her heart heavy with worry for John and the need to remain a pillar of strength for those around her.

Stephanie would arrive at the hospital every morning before dawn, her steps determined but weary. She would check with the night nurse for the latest update on John's condition. These briefings were a lifeline, providing her with the information she needed to cope and communicate with the others waiting anxiously in the lobby.

Anne always greeted Stephanie by her brother's side daily with hope and exhaustion. "Anything new?" she would ask, her voice a fragile whisper. Stephanie would hold her hand, offering whatever news she had, good or bad, with a reassuring presence. "He's stable," she would say, "but we need to stay strong. He's still fighting."

Stephanie knew her role was to bridge the gap between the medical staff and John's loved ones, translating complex medical jargon into digestible updates that could offer peace. She took meticulous notes during her conversations with the doctors, especially Dr. Patel, who appreciated her thoroughness and dedication.

One morning, as Dr. Patel explained the nuances of John's latest test results, Stephanie asked the questions she knew were on everyone's mind but were too afraid to voice. "What are the chances, realistically, of him waking up?" she inquired, her voice steady yet soft.

Dr. Patel looked at her with compassion, recognizing

303

the weight of her question. "It's difficult to say," he began, choosing his words carefully. "We're cautiously optimistic because he's stable, but we're in a critical waiting period. The next few days will give us a clearer picture. All we can do now is hope and support him as best we can."

Stephanie nodded, absorbing the information. She took a deep breath, preparing to relay this to the others. She knew the importance of maintaining hope while preparing them for possible outcomes. It was a delicate balance she was determined to manage with grace.

Stephanie became the unofficial spokesperson in the waiting room, delivering updates calmly. "Dr. Patel says we need to be cautiously optimistic," she explained to the gathered friends and family. "John is stable, but the next few days are crucial. We need to keep supporting him and each other."

She saw the ripple of relief and continued anxiety pass through the group. These moments tested her the most, seeing the raw emotions on the faces of those she cared about. She moved among them, offering hugs, words of encouragement, and sometimes just a listening ear. She knew that her presence, her ability to remain calm and hopeful, was a source of strength for them.

Stephanie facilitated small group discussions throughout the day, allowing people to express their fears and hopes. She encouraged them to share stories about John to keep his spirit alive in their hearts. "Remember when John helped organize that charity run?" she prompted one group. "He was so passionate about it, made sure everything ran smoothly." The stories flowed, each a testament to John's character and impact on their lives.

Stephanie also took time for herself, understanding the

necessity of self-care in her demanding role. She would retreat to a quiet corner of the hospital, taking a few moments to breathe deeply and center herself. During these brief respites, she reflected on her feelings, her deep connection with John, and the strength she needed to continue this journey.

In the evenings, Stephanie stayed with Anne, helping her manage the practicalities of life that still needed attention despite the crisis. They would sit together, discussing the day's events and making plans for the next. Stephanie provided a sense of normalcy in the chaos, helping Anne stay grounded.

Their conversations often turned to memories of John, moments that defined him and his relationships with those around him. "He's always been so resilient," Anne said one evening, her voice a mix of pride and sorrow. "No matter what life threw at him, he found a way to keep going."

"He's one of the strongest people I know," Stephanie agreed. "And he's got all of us fighting for him. That counts for a lot."

Stephanie's reflections during these quiet moments were intense and introspective. She thought about the journey she and John had shared, their progress, and the battles they had fought together. She realized that her commitment to John's recovery went beyond her professional duty; it was deeply personal. She cared for him, not just as a professional but as a friend; that bond fueled her determination.

Stephanie's role remained vital as the days turned nights and nights into days. She was the linchpin holding the fragile network of hope and support together. Her strength and compassion were the bedrock upon which the community leaned. As she sat by John's bedside, whispering words of encouragement, she believed that their collective hope and love would guide him back to consciousness.

Stephanie knew the road ahead was long and uncertain, but she was ready to face it. She would continue to fight for John, to be the beacon of hope for those around her. And in the quiet moments, when the world outside the hospital faded away, she held onto the belief that they could overcome anything together.

The town of Willow Creek had always been a close-knit community, but John's condition brought everyone closer together. News of his coma had spread quickly, and the response was immediate and overwhelming. The community rallied in big and small ways, each act of kindness a thread in the tapestry of support surrounding John and his family.

Sally's diner became the unofficial headquarters for organizing efforts. Usually filled with casual diners and laughter, the booths were now occupied by groups planning fundraisers and support events. Sally herself was a whirlwind of activity, coordinating meal deliveries to the hospital and ensuring that no visitor left without a warm meal and a kind word.

"We're going to have a bake sale this weekend," Sally announced one morning, her voice filled with determination. "All proceeds will go to help cover John's medical expenses. And I want everyone to spread the word. We need all the support we can get."

The bake sale was just the beginning. Local businesses donated goods and services for auctions and raffles, each contribution a testament to John's high regard. The town hall hosted a charity concert featuring performances by local musicians who dedicated their songs to John. The event was a resounding success, bringing together people from all walks of life, united by their concern and hope.

The high school students organized car washes, bake sales, and sports tournaments to raise funds. They created a giant banner filled with messages of hope and encouragement for John, which they hung outside the hospital. Each day, students added new messages, their words a vibrant display of their support and belief in his recovery.

Social media played a significant role in spreading the word and gathering support. A page dedicated to John's recovery quickly gained followers, providing updates on his condition and information about upcoming events. People shared their stories of hope and resilience, creating a virtual community of supporters who believed in John's strength and the power of collective hope.

Prayer chains and vigils became regular events. Father Thomas led nightly vigils at the church, inviting the community to pray. The sight of flickering candles in the church and windows throughout the town was a moving testament to the unity and hope that had taken hold.

In addition to emotional and financial support, practical help was also organized. Volunteers took on tasks such as mowing the lawn at John's house, caring for his pets, and ensuring his bills were managed during his hospitalization. These acts of service, though small individually, collectively alleviated the burdens on John's family, allowing them to focus on his recovery.

For Anne, the community's support was a lifeline. The constant presence of friends and neighbors, the meals and messages, and the practical help all provided a much-needed sense of stability and hope. She often felt overwhelmed by their kindness, tears of gratitude mingling with her fears for

John. "I don't know how we would get through this without all of you," she would say, her voice thick with emotion. "Thank you from the bottom of my heart."

Stephanie, too, found solace in the outpouring of support. She saw firsthand the impact of their collective efforts, each act of kindness a thread in the fabric of hope woven around John and his family. She worked closely with the volunteers, offering guidance and ensuring their efforts were coordinated and effective. Her background in community organization proved invaluable, helping to channel the outpouring of support into meaningful actions.

One particularly moving initiative was the creation of a community garden in the park across from the hospital. Volunteers planted flowers, herbs, and vegetables, each plant symbolizing a wish for John's recovery. The garden quickly became a place of reflection and hope, a living testament to the community's commitment to supporting John. People visited the garden daily, tending to the plants and finding solace in nurturing something new.

As the garden grew, so did the community's unity and purpose. Coming together to create something beautiful amid uncertainty was a powerful reminder of their collective strength. The garden was not just a symbol of hope for John's recovery; it was a testament to the resilience and compassion of the community itself.

For Stephanie, these days were a journey of self-discovery. She realized that her strength came from within and the community around her. Their hope and resilience became her anchor, guiding her through the emotions that threatened to overwhelm her. And in supporting others, she found a renewed sense of purpose, a commitment to seeing John through his fight.

As the weeks turned into months, the community's support did not waver. They continued to rally around John and his family, their collective hope a beacon of light in the darkest times. The bonds strengthened during this crisis would endure, a lasting testament to the power of unity and compassion.

The community's support for John was a living, breathing legacy of his impact on their lives. Each act of kindness, each message of hope, each moment of shared vulnerability added to the tapestry of resilience and compassion that defined them. As they faced each new day, they did so with the knowledge that they were not alone, their hearts united in the fight for John's recovery.

The practical support extended beyond the hospital and church. Neighbors took care of John's home, mowing the lawn, tending to the garden, and looking after his pets. They handled bills and other practicalities, ensuring Anne and the rest of the family could focus entirely on John's recovery.

One particularly moving initiative was the creation of a community garden across from the hospital. Volunteers planted flowers, herbs, and vegetables, each plant symbolizing a wish for John's healing. The garden quickly became a place of reflection and hope, a living testament to the community's commitment to supporting John. People visited daily, tending to the plants and finding peace by nurturing new life.

As the garden grew, so did the community's unity and purpose. Coming together to create something beautiful amid uncertainty was a powerful reminder of their collective strength. The garden was not just a symbol of hope for John's recovery; it was a testament to the resilience and compassion of the community itself.

For Stephanie, the outpouring of support was both heartening and humbling. She saw firsthand the impact of their collective efforts, each act of kindness adding to the fabric of hope woven around John and his family. She worked closely with the volunteers, offering guidance and ensuring their efforts were coordinated and effective. Her background in community organization proved invaluable, helping to channel the outpouring of support into meaningful actions.

The community's support for John was a living, breathing legacy of his impact on their lives. Each act of kindness, each message of hope, each moment of shared vulnerability added to the tapestry of resilience and compassion that defined them. As they faced each new day, they did so with the knowledge that they were not alone, their hearts united in the fight for John's recovery.

As the days turned into weeks, the community of Willow Creek settled into a new normal, defined by a constant undercurrent of hope and uncertainty. John's condition remained unchanged; he was stable but still in a coma. The initial shock had worn off, replaced by a deep, enduring determination to see John through this ordeal. The community's focus shifted to the future, grappling with the possible outcomes and preparing for the long haul.

Discussions about John's future became a common thread in conversations. Friends and family gathered in small groups, pondering what lay ahead. "What if he wakes up tomorrow?" someone would ask, their voice filled with tentative hope. "What if it takes longer?" another would counter, the question hanging heavy in the air. The uncertainty was a constant companion, a shadow that touched every aspect of their lives.

Stephanie continued her dual role at the hospital as a therapist and friend. She spent her days managing the ebb and flow of emotions among John's visitors, providing a steadying presence and a compassionate ear. She also closely monitored John's condition, liaising with Dr. Patel and the medical team to stay informed about his progress.

Anne, always by her brother's side, grappled with the unknown. She spent hours talking to John, telling him stories from their childhood, recounting funny anecdotes, and sharing updates about the community's efforts. "Everyone is rooting for you, John," she would say, her voice soft but firm. "You have to keep fighting. We're all here, waiting for you."

The community garden across from the hospital had flourished, becoming a place of solace and reflection for many. People visited daily, tending to the plants and finding peace in the simple act of nurturing life. The garden was a living symbol of their hope and resilience, each bloom and sprout a testament to their collective strength.

Stephanie took a break from the hospital one afternoon and wandered to the garden. She found Father Thomas there, his hands dirty from planting new flowers. He looked up as she approached, his eyes warm with recognition. "Hello, Stephanie," he greeted her, standing and wiping his hands on his pants. "How are you holding up?"

Stephanie smiled, appreciating his concern. "I'm managing," she replied. "It's not easy, but seeing everyone come together like this helps. It gives me hope."

Father Thomas nodded, his expression thoughtful. "Hope is a powerful thing," he said. "It can sustain us through the darkest times. And right now, it's what we all need most."

Walking through the garden, they talked about the future,

the community's resilience, and the strength they found in each other. "No matter what happens, we'll get through this," Father Thomas said, his voice filled with conviction. "Together, we're stronger than any challenge we face."

Back at the hospital, discussions about John's future continued. The medical team prepared for various scenarios, ensuring they were ready for whatever came next. Dr. Patel regularly met with Anne and Stephanie to discuss John's condition and outline potential next steps. "We need to be prepared for all possibilities," he explained. "John's recovery will be a long journey, but we'll be with him every step of the way."

The community echoed this sentiment, and their actions and words were a testament to their unwavering support. Fundraisers and prayer groups continued each event, reaffirming their commitment to John and his family. The sense of unity and purpose grew more robust, each act of kindness and solidarity reinforcing the bonds that held them together.

For Stephanie, the future was a landscape of unknowns filled with hope. She reflected on the journey she and John had shared, the progress they had made, and the strength he had shown. She believed in his resilience, the power of the community's support, and the possibility of recovery.

One evening, as the sun set and the hospital room was bathed in a soft, golden light, Stephanie sat by John's bedside, her hand gently holding his. She spoke to him, her voice filled with a quiet determination. "You're not alone, John," she whispered. "We're all here, fighting for you. No matter how long it takes, we're not giving up."

The room was quiet; the only sounds were the steady beep of the monitors and the soft hum of the ventilator. Stephanie's words hung in the air, a promise and a prayer. She knew that the road ahead was uncertain, but she also knew that they would face it together with hope and strength.

The community's discussions about the future reflected their collective hope and resilience. They faced each day with a mixture of anxiety and determination, their hearts united in their support for John. As they looked ahead, they did so with the knowledge that they could overcome any challenge together.

The legacy of John Miller was written not just in the past but in the present and future, and they were building together—a legacy of love, resilience, and unbreakable bonds. And as they faced each new day, they did so with the belief that, no matter what the future held, they would face it together, united in hope and strength.

The story of John Miller was far from over. His legacy was not just in the past but in the present and future they were building together—a legacy of love, resilience, and unbreakable bonds. And as they faced each new day, they did so knowing they could overcome any challenge together.

As the sun began to set, casting a warm, golden light across the hospital room, Stephanie and Anne found themselves alone with John. The monitors' soft glow and the machines' gentle hum created a serene, almost sacred atmosphere. They sat in silence for a while; each lost in their thoughts.

"I was thinking about the future today," Anne said quietly, breaking the silence. "About what happens if John doesn't wake up. I know we need to stay positive, but it's hard not to think about it."

Stephanie nodded, understanding the fear that lay behind Anne's words. "It's natural to think about all the possibilities,"

313

she said gently. "We have to prepare ourselves for every outcome. But right now, all we can do is stay hopeful and continue to support him. We have to believe that he will wake up."

Anne sighed, her eyes filled with a mixture of hope and fear. "I know you're right," she said. "It's just so hard not knowing. But seeing everyone come together, all the love and support, it gives me hope. I just want him to come back to us."

Stephanie reached out and took Anne's hand, offering her silent support. "We're all in this together," she said softly. "And we'll face whatever comes next as a community. We're stronger than we think, and we have each other."

Their conversation was a reflection of the collective struggle that everyone was facing. The uncertainty of John's condition was a heavy burden. Still, it also brought out the best in people, their compassion and resilience shining through. They found strength in each other, their shared hope, a powerful force that carried them through the darkest moments.

As night fell, the hospital quieted, the day's visitors making their way home. Stephanie and Anne remained by John's side, their hearts united in love and determination. They knew that the journey was far from over. Still, with the support of their community, they would continue to fight for John, holding onto the belief that one day he would wake up and return to them.

The story of John Miller was still unfolding, each day adding a new chapter of hope and resilience. And as they faced each new day, they did so knowing they could overcome any challenge together.

The community of Willow Creek has always been known

for its strong sense of solidarity. Still, John's situation brought out an extraordinary level of support and action. The initial shock of his coma gave way to a sustained, organized effort to assist in any way possible. The town mobilized like never before, turning their concern into concrete actions.

Sally's diner remained the hub of activity. An ever-growing number of volunteers attended her weekly meetings to coordinate efforts. The atmosphere was camaraderie and determination, each person eager to contribute. One evening, Sally stood at the front of the packed diner, her voice ringing with resolve as she outlined the upcoming plans.

"We've raised a significant amount from the bake sale and the charity run," she announced, eliciting a round of applause. "But we're not stopping there. We have more fundraisers planned, and we need all the help we can get. We're going to hold a town fair next month, with games, food stalls, and a raffle. All proceeds will go to John's medical expenses."

The response was immediate and enthusiastic. Volunteers signed up for various tasks, from setting up booths to donating raffle prizes. Local businesses continued contributing, offering their services and goods for the cause. The fair was shaping to be a significant event, a testament to the community's unwavering support.

Meanwhile, the nightly vigils continued to draw large crowds. The candles, once a tiny circle of light, now formed a wide arc around the hospital, their flames flickering in the night air. The vigils had become a cornerstone of the community's efforts. In this place, people could come together to pray, reflect, and draw strength from each other.

Father Thomas led the gatherings with a quiet grace, his words providing comfort and hope. "In times of trial, our faith and unity are our greatest strengths," he would say, his voice carrying over the crowd. "Let us continue to support John and his family with our prayers and our presence. Together, we are stronger."

Stephanie made it a point to attend these vigils whenever she could, finding solace in the shared sense of purpose. She was often joined by Anne, who found strength in the collective support. Seeing so many people united in their hope and determination was a powerful reminder that they were not alone in their struggle.

The community garden across from the hospital had flourished, becoming a symbol of hope and renewal. Volunteers tended to the plants daily, transforming the once-barren plot into a vibrant oasis. The garden was a place of peace and reflection, a tangible representation of the community's love and support for John.

One sunny afternoon, Stephanie and Anne visited the garden together. They walked along the neat rows of flowers and vegetables, their hearts lifted by the beauty and tranquility around them. "It's amazing how much this place has grown," Anne said, her voice filled with awe. "It's a living testament to the support John has from everyone."

Stephanie nodded, her eyes bright with unshed tears. "It's incredible," she agreed. "Every plant, every flower is a symbol of hope. It shows how much people care, how much they believe in John's recovery."

The garden was not the only place where the community's efforts were evident. Throughout the town, signs of support for John were everywhere. Businesses displayed posters and flyers about upcoming fundraisers, and homes had banners and signs wishing John well. The town's social media pages were filled with messages of hope and updates on the various initiatives being undertaken.

At the high school, students organized their events to contribute to fundraising. They held car washes, bake sales, and even a talent show, each bringing in much-needed funds and raising awareness about John's situation. The students' enthusiasm and creativity were infectious, inspiring others to get involved.

One evening, Stephanie and Anne attended the high school talent show, sitting in the front row as students took to the stage to perform. The event was a heartwarming display of community spirit, with acts ranging from musical performances to comedy sketches. Each performer dedicated his act to John, and his words reminded him of his impact on his life.

As the show ended, the principal took to the stage to thank everyone for their participation and support. "John Miller has always been a pillar of this community," he said, his voice filled with emotion. "Tonight, we've seen just how much he means to all of us. Let's continue to support him and his family in any way we can."

The thunderous applause was a testament to the community's collective resolve. Stephanie looked around, her heart swelling with pride and gratitude. She knew that these acts of kindness and solidarity were not just about raising funds— they were about showing John and his family that they were not alone.

Back at the hospital, the atmosphere remained one of quiet determination. The community's actions had created a foundation of support that carried everyone through the difficult days. Stephanie continued her counseling sessions, offering guidance and support to those who needed it. She knew maintaining hope was a collective effort, and she was determined to do her part.

One evening, as the sun set, Stephanie and Anne found themselves alone in John's room. The monitors' soft glow and the machines' gentle hum created a serene, almost sacred atmosphere. They sat in silence for a while; each lost in their thoughts.

"I was thinking about the future today," Anne said quietly, breaking the silence. "About what happens if John doesn't wake up. I know we need to stay positive, but it's hard not to think about it."

Stephanie nodded, understanding the fear that lay behind Anne's words. "It's natural to think about all the possibilities," she said gently. "We have to prepare ourselves for every outcome. But right now, all we can do is stay hopeful and continue to support him. We have to believe that he will wake up."

Anne sighed, her eyes filled with a mixture of hope and fear. "I know you're right," she said. "It's just so hard not knowing. But seeing everyone come together, all the love and support, it gives me hope. I just want him to come back to us."

Stephanie reached out and took Anne's hand, offering her silent support. "We're all in this together," she said softly. "And we'll face whatever comes next as a community. We're stronger than we think, and we have each other."

Their conversation was a reflection of the collective struggle that everyone was facing. The uncertainty of John's condition was a heavy burden. Still, it also brought out the best in people, their compassion and resilience shining through. They found strength in each other, their shared hope, a powerful force that carried them through the darkest moments.

As night fell, the hospital quieted, the day's visitors making their way home. Stephanie and Anne remained by John's side, their hearts united in love and determination. They knew that the journey was far from over. Still, with the support of their community, they would continue to fight for John, holding onto the belief that one day he would wake up and return to them.

The story of John Miller was still unfolding, each day adding a new chapter of hope and resilience. And as they faced each new day, they did so knowing they could overcome any challenge together.

The legacy of love, resilience, and unbreakable bonds would continue to be written, one day at a time. And as the night deepened, the quiet hum of machines and the presence of loved ones keeping vigil, the community held onto the belief that they could overcome anything together.

Afterword

Dear Reader,

As you reach the end of this book, I want to share a deeply personal and emotional experience with you. Writing John's story has been more than just a creative endeavor; it has been a reflection of my own struggles with mental health. Through his trials and tribulations, I hoped to shed light on the often-hidden battles many of us face with mental illness.

John's journey is a testament to the complexities of mental health, the profound impact it can have on our lives, and the critical importance of seeking help. His story, though fictional, is rooted in the harsh realities that countless individuals endure daily. It serves as a stark reminder that untreated mental illness can lead to devastating consequences, not just for the individual but for everyone around them.

In my own life, I have grappled with the shadows of CPTSD. The visual representations of inner thoughts, the audible sounds, and the overwhelming sense of isolation are not mere plot devices but actual experiences that I and many others live with. Therapy, support groups, and a strong network of understanding individuals have been crucial in my ongoing battle with mental health. It's a continuous journey that requires courage, patience, and, most importantly, support.

If there's one message I hope you take away from John's story, it is this: you are not alone. Mental health struggles are not a sign of weakness. They are battles that require immense strength and resilience. If you or someone you know is struggling, please ask for help. There are resources available, and there are people who care. Whether it's a trusted friend, a family member, or a mental health professional, talking about your struggles is the first step toward healing.

Creating a supportive environment is not just the responsibility of those struggling but of society. We must strive to foster understanding and compassion to break the stigma that surrounds mental health. Education and awareness are vital in creating a world where people feel safe to speak out and seek help.

John's legacy within these pages is a call to action. It is a plea for better mental health care, greater empathy, and a commitment to support one another through our darkest times. His story reflects the urgent need for change in how we view and address mental health.

To everyone reading this, I extend my heartfelt thanks for joining me on this journey. Your willingness to engage with this challenging subject matter is a step towards greater awareness and understanding. I encourage you to carry the lessons of John's story with you, to advocate for better mental health care, and to be a beacon of support for those in need.

Remember, we should not walk alone on the road to mental health. Together, we can create a world where everyone needs the support to thrive.

With deepest gratitude,
Magnum Tenebrosum

About the Author

In the dim-lit realms of horror literature, I, Magnum Tenebrosum, emerge as a shadowy architect of the macabre, navigating the labyrinth of the human psyche. A devotee of Lovecraftian Cosmic Horror, my tales plunge into the abyss of existential dread, madness, and the unfathomable unknown.

Fueled by an intense fascination with the morbid, my works have cultivated a devoted following among those who seek the darker corners of literature. These cosmic horror stories possess a peculiar ability to reach deep into the reader's soul, leaving behind an eerie disquiet long after the final page surrenders to the darkness.

My true identity remains a cryptic secret, yet the influence on the genre speaks volumes. With an ardor for crafting narratives that tap into the primal fears within us, I persist as Magnum Tenebrosum, a spectral guide inspiring a new generation of horror enthusiasts and those daring enough to explore the depths of my imaginative abyss.

You can connect with me on:

- https://darknessstudiosllc.wixsite.com/magnumtenebrosum
- https://x.com/Magtenebrusum
- https://www.facebook.com/MagnumTenebrosum

9 798330 295111